SUMMER INDISCRETIONS

TAMARA MATAYA

sourcebooks
casablanca

Published by Sourcebooks Casablanca, an imprint of Sourcebooks, Inc.
P.O. Box 4410, Naperville, Illinois 60567-4410
(630) 961-3900
Fax: (630) 961-2168
www.sourcebooks.com

Printed and bound in Canada.
MBP 10 9 8 7 6 5 4 3 2 1

Dedicated with love to all the amazing big brothers out there—especially mine, Bruce Pederson, who had the hottest friends. ;)

Tired of your life? Looking for a Switch? Free-spirited beach dweller looking to Switch lives with an outgoing urbanite for three weeks. Must love surf, sand, and plenty of Miami sizzle. Please call Shelby ASAP at the number below. Need the perfect getaway? Let's do this!

Chapter 1

Melanie

"Excuse me, do you know the way to the nude beach?"

"Uh, sorry?" Before I can answer the smiling stranger, my phone rings, buzzing against my leg and making me jump. I fumble to answer it, clumsy in my confusion.

It's the office. I'm on vacation. I shouldn't answer… but what if it's an emergency? And—

Hold on a second. *Nude beach?*

My phone rings again before I can gather my scattered thoughts enough to ask. Too late—the stranger's already walking away. I want to chase after him, but…I stare down at my phone. What if it really is an emergency? Shoving my thoughts into order, I start walking as I accept the call. Resentfully.

"Melanie Walker speaking."

"Miss Walker, I need you to set up a meeting between me and Nick in Editorial. He's been up to something. What exactly are we paying him for?" Thaddeus Mitchell III's voice slides up my spine and lodges behind my eyes—a migraine in the making.

"I'm not in the office, Thaddeus."

"Really? I hadn't noticed." The implication being that I do nothing at work. "There's a lightbulb burned out in the stairwell that you need to see to."

Thaddeus Mitchell III was hired at the online women's magazine *H2T* (*Head 2 Toe*) as a sales consultant one month ago and has been a raging pain in my ass for each of those thirty-one days. I'd say twenty-some days, allowing for weekends, but he basically went Miranda Priestly and has been contacting me outside of work hours as well. Much like he's doing now.

"Thaddeus, contact Maintenance about the light. Their number is in the company directory. I'm HR. If you want to set up a meeting with Nick"—who's doing nothing wrong—"you'll have to talk to Valerie directly or wait until I get back. I'm on vacation right now."

"You have your cell phone—a marvel of technology, will wonders never cease? Send an email. Let's get this show on the road."

This sarcastic, condescending asshole was hired directly by my boss, and what rankles the most isn't that he's woefully unqualified, or that he doesn't need the paycheck—and has bragged about it to anyone who will listen.

No. It's the way he treats me when no one's looking. More than that, it's the way I let him get to me instead of brushing him off the way I can everyone else. I dig my nails into my palm, annoyed as hell that stomping out my frustration is proving impossible because I'm wearing flip-flops on sand.

"No." I'm tired of him turning the place I love to work into a hell I dread entering. He's the main reason I needed to get out of New York for a break.

"*Excuse me?*"

I think I've finally gotten his attention. "Talk to

Valerie, or send an email and wait until I get back. Do not call me again at this number."

"You're going to regret this lack of professionalism."

"Have a nice day," I grit out through clenched teeth and end the call.

I'd like to lose a high heel in his ass, but *that* would be unprofessional. He's lucky I haven't complained to my boss, not that he's committed a fireable offense, but I refuse to let him invade my vacation.

I glare at my phone, hitch my beach bag higher on my shoulder, and walk faster, loathing Thaddeus's intrusion. I focus on my feet and concentrate on taking slow breaths. Even twelve hundred miles away, I'm not free from him.

You'd be free of him if you moved over to Editorial.

The thing is, I'm great at my job, and it's what I know. Then again, maybe I know HR a little too well and the luster's worn off. And that's part of the problem that's been steadily nagging at me with every new idea for an article I have—that I've worked my ass off to get to the wrong place in life and am fighting for a career that doesn't fit anymore.

Plus, in another department, I wouldn't have to deal with the petty crap people like Thaddeus dump on me every day.

I want to throw my phone when it dings in my hand, but this time, it's a text from my best friend, Bailey, who works as a features editor at *H2T*.

Bailey: What's your Switch partner like?

I text back as I walk down the beach.

Me: We won't meet in person until after the Switch, but if the photographs tacked to the corkboard in her bedroom are anything to go by, Shelby Kellerman's life is a cross between an imported beer commercial and an Abercrombie & Fitch ad.

Bailey: What?

Me: Effortlessly beautiful people having a great time no matter what they're doing. Drinking at the bar, smiling at a concert, running on the beach—each picture made me want to jump inside and spend time there.

Bailey: What did she look like?

Me: Leggy, blond, taller than I thought, freckles across the bridge of her nose that give her an air of innocence despite a body that wouldn't look out of place on the cover of Sports Illustrated or Victoria's Secret. Light-brown eyes, and her hair has natural highlights from the sun.

Not that I had been obsessing over those pictures or anything.

Bailey: I don't know if I should have a crush on her or hate her viciously. lol

Me: I know how you feel!

If I'd grown up here instead of New York, would I be like that? Shelby radiates happiness and serenity. Why would she want to Switch her breezy life for mine, even temporarily?

Bailey: How's the house?

Me: Disgustingly big. What's she going to think of my cramped apartment, stuffed with books and with stark-white walls I've never gotten around to painting? Every room in her place is a different color.

Bailey: It's all part of the authentic Brooklyn experience. lol

Me: I guess. But she gets a freaking sea breeze, Bails. The nicest thing the wind blows into my apartment is a sickly spiciness from the Thai place a few doors down.

Bailey: She didn't sign up to Switch apartments with you for three weeks to be in a place exactly like hers. It's about experiencing something new, same reason you did it, right?

Me: That's for sure. I had to flee the oppressive spaciousness and head to the beach.

Bailey: Awesome! Get some sun for me! You're OK, though?

Not even my best friend knows everything about my sudden need to escape my life.

Me: I'm fine. Adjusting to all the sunshine and personal space.

Bailey: I don't want to beach block you. Call me later! Remember—you're there for a fun time. Seize it by the short and curlies!

Me: I will.

Bailey's right. Fuck Thaddeus. Fuck the day from hell that sent me here. I spread my towel and settle on it, digging in my bag for the bottle of water I packed.

The breeze rolling off the ocean hits me, counter-acting the heat with a deliciously salty tang, and I put my cell away, determined to be fully present in *this* moment. If vitamin D is the feel-good vitamin, I'm going to soak up as much as I can. I *need* to feel good right about now. I'm doing the most adventurous thing I've ever done, and no one can take that away from me.

Walking up King's Point Drive to the beach felt like an adventure in a foreign land. People are friend-lier and wear less clothing in Miami—clothing in a dazzling rainbow of colors—and a lot of women seem to wear bikini tops instead of real shirts or tank tops. Is this why they seem happier in Florida, or is it all the space? Maybe it's just because it's so close to the beach.

Without the tall buildings reaching high above like back home, the sky is nearly oppressively open, and I squint up at it for a moment before my eyelids pinch shut against the brightness of the sun. Shelby's condo is on a little almost-island surrounded by water, with the Oleta River State Park on the west and the ocean a couple blocks to the east. I'm in Miami, but somehow I feel like I'm in an oasis away from it all.

I absorb the sultry thickness, blind to anything but that ocean scent, so unfamiliar and pleasant. I lie back on my elbows, relishing the pure sizzle of the sun on my skin…for about three minutes because, damn, it's hot. How do sun worshippers do this every day without feeling the need to hire someone to baste them every half hour? Either that or hire a cabana boy to fan them and hand-feed them peeled fruits. Screw grapes—I'd like someone to peel the white crap off my oranges for me.

I grin and look around for a hypothetical candidate.

Sweat beads on my upper lip and tickles my back. Maybe I should mosey to that little stand where they're renting oversize umbrellas to people who didn't bring one—like me.

The stand where a woman in her late seventies waits in line, completely naked.

Blinking hard doesn't make clothes appear on her body; her nudity isn't a mirage. But what the hell is she doing? Is she a vagrant or someone senile who wandered away from her family? Did the ocean knock her bathing suit off? Was it eaten by a shark?

I blindly grope—*grab*—for my bottle of water because maybe this is a vision or hallucination brought on by the heat. Why isn't anyone freaking out about Naked Grandma? Is it like staring at the sun? No one wants to see that, so a glance burns your eyes and you don't try again or tell anyone you did it because it's universally *not done*? Is everyone pretending they didn't notice so they don't have to make eye contact with her and tell her to put some clothes on?

She's just naked and loitering like she's waiting to check out at the grocery store.

Any minute now, someone's going to approach her and say, "There you are, Mildred! Let's get you tucked back into this caftan so you can parade around the beach with dignity and style."

Swallowing a mouthful of water, I screw the cap back on the bottle and finally take a proper look at the people on the beach. There are some bathing suits, but...

Oh my God. No wonder no one's saying anything to Mildred. My toes curl with embarrassment, even though I'm fully clothed with a long T-shirt over my tankini, because I'm somehow feeling exposed while covered up. Apparently, embarrassment through osmosis is a thing. I've never seen this much flesh in my entire life.

A topless thirtysomething woman applies sunscreen to her legs, her breasts jiggling with every motion.

Stop staring at her.

A naked man runs up the beach with a surfboard, flaccid penis bouncing around like one of those wacky, waving, inflatable, arm-flailing tube men.

Stop staring, Melanie!

An extremely muscular man jogs by, and my gaze zooms to his crotch with startling accuracy, like I've had years of checking out naked packages.

STOP.

The thing is, I've never really seen a flaccid penis before. In my experience, by the time I'm in close proximity, they're…ready for business, and who really pays attention after sex? You either get dressed or you're snuggling with the guy under the covers, not staring at his spent member. My longest relationship was seven months, but we never lived together, so I haven't experienced a naked, unaroused man casually strolling around my personal space.

A few more men stroll by, and I Can't. Look. Away.

I didn't know thighs could be so hairy.

Old guys, young guys, burly guys, and skinny guys strolling around in the bright, bright sunlight, unafraid of getting burned in vital places. I mean, they have to put sunscreen on, but how can they apply it without being inappropriate? Talk about indecent overexposure!

Sprays, maybe?

Huh. Penises are so much sadder when they're soft, sort of shrunken in on themselves like they're embarrassed. It's fascinating, and I absolutely cannot look at them without gawking. But the women are in the buff as well, letting it all hang out for everyone to see. Muscles ripple, booties jiggle, and I'm freaking mesmerized at how nonchalant everyone is about this.

Wow, that man's legs are hairy. It's like he's wearing fuzzy leg warmers.

Some people are wearing clothes, to be fair, but their suits might as well be invisibility cloaks. I'm blinded by flesh.

This has to be how teenage boys feel during a hormone storm.

A lady's ice-cream cone drips onto her. Oh my gosh,

that can't be sanitary. And is everyone fine with getting sand everywhere? The lady with the cone sees me staring and slides her sunglasses down her nose, peering at me over them and giving a friendly grin.

Oh my God, I need to get out of here.

I stand and stuff my things back into my bag, hightailing it out. I stop short, nearly grabbing a woman's boobs when I aim my hands for her shoulders. "Sorry!" Dodging around her, I keep my eyes down, but that makes my brain wonder feverishly if the toes belong to someone who's naked—and if their feet match what I think the bodies should look like, based on flip-flops and nail polish…or toe hair.

Preoccupied with a huge pair of men's feet and trying very hard not to look up, I collide with a fortysomething man wearing nothing but flip-flops and a gold necklace—and sprawl face-first on the sand.

"Whoops!" He squats down just as I turn my head to spit out some sand, and this is not his most flattering angle. He's slick with oil, and when he helps me to my feet, he leaves shiny patches on my hands and forearms. "You OK?"

"I'm fine." My voice comes out an octave too high, and I ooze out an embarrassed "thanks" and scurry away, still smelling like his coconut suntan oil.

Was that rude? Should I have stayed and chatted with him? How the hell do you chat with a shiny, naked guy? Flustered, I rush back the way I originally came, stopping when I find what I'm looking for.

This is where the stranger asked about the nude beach before. Now that I'm here again, I see the signs pointing to Sunny Isles Beach—where I was trying to go instead of Haulover Beach. Thaddeus's call must have distracted me.

I can't believe it, but the sign for Haulover confirms what the boldly bared genitals have already shown me.

I found the *nude* beach.

Chapter 2

Blake

I MAY NOTICE THE DIPS AND CURVES OF A WOMAN'S BODY, but once my hands are on her, she becomes muscles and tissue and body parts with Latin names I learned from anatomy textbooks. The only kinks I delve into with clients are the ones in their necks. I never mix business with pleasure.

My client winces when I work on her trapezius muscles. I pause. "Have you been doing the stretches I suggested, Carla?"

She hesitates, shoulders tensing ever so slightly. "Maybe not every day."

Or even every week. I push my thumbs up her spine and out over the knot between her shoulder blades. "It shows. You're going to end up with a stress hump if you don't start stretching more. Now, I'm not saying Quasimodo can't be attractive, but—"

"I hear you. They hurt though. I tried doing them, but it felt like someone was stabbing me."

"I know they suck, especially at first, but it gets better. They'd hurt less if you did them more often."

She sighs. "Fine. I'll do the annoying stretches."

I shake my head. So many injuries could be avoided if people would take better care of themselves. A massage will make them feel better for a while, but if they put in the work, the massages would make them feel even better. Too many people are looking for quick fixes, but if they weren't, I'd have less work. Then again, Carla's the type who has someone to do everything for her. If she could pay people to do her stretches, she would.

I rub more gel on my hands and work my way up her calves. My forearm twinges as I focus on a particularly tight knot, and I realize I'll need to do an ice bath on my arms tonight. I've been taking on too many clients lately because of my upcoming vacation.

She shifts on the table. "You have any plans for the summer?"

"As a matter of fact, you're my last client for two weeks." Five minutes to go, not that I'm counting down much.

"Oh, are you going anywhere?"

"Nope. I plan on staying in my apartment and doing as little as possible. What about you?"

"Well, Teddy and I are heading to our place in the Hamptons. His mother-in-law is having some work done in Switzerland at a very exclusive spa, so I'll be accompanying her…which should be interesting."

"Do you get along well?"

"No. I'm kind of hoping they pull her skin so tight she'll look like she's frozen in a wind tunnel and won't have the slack to sneer at me anymore."

We laugh at that mental image. "She sounds awful."

"She's the worst. But I love Teddy enough to put up with that crusty, old battle-ax." She tenses as I press firmly on a trigger point and wait for it to release.

She and Teddy always seem like partners in crime,

and a relationship like that appeals to me. Unfortunately, most of the women I've met lately seem more interested in being taken care of than being a partner. I'm not looking for a spoiled princess or someone so jaded and cynical that she assumes the worst of me right off the bat; I'm looking for someone to have adventures with.

I give Carla's hamstrings a quick work-over for the last few minutes of our session, and with that, my two-week staycation begins. "Alright, you know the homework."

She sighs. "Stretchy, stretchy. I'll book our next appointment when I get back from Europe."

"Have a good vacation." I wipe my hands off on a towel and toss it in the hamper in the corner of the room.

"You too."

I leave the room to let her dress, stretching the tension from my forearms before writing my notes in Carla's file. Then I scrub my hands and arms in the sink.

My best friend, Shawn, calls while I'm drying off. I toss the hand towel into the laundry basket before grabbing my phone from the counter and answering. "Hello?"

"She's lost her fucking mind."

"Who's lost her mind?"

He huffs into the phone. "My sister. You're not going to believe this."

I grin at his annoyance. The wildest thing his kid sister has ever done wouldn't make an elderly church lady blush. Melanie is way too responsible. Even when she was in high school, she acted like a scandalized nosy neighbor, tattling on us when Shawn and I snuck out to go to parties. "Lay it on me."

"She took a three-week vacation out of the blue."

I don't get it. "So? She's in a high-stress position. It is summertime. My vacation starts today too."

"Not done. She used some sketchy website to swap houses with a complete stranger for a couple weeks. This isn't a bed-and-breakfast situation. Trust me when I say something's wrong."

I grimace, feeling less casual about the situation. She's a bit of a control freak and not a spontaneous getaway kind of woman. Jetting off to Florida to stay in a stranger's house is completely out of character. "Mel's never been the 'feel free to put your feet on my coffee table' type," I admit.

"Never mind an unsupervised *stranger* living in her apartment. I don't know why she suddenly decided to do this, but it's not like her. Maybe she's on drugs. You hear stories about the fashion and publishing industries being full of drugs. Do you think she's gotten involved in that shit?"

"Not a chance. She's not the type—and drugs are more in the music business, not publishing. I've heard liquor is the poison of choice for writers. Maybe she just needed a break." I lean against the counter. "Agreed it's weird, but there's nothing you can do about it. She's an adult."

"Well, there's something we can do."

"*We?*"

"You've got to do me a favor and go to Florida, man."

I laugh. "I can't just go to Florida and spy on your sister."

He makes an agitated noise. "This is my little sister we're talking about. Mel? The girl who put the hyphen in anal-retentive?"

"I see your point. If you're so worried about her, why don't you check on her yourself?"

"Three reasons. One, she'd kick my ass for interfering—and if it all turns out to be fine and dandy, I don't want to trample the one time she's decided to do something outside her comfort zone. If it's all straightforward and safe, then this could be a good thing for her. Two, my boss won't give me the time off work."

"And three?"

He clears his throat. "The chick she switched houses with is a fucking fox."

"How do you know that?"

"I went over to Mel's as soon as I heard about this ridiculousness. I needed to see for myself the kind of person she was switching houses with in case they were some freak or a criminal just waiting to rip her off. I had visions of pulling up and Mel's apartment being empty except for the lightbulbs because her guest had cleaned her out or had thrown a raging party and trashed the place."

"Which wasn't the case."

He sniffs. "Not even close. But we got to talking, and you know how it is."

I shake my head. "And you've kindly offered to show her around the city?"

"Something like that."

"Something tells me you're still going to get your ass kicked by the end of this. One way or the other." I pause. "Mel really took off to Florida?"

"She did. If you go check on her for me, I'll even fly you down using my air miles."

I grin. "There *and* back."

"Damn, you caught that?"

"You blew it by being oddly specific."

"Fine, but you're paying for your own damn hotel!" He laughs. "Do we have a deal then?"

Two weeks in Florida, kicking up my heels on the beach, with only the small cost of checking on Shawn's sister? Maybe it's been a while since I've seen her, but Mel's the little sister I never had—and Shawn's like my brother. I owe it to him to make sure she's OK—and hell, I could use some time away from it all. "Text me the flight details."

············——············

Shawn emails me the itinerary as I'm walking into my apartment.

He has me on the first flight tomorrow.

It's short notice but worth it. I need the change of scenery, to be honest. I'm on my third and final year in my doctor of physical therapy program at NYU. I love massage therapy, but it's hard on the body. The past few years have been a whole lot of *all work and no play*. When I'm not studying, I'm working. Even the summers have been jammed with practicums in addition to my packed work schedule. I work full-time at one clinic and weekends at another. It's tight, but I want to come out of this degree with no debt.

I fill the sink with water and ice and plunge my forearms underneath, trying not to tense at the frigid temperature needling my skin. My body will thank me at the end of this—at the end of this summer too, when my practicum is done and my schedule downshifts from manic to hectic.

As I try to wind down, my mind keeps drifting to Mel. I haven't seen her in a few months. Doesn't feel that long, but there were times when she didn't make it to Sunday dinners or events with her family. Other times, she was there but I was away taking a seminar on Active Release Technique or whatever else that week.

She's the director of human resources at a magazine, and she recently did me a favor. I'd told her all about the hippies at Inner Space and the receptionist who may need a new job, based on a tense moment I walked in on. Sarah had looked like a deer in the headlights with Phyllis looming over her while Fern did nothing. I really should have asked Sarah first, but she confirmed my suspicions when she jumped at the job and aced the interview with Melanie.

Sarah seemed like a good person, so I'm glad I could help. Fern and Ziggy aren't bad people per se, but they do a lot of things that irk me—and I wouldn't be surprised if their main masseuse, Phyllis, is into some shady shit. With no questions asked, Mel did me a solid and gave Sarah a chance. I owe it to her as well as Shawn to make sure she's okay. The chances of Mel being involved in anything dangerous are next to impossible, but who am I to look a gift horse—with a plane ticket to Florida—in the mouth?

Chapter 3

Melanie

LAST WEEK, I HAD A DAY SO HORRENDOUS, I WAS TEMPTED to fake my own death. Six days and twelve hundred miles later, part of me wonders if it was really that bad.

But I know it was. Otherwise, I wouldn't be standing in a strange woman's apartment with my hands in her underwear drawer. I gnaw on my lower lip and stare at the tiny scraps of fabric—mostly thongs—tangled together in disarray. Shelby Kellerman's ass is way tinier than mine, probably from all the swimming she does. Her surfboard is propped in the corner of her bedroom, a silent *ta-da!* to her athleticism. It mocks me with its existence.

The nine hours a day I spend chained to my desk, plus two hours on the R train, have softened me considerably over the last few years. Shelby probably doesn't feel bad when she can only squeeze in the gym once a week. I bet her life gives her all the action she needs without an elliptical or a sadistic spin instructor named Nadia.

I bet she wouldn't have let herself be chased from a nude beach by embarrassment. She'd have cavorted with the best of them, probably arranging a beach volleyball game or water polo. Naked water polo where you sit on people's shoulders with crotches snuggled up to the backs of necks… And I can't even finish that train of thought.

I slept terribly last night, tossing and turning and regretting my overreaction at the beach yesterday.

The tiles are cool beneath my feet as I pace around Shelby's bedroom, soaking in the details of her life and the differences between us. Everything here is so… fresh. Buttery-yellow walls with white-painted trim. Light-silvery-gray sheets on the bed, covered with a turquoise chenille throw. A salty sweetness fills the air, and I still can't tell if it's the remains of her perfume or the ocean air wafting in through the huge window.

With an almost angry sigh, I move back to the dresser, scoop her tiny panties from the top drawer and drop them into the bottom one, and carefully arrange mine in their place according to type and color. They never felt boring until I found myself elbow deep in someone else's much more èxotic underwear. Wouldn't a pearl thong—I don't know—chafe?

I slide the bottom drawer open again for another voyeuristic glimpse. The first one I lift gingerly has two strings of beads that go way past thong territory up the front. Wouldn't these…*pinch* or get caught in pubic hair?

Don't be ridiculous, Melanie. Women like Shelby don't have pubic hair.

Annoyed with myself, I drop Shelby's thong back into the drawer and take my toiletry bag into her bathroom.

Sage-green tiles on the walls, white tiles on the floor, and there's sea glass in a dish atop the huge vanity. On the edge of her large tub must be thirteen different types of shampoos and conditioners. I crack the lid on a brand

I've never tried, admiring the musky vanilla scent. Is Shelby doing the same to my two lonely bottles that smell like toasted almonds and brown sugar?

I rearrange the hair products so the matching shampoos and conditioners aren't scattered all over and put the body washes on the opposite end. I pluck the towel lying by the sink and hang it on the rack. Staying in a stranger's house instead of a hotel is weird. It doesn't feel like my temporary sanctuary a thousand miles from home. It's like she just ran out to the store and will walk in any minute and catch me in her house, making it impossible to relax.

The fact that I'm alone and so far from home also makes me tense, but I had to get out of New York. I needed a break.

Straightening the living room helps. Shelby has a small collection of seashells on an end table, and I flip them around, admiring as much as displaying them to better showcase the delicate shades on the insides.

I know why I'm doing this—organizing things helps take my mind off the beach. But I came here to unwind, and isn't a nude beach the epitome of throwing your inhibitions and troubles to the wind?

"Why can't I just *relax*?"

Something orange flashes at the corner of my eye, and I whirl toward the open window. A tabby cat twitches its tail and stares at me with large, yellow eyes that seem to say *Bitch, get a grip*. Maybe Shelby doesn't talk to herself much.

"What's your name, buddy?" I walk over to the cat, who leans into my touch when I gingerly reach out. I've never had a cat, but my parents' neighbor had an

ornery, old Siamese that used to scratch me whenever
I tried to pet it. This guy's already way nicer. "Shelby
never told me your name." He must have hidden when
I was here earlier. He purrs when I stroke his forehead
with the pad of my thumb, realizing I'm not an intruder.
He looks like a Buddy. "I was about to make lunch.
You hungry, Buddy?"

Predictably, he doesn't answer, but he comes running when I use the can opener on the tuna I find in
the cupboard. I dish a portion into a small bowl and
smile at the little growly sounds he makes as he digs in.
I eat a sandwich one-handed while I organize the cans
in Shelby's cupboard. She eats a lot of chickpeas—or
doesn't, based on the seven cans I find. Lots of beans as
well, and lentils—something I've been meaning to eat
more of, but never quite get around to.

I lean against the counter and finish my sandwich,
eyeing the open floor plan. In square footage alone, my
apartment could fit into hers at least three times. There's
a door I hadn't noticed in the dining area that leads to a
shallow terrace with a charming wrought iron table and
matching chairs shaded beneath a turquoise umbrella.

All of this *and* an outdoor area that doesn't reek of
garbage? I may have to brush up on the rules of squatters' rights.

The cat bumps against my ankle, slipping through the
open door. No point worrying about him getting out; he's
obviously as free-spirited as his owner, so I leave the
door open for him, enjoying the smell outside anyway.

After washing my dishes and putting them away, I
wander back into the living room and sit on Shelby's
white couch. I've never seen a white couch outside of

decorating magazines and nightmarish tampon commercials. Maybe they're more common down here? The cat joins me a moment later and heads to a patch of sunlight streaming through the window.

I tap my foot against the floor and try to get more comfortable, but it's no use. I can't seem to settle into Shelby's perfect home, her perfect life. I'm haunted by the memory of genitalia flapping in the breeze. It's ridiculous that I'm this thrown off by some skin. I'm not a prude. I take the R train to work every day, and I've seen it all—sometimes on the same day. Naked people don't scare me. So what the hell am I doing hiding in this—admittedly very beautiful—place, still in my pajamas like I'm going to camp out on the couch for the rest of the day?

"I should just go back to the beach, shouldn't I?"

Buddy twitches his tail and stares at me, looking nonchalant and bored as only felines can. He turns back to look out the window. He's probably had a thousand adventures with his fun owner, doing fun things with fun people.

I sigh and check my phone.

The four missed calls from Thaddeus may have something to do with my desire to play hermit. He makes me feel vulnerable—and feeling vulnerable isn't good for a nude beach.

Shelby probably doesn't care about the lack of clothes while she's prancing up and down in the surf like a gazelle. Why have I let it bother me so much? What's one little, clothing-optional beach? Pictures aren't allowed, and while it's not crowded to the point of no privacy, there are enough people that no one really stands out. Only complete assholes would go there and stare.

Thaddeus and his messages can't chase me from my phone—because by locking it in a drawer for the rest of my vacation, I'd miss out on calls from Bailey. And I can't allow a little nudity to chase me from the beach.

Besides, it's not like *I* have to prance around without clothes.

Unless I want to.

If the mood strikes.

I get dressed, slipping my tankini on under a floaty sundress, pack another bag, and march out Shelby's front door and down the street. This time, I'm armed with knowledge and a big umbrella to block any excess flesh from my direct line of sight. I grabbed a large hat too, on the off chance someone slips past my first line of defense.

I normally dress more conservatively than a sundress, even when not at work, but that's nothing compared to what I'm about to do. This isn't about a bathing suit anymore; it's about redemption! I turn right and keep marching, determined to do this.

The last dregs of my pep talk fade when my feet hit the beach again, but I hold my head high and keep going. The key to survival is to block everyone else out. But try as I might not to look, ignoring blatant nudity is not in my wheelhouse.

I spread out my towel so my feet are pointed at the water and jam my umbrella into the sand at eleven o'clock, covering one side.

There. Simple.

I angle the wide brim of my hat down and pull out

my e-reader to focus on instead. Even with oversize sun-glasses and a hat hiding most of my face, I can't look at other people's bodies. It's rude.

And I don't want to get squawked at for being a creeper.

Soon I don't have to pretend to focus on my book. The story sweeps me up, and I chuckle at the woman going on an unexpected solo trip. Like me, but less tragic. Little by little, my muscles relax as the fresh air and soft crash of the waves work their magic. My legs stick out from the shade of the umbrella and start to warm from the sun, so I turn onto my belly to give my calves some tan time. Maybe I'll go home with a sun-kissed glow instead of a computer-screen pallor.

Not that it's likely to happen hiding in the shade. I tweak my umbrella, exposing more skin to the sun-shine, and I sigh happily at the warmth on my back. The sun feels different in Florida, more direct. In New York, the sun has to flirt with you, draw you out from the buildings to kiss you with its rays. Here, your body is frenched with heat. Everywhere.

How would it feel to let the sun touch me every-where? Nothing between the light and my skin but a thin sheen of sweat, right here on this beach.

What's really stopping me from being a little more… adventurous? I bite my lip, and exhilaration tingles through me. Could I strip down? I'm twelve hundred miles from home and leaving in a couple weeks. No one will ever know I got naked in public, surrounded by strangers.

But I'll know.

My fingers fumble with the button on my e-reader,

and I close the case and set it on the towel near my hip before flipping over once more.

I could have this experience living inside me when I return home, something secret I did for myself. A taste of being someone like Shelby—self-assured and confident. Doing it just to do it, not to impress anyone.

Not scared or inhibited. Not worried about what everyone's going to think and fretting over appearances.

To get my cover-up off, I have to remove my hat, but I leave the glasses on to hide behind. I slip the fabric over my head and fold it, hoping I look casual even while cringing toward my umbrella.

Sitting up and semi-hiding behind bent knees, I slowly slide the straps of my tankini top down my shoulders. Shit—that hinders rather than helps, so I pull them back up and grab the hem of my top, smoothly pulling it over my head.

Or try to, at least. The bottom of the shelf bra's elastic catches on my boobs, and a wrestling match ensues between the spandex and me. My shoulder twinges in protest as I finally wrench free and cover my boobs with my forearms, quickly flipping to lie on my stomach.

I'm really doing it. Nudity is happening!

OK, partial nudity, but still.

I squeeze my eyes shut behind my glasses. The towel is a little scratchy against my nipples when I shift my arms above my head to rest my head on them. No one would believe I have this in me. I hide my grin in the towel.

It's so audacious.

Well, it would be, if I opened my eyes and had more than my bare back exposed. People expose more on regular beaches wearing skimpy thong bikinis. My bottoms are boy-short style, maximizing coverage of my ample assets, but they might as well be a poncho compared to everyone else here. The point of this is to do something outside my comfort zone.

One, two, three. I turn and sit up before I have time to talk myself out of it. I fix the tankini top and fold it neatly over my cover-up, trying to focus on something other than the nearby beachgoers.

The blush scorching my face is so hot that I'm surprised it doesn't fog up my sunglasses. What would Shelby do in this situation? I don't know if nudity is her thing, but somehow I know she's brave and adventurous—even when other people are looking. Maybe especially then.

If I could survive the day from hell that drove me here in the first place, I can be shameless about taking my top off at a perfectly respectable nude beach. For heaven's sake, I'm not dropping trou on Fifth Avenue.

I turn toward my bag as though searching for sunscreen, surreptitiously checking over my shoulder to see if anyone's noticed the world's most awkward striptease.

Thankfully, no one's looking.

At all.

Huh. Come to think of it, I was probably more conspicuous covered up. The breeze feels incredible—maybe because I'm drowning in self-awareness, making my skin sensitive with adrenaline. Tiny champagne bubbles of giddiness rise inside me as the realization hits: I actually like this.

Pretending to look for sunscreen was a good idea now that more of me is exposed—tender parts that have never seen the sun. I take the sunscreen from my bag and slather more on my shoulders and belly. Then I'm rubbing lotion on my nipples. In public. But somehow it doesn't feel sexy or pervy. It just feels nice, and the coconut scent adds to the tropical escapism of the moment.

I lie back, taking in the surreal blue of the sky, and a ridiculous grin pulls at my lips. I've taken my top off, not discovered a miraculous cure for the common cold. As accomplishments go, it's nothing I'd speak of. Ever. And yet, it's so far from myself, it's like I've discovered a new person inside me. Someone who can do things she never thought herself capable of.

And it makes me want to do more. Push myself further.

My long hair is a curtain, and I gather it into a messy bun so it can't cover anything like a psychological security blanket. Might as well do this right, since I'm already committed. I slide my glasses off, removing the last hiding place I have. I blink until I acclimate to the brightness, until I get used to the fact that my face is as bare as my upper half.

Wild delight prances in my belly. I'm not about to invite myself into that group of college guys' beach volleyball game, or even talk to anyone, but one goal met leads to another challenge.

This sunscreen is waterproof.

I want to feel the cool water flowing over my warm skin.

Taking a deep breath, I stand and stride straight toward the water. Three steps in, I scramble back for my towel and slip my flip-flops on. Christ, the sand is hot.

The fact that I'm more worried about people judging my rookie mistake than my half-naked body makes me want to skip all the way to the water this time.

Instead, I walk slowly but steadily, focusing on the way my body moves, the way a simple thing like walking feels different. At home, I don't rush to get dressed, but even after a shower, I'm wrapped in a towel. Now, my unsupported breasts hang a little heavier, and I'm more aware of them with every footfall.

Maybe this is why some women don't wear bras. The freedom makes me more aware of my breasts, makes me feel more…I don't know, womanly? It certainly makes me pay more attention to my curves.

Wanting to feel the wet sand, I kick off my cheap flip-flops just before the waterline, gingerly stepping in to meet the waves that reach out to lap at my ankles. The water's warmer than I expected, and I keep going until it swallows me up to the waist. I duck under, up to my chin, and turn back to look at the way I came— also to make sure no one goes too close to the things on my towel.

Waving my arms makes little eddies around my body, tickling my skin in a pleasant way. I realize now that we miss out on so many simple sensate pleasures because we're always covered up in the name of decency. But what's indecent about the human body? We've all got similar parts. The same breast that a partner sucks to create pleasure can be suckled by a baby to take sustenance.

Why are women's nipples somehow obscene when men's aren't? Is it because women's can be used to create something? Are we covering our nipples to appease men's insecurities about their own jobless ones? If anything, that should be reversed. Women's nipples have a purpose. They're functional. Men's are there for decoration or pleasure. Theirs are the hedonistic ones that should be shamed into hiding.

I grin, making a mental note to suggest such an article to one of the columnists at the magazine. There was that craze too, where women covered pictures of their own nipples with cut out pics of men's before posting online. That could be tied into it as well. I should write this down or I'll forget. Maybe later—I'm enjoying myself too much.

I move so my breasts are bared, and rivulets of water tickle my body as they drip down. The breeze feels cooler than before, and my nipples tighten. Not every country is as prudish as America, but aren't we supposed to be the heathen, decadent exhibitionists? Sand coats my wet feet and trickles between my toes and under my soles, gently exfoliating my heels. It's not sexual—it's sensual. The same as the marvelous feeling of having the water and air and sun on my full torso. Experiencing these sensations in public is a new, simple pleasure.

Other countries don't devolve into anarchy because they're more liberal about their bodies and who sees what. Here, no one blinks an eye at violent movies, but if a woman breast-feeds in public, it's a scandal.

Is it all about context?

I tuck a few stray hairs behind my ear and reach up to tighten my bun.

That's got to be part of it. I mean—

"*Melanie?*"

Stuck inside my train of thought, I turn toward the

man, my emotional safety net of anonymity torn away as four realizations slam into me at once.

It's my brother's best friend, Blake fucking Wilde.

I still have a crush on him.

I'm completely topless.

And he's staring at my tits.

I cover my breasts with my hands and spin to run away, but the maneuver fails because sand is not your friend when you're attempting a quick getaway. I try to duck down to cover my chest and belly but go too far. Salty water splashes over my face and up my nose.

Panic sets in and I flail around, legs going rubbery at my sheer mortification.

Oh God, I'm going to die topless in front of Blake. It's so undignified. Salt burns my sinuses and I gag. Strong, warm arms grip my hips from behind and hold me steady while I cough out the last of the stinging water and flounder in the shallow waves.

"It's OK, Mel. I've got you. You OK? Let's go sit down."

"I'm half-naked!" Yes, point it out in case he missed your nudity the first time. *Idiot.* "I'm OK." I sniffle and wipe my face. "My towel's just over there." I nod toward it since my hands are busy covering my assets.

"OK, let's go. I promise I won't look."

Chapter 4

Blake

I TOTALLY LOOKED.

Fuck. *Me*.

This is Melanie. Pain-in-the-ass, uptight little Mel… but the sun glistening off her womanly curves is short-circuiting my brain and making it rebel against seeing her as anything remotely resembling a sister. She's soft and supple, and I want to feel her skin with my hands and mouth to see if it's as smooth as it looks. That is *not* why I'm here. The fact she took a spontaneous vacation was outside the norm for her—or so we thought. Now I'm not so sure.

I see her at her parents' house for dinners, but now it's like I've never seen her before. Maybe I haven't. Who is this fearless woman? Naked in public with the most perfect… Yeah, I'm going to hell for even looking.

"What the hell are you doing here?" She pulls away and crosses her arms over her chest, but the sight of her flesh spilling out from behind her forearms is one hell of a distraction.

I focus on her unique hazel eyes—a shade somewhere between green and yellow—but damn my peripherals and the way they show me things about her body I should not be seeing. I promised Shawn I'd check up on his little sister, not check her out. "Vacation. Shawn mentioned you were in town too, so I thought I'd find you and say hi, see what you're up to. Didn't know you're a fan of nude beaches, Mel."

"Melanie. Mel's a boy's name." Her usual response is automatic, but what's new is the way her gaze slowly crawls up my body, making me feel exposed even though I've got shorts on. My ego smiles when her lips curl into a smile. She nods at a towel and umbrella a little way away. "This is me."

I grab my stuff where I dropped it on the sand and follow her.

I look away while she puts her bathing-suit top back on. It's a relief not to have her ample tits in my face, but I can't help regretting their disappearance.

What am I, twelve?

"How'd you find me? Miami's a big place."

I shake my head. "Your friend Bailey sent me Shelby's address. I went there and you were gone, so I decided to hit the beach for a while. I called and left a message on your cell. You had a mission in your eyes when you were coming out of the water. That was how I knew it was you."

"Same scary glare?"

I spread my large towel out beside hers while she adjusts the umbrella to give us both shade.

"You always were intense," I say. I settle next to her on my towel, angling slightly away from her.

"I had an article idea for the magazine. Speaking of... Hang on." Mel digs in her bag for her phone and thumbs a note into it. "Done." She blows her nose into a tissue, grimacing before tucking it back into a pocket in her bag. "So, Shawn sent you to check up on me, huh?"

I shake my head. "No, I was just—"

"Cut the crap. You've been rumbled." She stares at me with a shade less intensity than a Cold War interrogator. "You decide to drop by in *Florida*? My brother and Bailey are the only ones I told that I'd be here."

"Well, I was on vacation too. Fine, he asked me to make sure you were OK." I don't mention the flying-me-to-Florida part.

"Why wouldn't I be?" She bites her lip.

I tilt my head. "Swapping houses with a stranger doesn't really sound like you, though I have to admit you look perfect... Seem fine, I mean." Where the hell did my game go?

She hands me a new water bottle and twists the cap off her already opened one while staring at the ocean. "I guess. Nothing wrong with shaking things up, is there? Getting away from it all? Taking a break from things to try something new?"

"Nothing wrong with change."

She regards me with that shrewd gaze. "When's the last time we saw each other?"

I think back. We've both missed a couple dinners at her parents' house, so it's been about three months. "Shawn's going-away party?"

She smiles. "He was so obnoxious."

"Insufferable. He really thought he was going to stay in Australia for the rest of his life."

"My favorite thing was how he kept dispensing advice about going for your dreams."

I laugh. "And then a month and a half later, he slunk back home, dehydrated and peeling—"

"And arachnophobic."

"Classic Shawn."

"He's always been a free spirit," Mel says. "Even now, in a way, he plays for a living."

"Programming isn't playing."

"I know." She sighs. "He just seems to have more free time to figure things out. But no one can ever be mad at him. Things seem to click into place for my brother."

She's the first to celebrate Shawn's successes, so I know this isn't as simple as jealousy about his freedom. His lifestyle doesn't seem like something she'd want. Maybe she just needed a break. Does her talk about figuring things out mean she's struggling with her job? Is that why she came here—to get away from her own life?

"His job's easier in a lot of ways," I prompt. "He's not managing HR for a whole company, for one."

She tucks her legs underneath her like a mermaid sitting on a rock, which only plays up the dangerous curve of her hips. "True. I do like having that power."

"Thanks for giving my friend Sarah a job there."

"I gave her a shot. So far, she's more than holding up her end of the bargain. You'd said she was in a tough place?"

I lean back on my hands. "It's not that they're bad people, but they're very 'to be here, you need to drink the Kool-Aid.' Sarah was working reception at the spa, and trust me when I say she needed to get out of there."

"But you're there," Mel points out. "Is it really that bad?"

"I'm only in on the weekends when no one else is. My interactions with the owners and other employees are minimal."

Mel narrows her eyes. "Are you and Sarah a thing?"

"No. She's got a boyfriend—a club owner slash DJ, Jack. He's a pretty cool guy. We've met a few times. Sarah and I are just friends."

"She's very pretty."

Something about the way she says that is too casual. Mel's not one to mince words. "She's cute, but she's not my type."

"Why not?" Her eyes meet mine with more heat than the hot sand.

It takes a herculean effort to keep my gaze on hers instead of it moving down her body. "I'm not really into waifs."

Her lips twitch like she's trying not to smile. "And the spa owners are awful?"

"They've got some weird ideas about things and they're extremely cliquey, but they're harmless if you're not a receptionist."

"What does that mean?"

"I'm an independent contractor with them, so I'm not technically an employee. I don't have to deal with them and their day-to-day operations as much. They're totally useless when it comes to running things smoothly. To make sure they understood, I left a note *and* told both of the owners in person that I'm on vacation for the next two weeks. They still keep scheduling appointments for me. My phone's blowing up with messages from Ziggy telling me about the new appointments, and others from the new receptionist telling me she's rescheduled those for when I'm back."

Melanie grimaces. "I've got a situation of my own like that. It's annoying."

"It is, but Fern and Ziggy pay well." I shrug. "I'm trying to get through this last year of school without crippling debt hanging over my head."

"Why not keep massaging instead of going into physical therapy? I thought you loved it."

"I do. People's bodies tell me so much more than they realize."

Her phone dings and she checks it, frowning before turning it off and tossing it back in her purse. "I'd like to pitch this phone into the ocean."

"I hear that."

"What do people's bodies tell you?"

I take another sip of water. "For example? I know your right shoulder is bugging you from the way you're holding your arm slightly closer to your side. Probably from the way you hold the mouse when using a computer. I can tell your back hurts right in the middle by the way you hunched your shoulders and stiffened when you adjusted the umbrella."

"You could tell all that from the few minutes we've been together?"

"I also know exactly how to make it feel better."

Her mouth softens as her lips part in surprise.

I smile. "I love massage, but it doesn't love me. It's too hard on the body. PT is still in the area of what I want to do, and it's something I can do full-time for a couple decades—even longer when people work under me and I can reduce my hours. Massaging as a career has a lit fuse, and I've already been doing it for nearly a decade.

"My hands have suffered and changed over the seven

years I've done it. There's a reason you don't see many older massage therapists. From the first massage we give, our years are numbered. My thumbs used to stand straight up; now they bend back more severely." I give her a thumbs-up to demonstrate. "Besides, the money's better in physical therapy."

Mel slides on an oversize pair of sunglasses, blocking her eyes. "Sounds like you've got it all figured out."

"Nah, but I have a solid plan and that counts for a lot. What about you?"

"What about me?" She crosses her arms, but it's more like she's trying to hide than be confrontational.

"Are you happy where you are?" I ask.

"Kind of heavy conversation for a day at the nude beach."

"Maybe. Still, are you where you want to be in life?" I gently prod.

Her chest rises and falls three times. "Right now, I think I am."

I need to see her eyes. She doesn't move when I lean in and slide her glasses down the bridge of her nose. I want to kiss her, but I don't. Her expression tells me she wants me to, but her brother would probably kill me.

So I swallow and sit back instead. "Good."

A volleyball hits the sand between us—which I take as confirmation to back off. Mel grabs it and looks around for the owner before bumping it over to her.

"Hey," the tall, blond woman says. "You want to join my boyfriend and me in a game of doubles?"

Mel shakes her head. "I don't really play."

I stand and brush the sand from my shorts. "Stop trying

to hustle the woman, Mel." I look at the woman while offering my hand to Mel. "She played in high school."

Mel reluctantly takes my hand. "Not beach volleyball."

I shrug and pull her up. "So maybe they'll have a chance."

She shakes her head all the way to the net, where we shake hands with Ruth and Xander—our competition. Mel tells me to go up front, so I do.

Her assertiveness is kind of sexy.

Ruth serves a hard one to the back of our side. Mel bumps it up to me and yells, "You!" which makes me pause, and the ball hits the ground on our side.

She laughs. "What was that, Wilde?"

"You?"

She tosses the ball back to Ruth. "That means it's yours. You were supposed to set it up so I could spike it."

"I know. It's just that your Amazonian cry startled me. I thought we were going for a slow hustle by lulling them into a false sense of security."

Mel moves back to her position. "You know what I've realized about myself? I don't like playing games. I like winning them."

My own competitive spirit rises to match hers. I also played a lot of sports in school, so this should be interesting. Ruth lobs one that Mel smacks toward the net, and I set it straight up just in time for Mel to come screaming up to spike it beside Xander. We slam a vicious high five and get back into position.

We don't get a point, but we get to serve.

I'd forgotten how intense Mel can get. Her focus is like a laser beam, and she throws herself around the sand with reckless disregard for her own well-being, but it is something to watch. No hesitation. She goes for it all, outmaneuvering me—and I'm definitely not a slouch physically. Soon we're both glistening with sweat and five points up.

I can't help but notice how well we work together after that initial misfire, angling around each other without a word spoken like we're made of magnets that snap automatically in place, or pushing each other where we need to go with a single touch of a hand on a shoulder or hip.

Xander counters Mel's blistering serve with a bump that brings it back to our side instead of setting it up for a spike. It soars through the air in a lazy arc.

We shout "mine" at the same time and collide, ending up in a tangle of limbs on the ground with me on top, pressed fully against her. Her face is flushed from the game, and we're both sweating… And all at once I can no longer keep myself from seeing her as the strong, vibrantly beautiful woman she is instead of who she's always been to me.

I lick my lips and her smile softens, her hands caressing my shoulders.

I *definitely* can't kiss her.

Chapter 5
Melanie

I WANT HIM TO KISS ME.

The sand burns my back and Blake burns my front, and I want him to make me feel good with those hands and that amazing attention to physical details. With barely a glance, he knew every ache in my body earlier. Well, every ache except the very insistent one between my legs. It hammers away at my common sense, demanding I remove every stitch of our clothing and explore his body with my tongue. Kiss me? No. I want him to *make love* to me.

From the way he's looking down at me with his pupils dilating even in this light, I'm pretty sure he wants that as much as I do, but something holds him back.

He gets up and helps me to my feet. We thank Ruth and Xander and excuse ourselves from the game while brushing sand off our bodies. As we head back to our towels, all I can think about is how good he just felt.

I smile at him, hoping to keep it friendly and not raise suspicion—at least until we're behind closed doors. "You should come over for supper. Check out my Switch partner's house."

"Yeah? What are you having?"

You? In my dreams. But hey, I sat topless on a nude

beach. Maybe today I can do *other* things I always assumed were impossible. A slow, wicked smile crawls over my face. "I'll have to see when we get there."

We pack up the towels, and he insists on carrying my bag back to Shelby's. I pretend I'm enjoying the silence. Really, I'm afraid I'll fall back into old habits and chicken out if we talk too much.

And I need this to happen. New York Melanie would never ignore calls from work. New York Melanie would never take off her top in public.

New York Melanie is way too responsible and level-headed to sleep with her brother's best friend—no matter how hot he is, with his six-pack and pecs and chiseled V-muscles. And that smile that's made me tingle since middle school.

But I'm not in New York. I'm on vacation. I've Switched.

Maybe it's the heat, or maybe it's the nudity going to my brain, but I'm not going to chicken out of this.

He clears his throat. "Shawn seems impressed with your Switch woman."

"I'm impressed with her." I unlock the front door and lead Blake inside. "There are these pictures in her bedroom—I'll show you." I walk him through the living room, not pointing out all my handiwork that suddenly seems fussy and uptight.

"Wow, it's bright in here. Airy."

I grin. "Like a furniture catalog. I can't believe how much space they get down here. It nearly makes me agoraphobic."

"I'm used to being crammed in tiny rooms massaging people. This much space is obnoxious. I'd become a compulsive hoarder, buying things just so I didn't feel so exposed."

"I know what you mean." I walk faster and face forward so he can't see my silly smile. His presence here feels like a sign, a gift. One I hope to unwrap in the very near future.

God, maybe vitamin D enters the nipples and goes straight to your brain. "Bathroom to the right, an office in here." I swing the white door open to reveal yet another huge room with a desk and shelves in complete disarray. I won't touch this room. Going through some-one's personal files and papers is inappropriate.

Not to mention that there definitely isn't enough space in those drawers for this much paperwork. If I started, I'd be collating and sorting for weeks until I was forced to buy her more furniture for storage.

Finally, I push open the door to the bedroom and walk to the pictures on the wall. "Here we are."

"Surfboard in the bedroom? Kinky."

I laugh. "Grinding on that wood like Beyoncé? It's not just for decoration." I point at one of the many gor-geous shots of Shelby. "There she is."

Blake's body heat radiates against my arm as he moves closer to look at the pictures. "Ah, yeah. She's definitely Shawn's type. I can see why he's so interested in playing tour guide for her."

Jealousy twists in my stomach like a shrieking eel, but I keep my voice level. "She's gorgeous. She could be a model. She eats like one too."

"Fridge full of twigs and berries?"

"Yeah. Maybe I should start eating those things."

"Only if you like the taste. It would be a crime to lose those curves because you think you should."

Pure lust radiates from his eyes, and I step toward him—but he shakes his head as though clearing it and smiles blandly at me. "So, what's for supper?"

Looks like I'll be having sexual frustration. "Let's go have a look in her cupboard."

I grabbed a few things—mostly carbs—at the store yesterday after the beach. Nothing makes you feel better about a nude beach fiasco than stress eating mini cupcakes over the sink. I also threw together a light pasta salad for supper today.

I dish the pasta onto our plates while Blake tears up greens for a salad. God, he's got nice hands. Powerful, large, and yet elegantly shaped instead of being meaty mitts. Who am I kidding? They could look like he was wearing ham hocks, and I'd want them all over my body.

"Do you like it so far?"

I blink, shaking away the image of his hands sliding up my thigh. "What?"

"Florida."

My shoulder twinges a little when I reach for two plates. "It's different."

He bumps his hip against mine. "You're overwhelming me with details."

I'd give more, but my head spins from his casual proximity. "The people are different. They're not manically rushing from place to place and fighting for another inch of standing room on the train. I didn't think ambling happened outside Western novels, but it seems to be the default pace."

He laughs and dishes the salad onto our plates. I hold up a bottle of sparkling wine and he nods, so I pour us each a glass. "Do you want to eat in here or on the patio?"

"She's got a patio too?" He shakes his head. "She's got to be shrinking in on herself, trying to combat the claustrophobia of your apartment."

Shelby's place feels cozier now that Blake's here. I grab my plate and head to the patio. "It's cramped, but it's homey. Besides, you only saw it once for about three minutes when Shawn helped me move."

"And you've probably got even more bookshelves crammed in there now." He pauses and adds, "What a view."

I follow his appreciative gaze to the sliver of ocean peeking through the buildings, crowned with a section of blue sky being painted ombré by the sunset. "Yeah, I'd be OK with keeping this view. How's your hotel?"

He shrugs and digs into his pasta. "It's OK. Nice pasta, by the way."

"Thanks." Everything he does makes my thighs clench and makes me wish I was what he was touching, tasting.

Putting in his mouth.

I can think of a few things I'd like him to put into mine.

My cheeks flame and I focus on my plate, unsure how to act on these feelings. I've known Blake for so many years, and I'm sure he's never seen me as more than Shawn's annoying kid sister. Despite my vicious crush on him, I used to tattle on them to Mom and Dad.

I sneak glances at him while he eats and enjoys the view, wishing for a bridge from "annoying teen with a crush" to "bold temptress." Even when interviewing Sarah, I got tongue-tied thinking about him. I ended up telling her we hadn't seen each other in years, which wasn't correct. I was trying to downplay and that came out. It's ridiculous how he makes me feel like an awkward kid. I felt so confident at the beach. How is that possible? I was half-naked, but now I'm way more awkward and vulnerable with my clothes on.

Is that the solution? If I stood up and took my top off, giving him a sensuous striptease, there'd be no mistaking my signals.

And I'd die of mortification if he wasn't into me.

But letting this go isn't the answer either. My breaths increase. I can do this. I can be the temptress.

Waiting until he makes eye contact again, I slowly stretch my arms to the sides and bring my hands back to my hair, lazily, sensually touching the nape of my neck.

"Shoulders bothering you again? Look, I can see you're hurting. I'd be an asshole not to offer you a massage." He holds his hands up. "Purely therapeutic."

Whomp, whomp. So much for sexy.

But he'll be touching me. I'd prefer a massage with a "happy ending," but the battle's not over yet. "Well, you've already seen my breasts today. A massage can't be any more embarrassing than that." I carry our empty dishes back inside and set them on the counter to deal with later.

"*Embarrassing* isn't the word I'd choose." His voice comes out an octave lower than normal.

My belly flutters at the want in it. "What word would you use?"

"I...shouldn't say."

Shivers crawl up my back. Maybe I should turn and kiss him, but a strange new part of me wants to drive him a little wild and draw this out. I've wanted Blake for, well, ever. I move to Shelby's couch and peel off my top, keeping my back to him. I lower myself to the cushions. "I'm ready." I don't hear him move closer, so I wiggle my ass, ostensibly to get more comfortable. Hopefully this looks more tempting than it feels. "Blake?"

"Yeah." He stands to my left side. "So, sometimes we get pain in one area because muscles farther away are tense, and it pulls everything slightly out of alignment."

"OK."

"I'm going to start on your legs and work my way up."

"Whatever you think is best. My body's yours." Was that too lame and obvious? I press my face against the pillow, hiding the blush. Does he understand how much I want him? I'm being as brazen as I can be.

He slips a pillow under my shins and lights my calves on fire with strong, steady strokes of his hands. Now that his hands are on me, sending jolts of heat through my core, I realize how deeply in trouble I am.

I smile and try not to purr. By the time he moves up to my hamstrings, I'm basically a puddle.

An incredibly horny puddle.

"Is it tender there?" His fingers knead my inner thighs, and my breath catches in my throat.

"What?" I croak, paralyzed by his hands. I want them on every inch of my skin.

"You're tensing up. Does it hurt there?"

"A little," I say. It's easier than the truth.

"Do you want me to stop?"

"No." I look at him over my shoulder. "Don't stop."

Chapter 6

Blake

TOUCHING HER WHEN I FEEL THIS ATTRACTION ISN'T RIGHT. It's a false pretense. I know her shoulder hurts and I want to ease that, but I also want so much more. She accepted a massage, nothing more. I'm going to keep the rest to myself.

But what if she wants more too?

No. I'll give her a massage, but I definitely won't kiss her. That would be crossing a line, and I'm a professional. There's no reason this can't just be like another day at the office. I've seen hundreds— *thousands*—of nearly naked women on my massage table. It's no big deal.

Except she's got the cutest little dimples on her lower back, right above her heart-shaped ass. God, I love a woman with curves. I press my thumbs gently into the dimples and roll them up her spine. She arches against me like a cat, and my cock stiffens.

It's just Mel. She's not a real woman—she's basically family. She annoyed me half to death at least three hundred times growing up, just like a real sister. It doesn't matter that I haven't seen her for a few months. We know each other too well for this to be sexy. We're *friends*. It's just skin and muscles. Focus on the trapezius.

But she doesn't feel like family, and on the other side of the soft skin I'm touching on her back—pressed against the couch—are her breasts. All I want is to see how they fit the palms of my hands, and then I want to claim those Cupid's bow lips with my own and feel the vibration of her moan against my mouth.

I blink hard. No, I don't want to claim anything. I'm just giving her a massage, working the tension out of her muscles.

"Mmm, that feels so good."

Her throaty moan slams me low in the belly, and my abs tense. I lean lower with the intention of kissing the back of her neck, but pull up short just in time. My rapidly dwindling self-control shrugs, leaving me alone with my hands on the softest skin I've ever felt.

"Your skin's gorgeous." The words just slip out.

"Your *hands* are gorgeous. This is the best back rub I've ever had."

I blow out slowly. Back rub, that's all.

Does she want this to be more than a therapeutic massage? Is she into this being more? "I could make this feel even better, Mel." I move a little closer to her, kneeling near her waist.

She shifts her hips a little and turns her face toward me, looking back over her shoulder. On the beach, she was as exposed as she is right now, but her expression was surprised and shocked. Now, with this heated invitation sparkling in her eyes, it's much more devastating.

All of the blood in my body is rushing to one place, and it's not my brain.

Reaching back, she traces the top of my shorts, where the fabric meets my belly. She drives my nerves crazy with that tentative touch—a complete contrast to the decisive expression on her face—and I swallow hard, my self-control ground down to a nub, but fuck it. "Mel, would you like to turn over?"

She nods and slowly spins around, covering her breasts with her forearms, a faint blush darkening her cheeks.

I take my time drawing my hands down her ribs, pausing on her hips as I lock my gaze with hers. "You're so beautiful. Don't hide yourself from me, OK?" She nods and moves her hands, goose bumps forming beneath my fingers as I draw them up between her breasts to trace her collarbones and the elegant slope of her neck.

Her breaths come faster, and I hold off as long as I can before palming her breasts and feeling the nipples harden into stiff peaks. Bending to kiss her ribs, I gently squeeze and then kiss my way to her right nipple.

She sighs when I suck it into my mouth, swirling my tongue across the sensitive bud. Her fingers find the back of my neck and pull me closer, so I follow her cue and suck harder until she moans. Then I switch to the other nipple. I lavish it with the same attention until her fingers clench my hair.

"Kiss me."

The second word is barely out of her mouth before I crush my lips against hers, melding her lips to mine. She wraps her arms around me like she's scared I'll try to escape, but I couldn't pull away if I wanted to. She's like raspberries and something sweeter, and I taste her mouth with my tongue, plunging it deep inside. Her lips are so damn soft, but they return my aggressive exploration, matching me perfectly. I want so much more.

I'll kiss her, but that's all. I'm not going to take advantage of this situation.

Her breasts spread against my chest when she pushes up against me. I nip her lip and circle her nose with mine before going in for another taste. Her kisses are bold and direct, and they drive me fucking crazy—just like she does. She doesn't tease me or hesitate with a tentative tongue.

I pull back and kiss her jaw before nibbling the delicate shell of her ear. She shivers beneath me—when did I climb on top of her?—but her legs squeeze my waist with firm pressure. I want to taste her neck, so I do.

If this is wrong, it wouldn't feel so goddamn right.

I bet all roads to hell start with a similar sentiment, the same hollow justification. I kiss her one last time, sweetly, and tuck an escaped curl behind her ear. I clench my teeth in an effort to gather my control and pull back.

She burns me with a hooded gaze. "Blake. I want you."

I scoop her off the couch in one fluid movement and carry her down the hall to the bedroom.

I'm a good guy, not a stupid one.

When a woman like this tells you she wants you, you consider yourself lucky and give her everything you've got. No holding back, no hesitation.

She breathes into my ear, nibbling the earlobe with her teeth while I walk us to the bed and set her on it. Mel reaches for me when I stand up.

"Come here."

I shake my head. "Take off your bottoms. I want to see you."

She bites her lip, but I keep my gaze on hers, not hiding my physical appreciation of her. After a moment, she eases the boy shorts over her hips. I need to see her naked. Now. Too impatient to wait for her to continue removing them at this glacial pace, I snatch the shorts from her hands and draw the fabric down her thighs and off. I ball up the bottoms and toss them away without a glance, leaving her naked on the bed.

The soft, fading sunlight streams through the window across the room, reflecting light onto her. It highlights everything I want to taste and touch, but she presses her legs slightly together and I frown.

"Are you trying to hide from me?"

She swallows hard and lets her hands rest on the bed at her sides. "No."

"Good." I slowly strip off my shorts. Her gaze sharpens, so I take my time.

They say size doesn't matter, but I've never heard any complaints.

When her eyes widen and she licks her lips, I grin. "Like what you see?"

She nods, and I slowly stroke myself a couple times. Her gaze flicks from my cock to my face like she's embarrassed to look for too long or it's dirty or wrong but she can't resist. Her thighs rhythmically squeeze, stimulating herself, but I want to be the one making her feel good. I trail my hands up to her knees, gently spreading them.

Her dark curls hide her arousal from me, so I kneel on the bed and flutter my fingertips, drawing the wetness up to rub her clit, teasing her with barely there touches. Her hips chase my hand around, and she grinds out a half hiss, half groan of frustration before sagging back on the mattress.

I want to go as hard and fast as I can, but this isn't a race. Now that we've decided to do this, I'm going to do it right, savoring her like she needs to be. It's been a few months for me, so I want it to last.

I grin. "I never did see to that shoulder. Turn over."

"But—"

I flip her so her ass is in the air and caress her outer thigh and one cheek. "What is it about this sexy ass you're ashamed of?" My belly tightens, the sudden blood surge making me ache. "Do you know how hot you are? How much I want you?" She tenses and then relaxes under my hand when I knead the other ass cheek and bend to lick the dimples on her lower back. She tastes salty like the ocean, and she shivers when I gently blow across the dampness I created. "I promise I'll make you feel good, Mel."

"Mel's a b—"

Her words cut off as my teeth sink in.

Her hips twitch. "Did you just bite my ass?"

I softly rub the place I indeed just bit. "Mmm-hmm." I do the same to the other side, and she moans.

"I think I like it."

"You think?" I slide a finger inside her and smile. "Yeah, you do." She gasps and grinds against the bed.

I bend her knee and lift her thigh, replacing my hand with my mouth as she rolls over to her back and grants me complete access.

Her legs tense and kick in slow motion, and her breath stutters. A thin, high-pitched whine resounds in her throat when I finally circle her clit with my tongue and tease it with quick, soft movements.

Her hand flaps toward my head, trying to hold me

in place. With that, I know it's time. I lock my tongue against her and relentlessly lave her with deep, steady, hard licks. Her belly tenses until she's almost sitting up, but she flops back down.

"God, oh my God, Blake."

It's a one-sided conversation. My mouth is a little busy.

She rocks her hips harder. She's close, so I keep it steady, not changing a thing, except for the two fingers I plunge in to pulse against her G-spot.

Her arousal drips down to my palm, and I want to lick her clean, but there's no way I'm stopping now. I want to show her how beautiful, how amazing she is.

Her toes alternately curl and point, and her body tenses.

Close, so close.

With a wrenching cry, she shatters around my fingers, under my tongue, squeezing in a way that makes me wish I'd been inside her when she came.

Next time.

Chapter 7

Melanie

HE'S TURNED MY BLOOD TO WARM CARAMEL. IT OOZES slowly through my body, leaving nothing but sweetness pulsing to the beat of my heart. I feel…delicious.

Blake's hands have nothing on his tongue—and his hands are sinfully devastating. His lips burn a trail, inch by inch, up my belly. Sated as I am, when he reaches my collarbone I'm lit up with the need for more of that mouth. More of those hands.

More of everything.

His body blankets mine, skin on skin. It covers me with his warmth and the weight of a thousand imagined fantasies finally come to life. His dark eyes melt me, and the proximity and the light streaming into the room kick up flecks of gold and green I've never noticed before. I'm about to idiotically mention them when he buries his hand in my hair, cradling my head and lifting me into a deep, unhurried kiss. Heat unfurls slowly in my belly, like the petals of an exotic flower I've only seen in pictures and never touched until now.

I uncurl under his touch, against his body, opening for more.

How many times did I dream of these hands meandering up my thigh and touching me? How many nights did I lie in bed, tortured by the lilting cadence of his voice just next door in Shawn's room and pretending Blake was whispering sweet nothings in my ear?

Pretending he was hesitating outside my room, and any moment he'd come inside and gently shut the door if only I wished hard enough.

Padding across my beige carpet, losing articles of clothing as he progressed.

Whispering my name as he sat on the edge of my bed.

Crawling under the covers with me when I lifted the blanket in invitation.

Spooning me from behind, gently petting my skin with those hands that had always seemed too large for his body.

Turning me over and slipping my nightie over my head.

Lips gently meeting mine and teasing them apart while his hands did the same to my legs.

God, I hope there are some condoms in Shelby's nightstand.

"Unless you've got condoms, you should check the nightstand." My voice comes out breathy and deep. I should have had him check before he got me off, but the postorgasmic haze makes it hard to care about balance. I'm OK with owing him one.

I just want more.

He nuzzles my neck. "Are you in a hurry?"

My nipples tighten. A strange boldness sizzles through my core and cuts off all sense of aloofness. "Blake, I've wanted you since the first time I came home and saw you playing video games with Shawn. I've basically had ten years of foreplay."

"Ten years of foreplay, and I only got you off once?" He shakes his head. "I can do better than that."

"What?"

He drags his teeth across my nipple on his way back down.

"Where are you going?"

He kisses down my belly. "Way I see it, if there are condoms in that drawer, I won't be able to wait to put one on and sink inside you." He circles my clit with his tongue. "And if there aren't any condoms in the drawer, I'll have to leave and find the nearest store so I can get back here as quickly as I can and sink inside you." He laps his way down and then slowly back up to my clit. "Either way, it's going to end the same."

My head spins. "Sounds like a happy ending to me."

"Maybe." His fingers deftly probe my slit, getting coated before sliding back inside. I arch my back. "But if I don't look in the nightstand, I can keep doing this."

"What are they, Schrödinger's condoms?"

He groans and sucks at me. "The fact you know about that"—he moves his fingers faster—"is so damned sexy."

My response is stolen by the white-hot stabs of pleasure that shiver through me. They undulate out in waves that make my hips shake. I clench around his fingers again, violently, suddenly coming. "*Please.*"

"You're so wet, Mel, and you taste so good. I almost don't want to stop." He sits up, stark want on his face. "Almost." He reaches for the nightstand, and I swear to God, I cross my fingers, toes, and labia that there are condoms in that drawer.

Please, please, please.

Blake pulls out a gold foil packet, tears it open, and unrolls the condom over his rigid length. He's so thick.

The fleeting fearful thought about his size evaporates as his thighs touch mine, nudging them open wide, wider. He reaches down and rubs the tip of his cock around, getting nice and wet before pausing at my entrance.

His gaze smolders when it meets mine, and he gently brushes the pad of his thumb over my cheekbone. His lips barely graze mine.

Then he enters me with a long, fluid thrust, stretching me with his girth. If he were any bigger, it wouldn't fit, but I'm so turned on that the tight fit is perfect. I whimper and clutch at his back.

He knows I like it, and he circles his hips, languidly grinding against me as he fills me completely.

I wrap an arm around his neck, intent on pulling him down, but he's so strong that I end up hanging off his neck with my back a few inches off the mattress.

He slides one hand up my spine and down my arm to take my hand, twining our fingers together. He props himself on his elbows, pressing our chests together. With my free arm around his neck, it's like we're dancing—only this dance is driven by the rhythm of our hips grinding together, moved by the pulse of his thrusts.

I hold him so tightly that my arms ache. My thighs hurt from clenching his waist so hard.

I drop my legs to the mattress, reaching behind him to grab his ass. My eyes roll back at the way it tenses and flexes.

"God, Mel," he grinds out. "So goddamn good."

His hips are tireless, driving into me, pounding my

body with a relentless pleasure that weighs my limbs down until all I can do is hold on and meet his thrusts. His tip stimulates my G-spot, and I twitch when new muscles start to tighten deep inside me.

"Blake," I whisper, instead of screaming every obscenity in my vocabulary. I turn inward as everything stops for an infinite, trembling moment that pierces through my consciousness and shreds me.

Blake's thrusts become wilder, faster, and he stiffens and moans, nipping my shoulder with his teeth. I come through the other side shaking, sweaty, and feeling like the most beautiful creature who ever lived.

Feeling like my bones have been replaced with warm water.

It was even better than my wildest dreams. Granted, I had zero experience and a rigid imagination back then. But I couldn't have predicted the pure, unadulterated satisfaction rolling through me right now.

In Shelby's bed.

Oh God, I used one of her condoms. Who am I even?

Blake pulls out and rolls onto his back beside me, his heavy breaths matching mine. He did most of the work; I don't know why I'm breathing so hard. I grin.

He nuzzles my neck. "What's so funny?"

"I was just thinking how you probably burned off way more calories than I did."

He smiles. "That's a cardio program I could get behind."

"Screw leg day. Every day is genital day."

He wraps me up and pulls me to his chest. I'm too floaty to resist, though I feel like I should. "I forgot how funny you are." He gives me a little squeeze.

"I haven't been funny in years," I admit.

"I know all your secrets. I know you. You're an ass-kicking, take-no-prisoners smart-ass."

"Maybe I was." I sigh. When was the last time I felt like that?

"You *are*," he insists. "You had a comeback for everything. No one could burn you when you were younger. It was awesome. I always loved how you took zero shit from anyone."

"I did a lot of faking. I was an insecure kid." I hate how he talks about me like I was something amazing. It makes me feel like even more of a loser now. "I'm still not that confident."

"Really?" He pushes up to rest on his elbow. "Because today I saw you topless on a nude beach. In public. With plenty of other people around. And you weren't shy at all. In fact, you were charging around in the water like a mermaid who'd just gotten her legs."

I giggle. "That was different. I had an idea for an article and didn't want to forget it."

He walks the tips of his fingers up my arm. "Yeah, you're right. You're a total shrinking violet."

"I was, um—" His lips press against my neck, and words float away, just out of range. "Blending in."

"Mel, you couldn't blend in if you tried. You're an original, kid."

"Kid?" I sit up. "Do I look like a kid?"

His gaze darkens as he looks at me. "Fuck no."

"Good," I say and settle back against him.

Maybe I'm not the firecracker he always thought I was. But that doesn't mean I can't pretend to be like her now. After all, I'm twelve hundred miles from home in a stranger's house with a man who knows how to use every appendage on his body to its full potential.

What's the harm in giving my insecurities a vacation as well?

Chapter 8

Blake

I wait for a bolt of lightning to strike me down, but the truth is that Mel feels too damn good in my arms. Shawn's going to kill me if he finds out. Still, there's no room for regrets. Christ, I'm glad there were condoms in that drawer, because I probably would have been arrested for public indecency otherwise.

She's dozed off with a tiny smile I want to devour, but I let her sleep. She looks so peaceful compared to the passionate lover who took my breath away less than an hour ago. I teased her a little, and she smacked me with a pillow. I discovered she takes pillow fights way too seriously. We kissed for a while, and then she fell asleep in my arms. She nestled against me like she was carved out of my dreams, made to fit there.

I shake my head. Poetry already? What am I, new? She's sexy as hell and sort of awesome. Any man would be a little starry-eyed after the sex we just had. But I wasn't expecting to feel so damn comfortable with her. I guess it shouldn't be a surprise; we've known each other forever. Maybe relationships are better when you start off as friends.

Not relationships. We're not… I don't know what we are, but it's too soon to go stampeding toward definitions or expectations. We had sex. That's all. Maybe we'll have it again. Who knows how she'll feel about things when she wakes up and the sex haze has worn off?

Not to mention that she's my best friend's little sister and should have been off-limits.

The guilt fades when she sighs in her sleep and nuzzles closer, the sheet tucking tighter around her like a second skin. She's her own woman. No one's being taken advantage of here, and treating her like a kid sister instead of a person I'm attracted to isn't right.

Is that a way to justify wanting to make her come again, six or seven times?

Maybe she's slept long enough.

························

"Blake? This is Ziggy. I'm not sure if Fern already called you or not, but we scheduled a massage for you for tomorrow morning. Thanks. Talk to you later."

I roll my eyes, annoyance stuttering through me. How hard is it to understand that I'm on vacation and won't be back for two weeks?

I finish my room service burger and delete the message. I listen to the next one while looking at a brochure. I want to find an ocean activity to do with Mel the next time I see her.

"Ziggy again. Just wondering if you got my message about the appointment. Thanks."

For real? Delete.

"Hey, disregard Ziggy's message." The last urgent, whispered message is from Laina, Inner Space's new receptionist. "I know you're on vacation, even if he and Fern don't. I've rescheduled the appointment for when you're back, and I'll keep doing so. I just didn't want you to worry about it." She's good but probably won't last another month at Inner Space. Fern and Ziggy aren't the easiest to work with. If I had to spend hours at a time with them in their little cult land, I'd go nuts.

As it is, Inner Space will be the first place I quit as soon as I finish my practicum. I won't miss any of them—especially not Phyllis. She took an unfortunately long time to get that I wasn't interested. From the stories Sarah shared when we hung out at her boyfriend's club, Phyllis has a vicious streak too. Glad I never had to experience that. I think her residual attraction for me keeps her civil.

I flip through the channels, settling on a *Supernatural* rerun.

When I eventually open my own clinic, I'm going to have a couple massage therapists, but I'll focus on the therapeutic side rather than on hot-stone massages and spa treatments. I want to make a real difference in people's daily lives, rather than make more money catering to rich clients who don't need the help.

I'd love to be more selective about clients and hours if I keep massaging—though that will be on a limited basis for older clients who have been with me for a while.

I don't crave money as much as the stability and the security.

Security like I used to feel hanging out with Shawn and Mel. I don't know where my parents are. I grew up with foster parents who didn't care about me beyond the checks they got from the government, but I always felt accepted at Shawn's house. Like I mattered.

If I'm honest, I thought Mel was cute when she was eighteen, but if we'd gone out and broken up, I would have lost her and my second family. And she was still so young. Growing up so sheltered, she had an innocence that I loved watching from afar. I felt protective of her, not attracted.

I hadn't seen much of that in my life. I relied on her family so much for emotional support that losing them would have devastated me. The fact she and I have slept together now doesn't change any of that…does it?

My phone rings. Shawn. A flash of nausea hits as an abridged sexy montage of all the things I did last night with Mel flashes through my mind. "Hello?"

"Hey, man. So? How was she?"

"What?" How did he find out? And what a weird fucking question to ask about his sister! I mean—

"Is Melanie OK? I'm assuming you found her. Has she alphabetized Shelby's house yet?"

Relief punches a hole in my lungs, deflating some of the awkwardness that had filled them. Of course that's what he meant. *Guilty conscience much, Blake?* "She's OK. I think this place is really good for her. She's relaxed in a way I've never seen." That's not a lie…

"Awesome. Maybe she'll keep a little of that when she comes back."

"How's Shelby?" I steer him off subject. "Didn't you have a date to give her a tour of the city?"

"Shelby is wild. Total hellcat with energy for days. We went out to a club, and not only did she charm our way in, but we hung out with the owner until four in the morning. He's flying us to Las Vegas in his private jet tomorrow to watch a boxing match."

"No way."

"Yeah." He sighs. "She doesn't even act sexy to get something. It's not a ploy or a game. She's so friggin' guileless and straightforward. There's this thing about her I've never seen before. She's fun and fresh and—"

"You want to give her what she wants just to see her smile." Melanie pops into my mind.

"That's exactly it," Shawn exclaims. "It's like she's a magical creature who appears out of nowhere to tempt you away from the boring reality you've resigned yourself to."

I snort. "When have you ever resigned yourself to anything boring?"

"I buckled down once. How did you know she's like that?"

"We've all met a woman like her. Someone you never saw coming who turns your world upside down." *Man, I need to knock it off.*

Shawn pauses. "I don't know about that. We only met the other day."

"Ah." He's a goner. There'll be no living with him when Shelby leaves.

"Anyway, thanks again for going down there. Hope you're not too bored."

"It's Florida. I'll find something to do to occupy my time." If he knew I was doing his kid sister, he'd lose his shit. Flaky or not, he cares about his family, and he's loyal as hell. And I care about them like they're my own.

We hang up, and I ponder that. Am I making a mistake?

Maybe. But if Mel doesn't want me around, that's up to her. I've had a hell of a time with her so far. I'm not going to overthink it or try to take the decision out of Mel's hands.

My attempts to focus on the TV are a complete waste of time. When my favorite show can't distract me from the thoughts running around my head, I decide to put an end to it.

I dial Mel's number.

"Hello?" She manages to sound sexy, impatient, and curious all at once.

I go for a cheap laugh. "What's a guy gotta do to get a date around here?"

"Troll nude beaches for mysterious women from his past?" she suggests.

I bite my lip. "Nah, I did that yesterday."

"Me too."

That earns a laugh. "What's her name?" I ask. "I'm a better time than she is. Give me a chance to win you back."

Her soft laughter patters through the phone. "Nerd. What did you have in mind?"

"Something beachy. Might as well cash in on the local scenery, right? A good time is mandatory, and clothing is optional but recommended in the interest of not getting arrested."

"Ah, so not our nude beach?"

I pace around the room, interest revving my blood now that we're talking again. "No, another little spot I heard about."

"Never thought I'd have a nude beach with someone."

I scrub my hand down my face, realizing I need a shave. "Stick with me, and the glamour never ends."

"Is that right? What's next, cow tipping?"

"I think we'd have to settle for sea cows down here," I note.

"Oh, the huge manatee! What time?"

"I'll pick you up at four." Three hours from now.

"A day date?" There's a smile in her words. Mel's teasing me? I like this side of her.

"Yeah, but if you play your cards right, I'll let you cop a feel."

She sighs, and I can picture her rolling her eyes. "See you soon."

"Oh, and Mel?" I can't wait to see the look on her face. "Bring a change of clothes."

Chapter 9
Melanie

PERPAPS TELLING ME TO BRING A CHANGE OF CLOTHES WAS presumptuous on his part. Sleeping together once doesn't mean I'm going to do it again, but since that's precisely what I want to do, I pack a bag. No sense cutting off my nose to spite my face.

I ache in all kinds of places today. Maybe sex is a better workout with a partner like Blake, but I can't remember ever being this sore from doing it before.

My phone rings just as I'm pouring three kinds of bubbles into the tub. "Hey, Bails."

"Did you know there's a conspiracy theory that the CIA invented dinosaurs to discourage people from time traveling?"

I slip off my robe and ease into the hot water. "That can't be."

"It is!" She cackles. "I'm writing an article about it. People believe weird things, Mel. Flat earth, Scientologists, nanobots in fruit. If I were six percent more impressionable, I'd be in trouble. Did you know that baby carrots are a lie?"

"Uh, what?" I put her on speaker so I have both hands free to lather and exfoliate.

"Yeah! It's outrageous. Baby carrots are just regular carrots that have been ground down into tiny nubs."

"Huh. That feels like false advertising."

"You're telling me! No one likes a tiny nub."

"Speaking of nubs…" I trail off, face burning.

"Oh my God, you finally got some! Tell me you've participated in some shenanigans! Spill everything!"

I grin at finally having something salacious to tell her. "Oh, you know. I'm sleeping in a stranger's bed, and the other day I went topless at a nude beach."

She gasps. "You did not!"

"I did."

"Did I dial the wrong number? Who am I talking to? That's wild. I'd say I wish I'd been there to see that, but there's such a thing as TMI when it comes to full frontal between besties."

I scoff. "It wasn't full frontal; it was full upper. And that isn't even the craziest part."

"What?" Bailey's voice is a strangled squeak, and her breathing increases. She's so expressive and empathetic that telling news to her is the best. She gives good reaction, and she always cares about what you're saying. "Tell me."

"Blake Wilde showed up."

"He did not! What's he doing there? Wait. Did he show up when you were naked on the beach?"

"Yes, when I was on the beach. No, I wasn't naked, Bails. I was—"

"You had your tits out, and he saw them. Oh my God, I'd have *died*. So what happened then? Was he naked too? Did you finally get to see everything?"

"He had shorts on. We hung out for a while on the

beach, then came back to Shelby's place, and he gave me a massage."

"Oh my gosh. Did you still have your top off for this part?"

"It was after supper, and I'd dressed again when we were still at the beach. But then I took the top off for the massage." I blush but continue. "And then, we, uh…we slept together."

Incoherent sounds of joy pierce my eardrum. Bailey's the only one who knows all the awkward details about my vicious crush on Blake. "How was it? Was it everything you'd dreamed it would be? Oh my God, I can't believe it finally happened. Did he make the first move, or did you? Is he a good kisser? What happened after? Is he still there?" She hisses the last part.

I laugh and revel in her enthusiasm, glad to release these happy feelings that might make my chest explode at any minute. "Slow down. It was amazing, way better than anything I ever imagined. His *hands,* Bailey. You don't know the things that man can do with his hands, and he's even better with… Well, never mind that. I think I made the first move, but I was getting signals that he was interested."

"I'm sure that after seeing your tatas, he couldn't help himself."

"You're my favorite."

"Pretty sure Blake is, but I'll get over it. Are you seeing him again?"

"I'm in the tub now. He's surprising me with where we're going on a date this afternoon."

Bailey makes a sympathetic noise, knowing how I

feel about surprises. "I'm sure it will be awesome. Call me later and tell me everything."

"I will." I hang up and just soak for a few minutes before shaving and exfoliating so I'll be nice and smooth when I see him again. If someone had said this would happen to me, I'd have laughed in their face. Everything about my time here has been so far from myself that I barely know how to feel about it.

I hesitate with the razor at my crotch. Should I try shaving again? Blake was more than fine with what I've got going on, and I don't want to act like someone I'm not just for a man's approval. I like myself this way, and if he doesn't, too bad. Pubic hair, don't care.

After rinsing, I emerge from the tub, smelling like mandarin and roses and feeling like a million bucks. Maybe there's something to be said for Shelby's menagerie of products. Plus, if I'm going to spend more time in the ocean while I'm here, it's probably a good idea to use lotions and potions to protect my skin. In her pictures, Shelby's skin looks nice and soft despite her obviously spending time in the water and in the sun, out there living large without hauling a huge umbrella with her. If she's hanging on the beach all the time, she should resemble a catcher's mitt, but she's creamy and glowing.

I'll trust in her skin care regimen.

Blake and I head up the beach to a spot I hadn't made it to yet, where people are fully clothed and a little more active. There are more kids here too, screaming up and down the surf, burying each other in wet sand. A couple badminton games are in progress, and I remember that Blake used to play.

I nod toward the game. "When was the last time you played?"

He follows my gaze and smiles. "It's been years. These days I only have time to squeeze in a quick racquetball session at the gym—if I find someone to play with."

"I'll play with you."

"Yeah?"

"I'm handy with a racket."

He snaps his fingers. "That's right. You were in the tennis club, weren't you?"

"Badminton. Yeah, all freshman year I'd go to school an hour early to play with other people. My secret move was a backhand serve that just skimmed the net and landed in." I'd loved the sport. "I tried tennis but didn't have the control or accuracy. I liked how with badminton I could just smash the birdie as hard as possible. I tried that in tennis and kept knocking the ball out of the court."

"Why'd you stop?"

"Lack of interest. Not on my part—I loved it. But there were only three of us, and if someone didn't show up, it got boring."

"You played volleyball too."

I nod. "I did. Through middle school, and then a year of JV." It suited my competitive nature, and giving it up had almost killed me.

"Why'd you stop? You light up when you talk about it, and you kicked ass at it. You have a killer serve. Remember the time you smashed me in the face with the ball that Fourth of July?"

He'd bled onto his white T-shirt. Mom had whipped it off to put in the laundry, and I'd gotten exhilarated at the sight of his abs. I bite the inside of my cheek. "I just wasn't into it anymore."

"I don't believe that. Did you try out and not make it? I'm not judging you if that's the case. Our school always had the best players, and there's no reason to feel bad for not making the cut. We went all-state, and—"

"I made the cut. It was the uniforms, OK?" The words stampede out of my mouth, angrily running away from me. I'm powerless to stop them. "Do you know what it's like to pour yourself into those tiny fucking shorts and know that everyone's laughing at you, staring at your ass? Comparing it to the other teammates' and how they look way better?" My face heats and I try to walk faster to get away, but stomping on sand is impossible. Even more frustration builds. "It makes it impossible to focus on the game."

"Mel." Blake grabs my bicep, and I turn to shake him off until his eyes burn me into stillness.

"What?"

"You don't still feel like that, do you?"

The sand softly abrades between my toes when I dig one foot deeper. "I don't know. I hate that I let something so stupid get in the way of doing something I loved." And I *do* still feel big and clumsy compared to the couture giraffes picking their way down the street on Fashion Week. My corner of New York has higher standards of black-clad conformity than other places.

Yet we have the best restaurants in the world as well. How are women like me supposed to win with that working against us?

Blake drops the bag and grabs my hands, putting my palms flat against his chest before wrapping his arms around me. "I can't imagine anything ever getting in your way when you truly want something. You're a force to be reckoned with, Mel. Never let anyone tell you otherwise."

He hasn't seen the way I fade around Thaddeus and take whatever he dishes out because I'm afraid I'll be fired if I stand my ground. "Sometimes I feel like that. But sometimes I feel like a side character in my own life. Like I'm not the star, and it's all my fault. If the audience was screaming at me to do something, I don't even know what they'd be yelling. Hell, they've probably already changed the channel to find someone a little braver and more exciting. I hate that I quit back then, and I hate that I still feel like this now, when I'm older and smarter and should know better." Telling Blake I wanted him was the most assertive thing I've done in a long, long time.

Blake smiles and leans in. His lips are soft on my cheek, making me shiver all over. "Let's see what we can do about making you feel a little more badass right now." He leads me to a dock, where a fiftysomething man with long, thin hair scraped back into a skullet waits with a clipboard.

"What's this?" I take the proffered clipboard and flip through the one page of miniscule writing—a release form.

"We're going to do that." Blake points toward the ocean where a couple of people are zooming through the air and diving under the water like dolphins, propelled by jets of water attached to their feet.

"What is that?"

"Flyboarding. Doesn't it look awesome?" Blake grins but keeps his eyes on the people doing it.

That's one word for it. They're out past the harbor, in deeper waters where I'm sure a few sharks are circling their feet and licking their lips in anticipation.

Do sharks have lips?

I fiddle with the page covered in legalese. "Why do we have to sign these? Isn't it safe?"

Skullet shakes his head. "It's perfectly safe, but sometimes certain people ruin things for everyone. Spring breakers. This is just a way for the company to cover ourselves in case some dudebro decides to get fancy and hurts himself—or someone else—in the process. But we've never had an injury."

I try to keep my voice even. "And how long have you been operating?"

"Eight months. But it's a fairly new thing, so…" He turns back to his boat, fiddling with some cables.

The waiver's bold type and shouty caps warning that this activity can lead to injury or death don't exactly give me warm fuzzies—especially when paired with the unconditional release of the company and its employees. I scan the page, and words like *indemnification* and *damages* jump out at me.

"Hey. You still reading that?" Blake nudges my shoulder with his.

"I like to actually read the things I sign." Or pitch into the ocean without signing.

He smiles. "I bet you're one of those people who reads the terms and conditions when downloading music, aren't you?"

I sniff. "Of course. Who knows what you're signing away? They could slip in a clause about taking your kidney or giving your download details to a reality television show that you didn't realize you were signing up for."

"Because that would hold up in court."

"Shut up and let me finish." Why can't I keep a straight face around him? I focus on the page again, hoping he doesn't notice my stupid smile.

He taps the signature line with his pen. "These waivers are standard. Same as when you go zip-lining or for a routine procedure at the hospital."

"I've never done either."

He smiles. "And you won't today, either. Come on, we can stay perfectly safe in our boring little bubbles, or we can get out there and tear things up."

I follow his finger, which points at the people already in the water. A little girl, no older than seven or eight, flips in and out of the water like a dolphin. She cuts graceful arcs in the air, squealing with delight while her grandmother floats twenty feet in the air on a jet of water. It looks like so much fun.

I sign with a flourish and hand the clipboard back to the man on the boat, turning to poke Blake in the chest. "OK, but if I break something, *you're* getting something broken."

Besides, if grandmas and little kids can do it, how hard can it be?

<hr />

I'm going to drown with my ass hanging out of my shorts.

My feet are locked into the heavy jet boots that are powered by the Jet Ski's motor. The boots float, but they pull at my feet in a way that has claustrophobia nipping at my heels. The life jacket keeps me above water, but this is impossible. I roll to my back again, trying to hide my ass. I pull at the wet fabric of my surfer-style bathing-suit shorts, but the waistband clings to my hips for dear life.

"Roll over!" Skullet calls, but the last thing I want is to be shot out of the water like this.

The motor's not as loud as I expected, but the vibrations are probably the only thing scaring away the ocean's predators, so the rumbling sensation is vaguely comforting. Or it would be, if the force of the jet propulsion hadn't torn my shorts down my hips.

A shark's going to bite off half my ass, and I'll bleed to death in the ocean with an asymmetrical posterior. The thought drives my desire to make the jets work as soon as possible, so I renew my struggle—but the more I flail around trying to cover myself, the more power goes to the jets. Soon I'm being shot out of the water and slapped back against the surface like an orca having a seizure.

Fortunately, one last violent tug gets my shorts firmly back in place, and the next thrust of the jets hits when my body is rigid—which is apparently the secret to flyboarding. I go from skimming the water like a torpedo to standing straight up.

It's like floating.

Steadily, like a deep inhalation, I'm raised fifteen feet in the air and held. Holding perfectly still lest I screw it up, I cautiously meet Blake's impressed gaze from the back of the Jet Ski. He went first, so he knows how difficult this is, but I wish we were both able to go at the same time…mostly because then there'd be less focus on me trying to do this.

I bet you could see a lot of sharks from here.

Shit! I flail, trying to see any sharks in my vicinity, and smack back to the water. It stings my skin and tweaks my neck hard enough to bring tears to my eyes.

I hate water, and I hate the operator, and I hate the grandma and child who made this look so damned easy.

I hate the way I want to give up.

I'm not a quitter. I never used to be. Maybe the past few years have seen some compromises that would make my younger self cringe, but that stops right now. I can do this.

Frustration bubbles up and washes over me, and I use that emotion to straighten my legs and tighten my core. I soar twenty-five feet above the surface, holding steady until my celebratory air punch sends me shooting to the side, dunking me under the water again.

I cough salty ocean water out of my lungs—eyes streaming, nose burning—and smooth the soaked tendrils of hair back toward my ponytail.

Blake's smile sends sparks skittering across my skin. I probably look like a drowned rat, but I've never felt more beautiful.

Chapter 10

Blake

I STILL CAN'T WRAP MY HEAD AROUND MEL'S CONFESSION. She attacks life—and she proved it just now with the way she threw herself into flyboarding and crushed me at it.

It's hot as hell.

By the time we get back to my hotel room, the salt and sand have dried on my skin, making me feel more than a little crusty. I swipe the card and lead the way inside, thoroughly uncomfortable.

"Nice room." Mel trails her hands over the table, the dresser, the foot of the bed. She does that a lot, I've noticed. A tactile woman.

"Thanks." Since Shawn paid for the airfare, I decided to treat myself to a little nicer room, but not swanky enough to break the bank. Still, the thread count is unbelievable, and I'm suddenly gripped with the urge to lay Melanie naked on the sheets.

Focus, Blake. She said she was hungry on the way over here. She didn't specify food, but that goes without saying, so I hand her the room service menu and try not to think with my dick. "They've got some awesome burgers here."

"Nice." She fidgets with the menu but doesn't look at it.

"You could order something and have the shower while you wait. Or…" I trail off.

"Or?" I can't tell if the pink on her cheeks is from too much sun or a new blush.

I take in her body—from her eyes to the tips of her toes and back again. I'm hard by the time my gaze meets hers. "Or, we could shower together and then eat."

She tosses the menu onto the dresser. "Showering together would save water."

"It's pretty much the only responsible choice." I walk close enough to invade her personal space.

She bites her lip. "Conserving water saves innocent little sea creatures."

"Conservation is sexy as fuck." I pull her close and slant my mouth over hers, tasting the salty warmth of her lips. I stroke down her spine and haul her hips against mine, pressing my hips against hers. She sighs like it's a relief.

Her fingers slip under my T-shirt and dance across my back with a lightness that makes me ache with want. I knead her ass, teasing the crease where it meets her thighs, frustrated by the clothing separating her skin from my touch.

She must feel the same way, because she pulls back and tugs impatiently at my shirt. I strip for her and she kisses my chest, licking her way to my nipples.

When her hot mouth takes one in, I freeze a little. I'm unused to this, but she could put that talented tongue anywhere on my body and I'd let her do whatever the hell she wanted.

She's warm against my palm, and I gently work her through her clothes until her breath catches. I peel off her shirt.

"Let's go into the bathroom," she suggests as she undoes my trunks, and I pull her shorts down in response. Her eyes lock onto the head of my hard shaft as she removes my last article of clothing. She licks her lips and my cock twitches.

"What are you thinking, Mel?"

She takes off her top and frees her breasts, now paler than her arms and chest from all the sun she's been getting. "I want you in my mouth. I want you inside me." Her gaze meets mine. "Anywhere."

Christ. "Get in the shower. Make it whatever temperature you want."

She frowns. "What will you be doing?"

"Grabbing all the condoms and joining you."

She grins and dashes into the bathroom. I grab the condoms I bought earlier. I take them to the bathroom in time to see her slip inside the glass stall. Steam rises and fogs the glass as the water pours down, hiding her body from mine.

Fully aware I'm watching, she grabs a bottle of body wash and lathers it in her palms. She rubs it all over herself, making the air smell like almonds, and my erection grows even harder.

I open the door to admire the show without a foggy piece of glass obscuring the suds slipping down her skin, slicking her breasts and thighs, dripping to the floor.

Setting the condoms on the ledge, I pour some of the gel into my hands, then hold my hand out to capture some water. "Turn around."

She bares her back to me, and I massage the sweet-smelling foam all over it, mesmerized by the bubbles slipping down the crack of her ass.

"Spread your legs."

She does, and I rub my slick hands up her inner thighs and over the swell of her ass. I push her forward to rinse the suds clean and turn her to suck the droplets of water from a pert nipple. She moans but pushes me back until I'm standing straight.

She pours the body wash straight onto my chest. "You're still dirty. My turn." Her hands work steadily over my pecs and down my abs. A grin plays at her lips when she wraps her soapy hands around my shaft and slides up and down. "Mmm, Blake, you're really dirty right here."

I grit my teeth. "Pretty filthy."

Continuing the hot, wet friction, she drops one hand to caress my balls. She slides her palm beneath them, stimulating the sensitive skin until they harden too.

She pulls me forward into the stream of water, rinsing the soap away while she keeps working me until there's not a bubble left on me. Her confidence is almost as sexy as the things she's doing to me. She lowers herself to her knees and takes me in her mouth, keeping her gaze on mine, and I can't look away. I grab her ponytail, winding it around my hand, but I let her set the pace and depth.

God knows she's doing just fine.

"Melanie."

She sucks harder and raises her eyebrows in response. I'm glad two of the walls are tile, because the way I'm going to fuck her against them, glass wouldn't stand a chance.

"Stand up. Now." My voice is raw and deep, and she trembles to her feet.

I turn her so she's facing the spout and caress her from behind, wrapping myself around her. I take her wrists and set her palms against the wall above her head before slipping my hands down her arms and working her nipples into tight buds. "Keep your hands there."

She nudges her ass against my cock but keeps her hands where I told her to.

I nuzzle her neck. "Spread your legs for me, baby."

She does, and I take a step back to get a nice look while putting the condom on.

Her skin glistens, and her legs shake just a bit in anticipation. The way her arms are raised exaggerates the curve of her back, sticking that ass out. This woman does things to me.

She moans when I kiss the back of her neck as I reach past her to grab the detachable showerhead.

"What are you doing?" She keeps her hands splayed on the wall, but she turns so her eyes blaze a few inches from mine while I test the water's temperature on my wrist.

"Making you feel good." Satisfied with the temperature, I wrap an arm around her hips, position myself at her entrance, and press inside her as I turn the stream of water toward her clit.

Her pussy quivers around me and her hips buck. "Oh my God."

I want to bury my face between her legs and devour her, but I want to feel her come around me more. I pull almost all the way out and fill her again, keeping the jets trained on her clit.

"Holy shit." She sags against me, spreading even more, letting me go deeper.

With the water hitting her, I don't have to bother with anything fancy. I keep the jet going where it's supposed to and fuck her steadily, hard. Maybe too hard, but she slams back against me and moans every time, so I'm pretty sure she likes it.

I snag one of her earlobes between my teeth and suck it, gently breathing into her ear while I pound and circle the stream of water over her clit.

The way her legs keep tensing, I know she's not going to last long. But I want to come with her, come inside her when she does, so I grind harder. My balls ache and tighten.

So close.

She goes rigid against me, not even breathing, and cries out. Her body rolls against mine.

I get in three more thrusts before coming too. I drop the showerhead and wrap my arms around her.

She wraps her arms around mine, holding me close as we breathe and come down joined together.

She recovers first and reaches out to turn the water off. I hold the condom on and pull out. She moans when I do, and I kiss the top of her shoulder.

"That was amazing," I say.

She stretches her arms. "I've never showered with anyone before."

"Really?" It somehow pleases me that she chose to have this experience with me.

"Mmm." She turns, and I kiss her slow and deep. "I think I've been missing out."

I lean and toss the condom into the trash can. It's not always like this. Hell, I can't remember shower sex ever feeling this good, but I smile. "Yeah, you have."

"Can you hand me a towel, please?"

I open the door and hand her a fluffy white robe from the rack, wrapping a towel around my waist. She wraps her hair up. "You still hungry, Mel?"

"Famished."

God, she's cute like this. We emerge from the bathroom with a cloud of steam, and I cross to the menu and sit with it on the bed. "I'm still in the mood for a burger."

She flops next to me, tucking the towel tighter on her hair. "I could definitely go for some red meat. Shelby has mostly seeds and things." She reads over my shoulder and points at the classic bacon cheeseburger. "That one. No onions. Are you getting onion rings or fries for a side?"

"Why?"

"I want some of both, and if we each get one, we can share."

I can't fault her logic. "Sounds good." I call down and place our order while she flips through Netflix, looking for something for us to watch.

"What are your shows?" she asks as soon as I hang up.

"I haven't really had time for much lately. I've been working a lot."

She rolls her eyes. "Are you one of those assholes who makes pretentious declarations like, 'Oh, I don't watch television. Oh, I don't eat salt'?"

I toss a pillow at her. "You know I'm not. The last couple months have kicked my ass, but they're almost done. Then I'll glut on all the shows I've put aside."

"And those shows are…?"

"I've got a few seasons of *Supernatural* to catch up on, and I've been meaning to see *Sense8* but never quite get around to it. I've heard some great things about *Orphan Black* too."

"Oh, that's an awesome show! I can't believe how talented that actress is. She should win all the awards for basically acting by herself. We should watch that!"

I shrug. "Don't see why not."

I settle on the bed and open my arms in invitation. She snuggles against me, and we watch *Orphan Black* until the food comes.

Then we eat.

And digest.

Her back and neck stiffen from falling in the water today, so I grab some oil and work the tension from her body head to toe.

And then we're too busy watching each other to pay attention to the television.

Chapter 11

Melanie

MY PHONE RINGS, AND WHEN I SEE THE NAME ON THE CALLER ID, I answer immediately. "Hey, Bails. What's up?"

I lie on my stomach on Shelby's couch. Buddy immediately jumps beside me, snuggling against the curve of my hip. He purrs like he knows I'm happy and wants to share in the moment.

"You tell me. You never called me. I was left here wringing my hands, worried that someone else would hear the salacious details of your date before me. Now, I know I'm supposed to play it cool and wait three days for you to call me, but—"

I laugh. "Except for that last bit, you sound like my mom. We went out again yesterday and had an amazing time. I stayed at his hotel room last night—"

"And boy, are your hips tired?"

"Ha-ha. Seriously, I can't believe everything that's happened in just a few days." It's all got this surreal edge around it, framed by fluffy sand and skies too pretty and bright to be real. "It's a fantasy come to life."

"But? You're sounding a little flat about it."

I stroke Buddy's back, and he rewards me with a purr. "I mean, it's not like this can go anywhere, right?"

"Even if that were true, which it isn't, who says it

has to go somewhere? How long have we known each other—seven years? I love you, but when have you ever cut loose and done something fun and frivolous for the sake of doing something fun and frivolous?"

Searching my memories doesn't immediately offer up a rebuttal, and I'm forced to admit she's right. "That's true. Those f-words aren't really a part of my vocabulary."

"Five-year plans are so five years ago. What's stopping you from grabbing the moment? Seizing that sexy man and having a good time? Really sinking your teeth into his—"

"I get it." I laugh. "I'm the one stopping me, I guess."

"So get out of your own way for once. Stop putting limitations on it. Who cares how it ends? You're supposed to be *starting* something. Starting something and then actually enjoying it. Life's about the journey, not just the destination. You're skipping ahead, but skipping ahead like that means you're missing the part where it actually happens."

I smile. "I know you're right. Maybe I'm thrown off because I've wanted him for so long that I talked myself out of him ever noticing me."

"I think that's exactly it. Embrace this, Melanie. Take one for the team, for the girls on the bench wishing their crushes would tap them to get in the game."

I release the breath I wasn't aware I'd been holding. "You're right. I'm overthinking it when I need to jump in."

"Yeah, you are. Repeat after me: what happens on vacation stays on vacation."

"'What happens on vacation stays on vacation,'" I dutifully parrot.

"Excellent. Now, if you could 3-D print one thing, what would it be?"

I chew my lip. Bailey's random questions are usually prompted by topics for articles she's thinking of doing. "The only things I can think about printing are completely inappropriate. My mind's still in the gutter. Why? What would you print?"

She pauses for a minute. "OK, there was this dog. And he had no front paws." She stops, and I know if I saw her right now, her big eyes would be filling with tears. "And they made him paws. And they filmed him running, and ugh, I'm getting misty again just thinking about it."

"You're the sweetest."

She sniffs. "It's ridiculous, but it hit me right in the feels. Anyway, how are you, other than this? You never really said what prompted the Switch in the first place."

I stroke Buddy's forehead, tensing as memories of the day from hell that drove me here float back to mind. "Fine," I answer a little too tersely.

"If you need to talk—"

"I'd rather think about fun stuff right now, if that's OK."

"Of course it is." Her voice softens. "You're going to see Blake again soon?"

"He asked if I wanted to go dancing and I sort of begged off, saying I was tired. But you know what? I'm going to call him back and say yes. But maybe for a date tomorrow instead of going out tonight. He thoroughly wore me out."

"Yay! Do you have anything to wear? Want to send me pictures and I'll help you?"

Bailey has amazing fashion sense. She can make the

simplest outfit seem unique and fresh with some kind of voodoo I don't possess. I chew my lip and glance toward the bedroom. "Not really. But I bet Shelby has something sparkly I can squeeze into."

"I want updates. I'm glad you're sounding better."

"I'm feeling a bit better. Not there yet, but this is helping."

"Call me when you can, but no pressure. If I don't hear from you, I'll assume you're ravaging Blake on a beach somewhere."

"You may not be wrong about that."

She squeals, and I hang up feeling better because she's right. I overthink and put limitations on life, talking myself out of trying because things might not end well. How many things have I missed out on, not daring to start because I was too busy worrying about how they'd end?

I've already dialed Blake's number when I realize I forgot to ask Bailey how work is going. It doesn't matter. I'm on vacation, and work is the last thing I should focus on. Besides, even if something is up, there's nothing I can do about it here.

"Miss me already?" Blake's voice has a smile in it.

"Parts of you, maybe." I cannot believe I just said that.

"Which ones?"

"Your hands. And feet."

"Kinky."

I snort. "You did say you wanted to take me dancing. Is that still an option?"

"Mmm. I thought you were tired."

I roll over onto my back, careful not to push Buddy off the couch. "For tomorrow night. You in?"

"Definitely. I'll pick you up at nine and we can grab a bite first, if you like?"

"Sounds great." I smile and hang up, hoping Shelby has something in her closet I can wear. If not, I'll need to go shopping tomorrow. Is it weird to borrow something from her wardrobe? How would I feel if she was wearing my things?

I shrug and head to her room. If she really needed it, I'd be fine with her borrowing something—as long as she returned it in the same condition. What's she doing right now? Has she eaten at the dodgy bodega down my street? I should have warned her not to order anything from there except the cheese pizza.

Then again, if she'd told me that beach was clothing optional, I probably would have avoided it and missed out on all kinds of fun. Sometimes it's better to negotiate awkward situations without a road map. If you end up in trouble—or on a beach with your nipples in your first crush's face—at least it keeps things interesting.

Shelby's closet has everything from a gorgeous toga—in ombré from cream to light blue—to jeans to an evening gown. I feel a little guilty about flipping through her hangers and judging her clothes, like I'm raiding my cool older sister's closet while she's staying at her friend's. The hangers make little *snick-snick-snicks* as I rapidly dismiss dresses for being too small, too provocative, or too stiff for dancing.

Then I see it. A black-and-silver, sleeveless, beaded satin dress near the back of the closet. It's heavier than I expected from the beading, in flapper-style layers, but I lay it on the bed, undress, and slip it over my head before I can talk myself out of it.

It's modern and probably roomier on Shelby, but it fits. My curves bring the hem to upper thigh, but the fringe extends a couple inches lower, tickling my skin with strings of cool beads. The neckline plunges a bit, and I won't be able to wear a bra with it, but the beads hide my nipples.

And it looks amazing. It plays up my curves while the beads create movement. I look like a bombshell, and I sashay to the mirror, shaking and shimmying to see what it looks like from all angles when I move. Spinning around makes the beads rise, showing more leg than I'm normally comfortable showing, but it's OK. I've Switched.

I pull my hair out of its bun, and it falls past my shoulders. The way it brushes against my back reminds me of the hem, so I decide to leave my hair down and free tomorrow night.

The top is more silver than black, and I brought a strappy pair of black sandals that will go perfectly with this dress. I'd feel weird wearing someone else's shoes, so I grab mine. I slip them on and dance to the bathroom to experiment with a little more makeup than I normally wear—a practice run for tomorrow night.

This dress *screams* for smoky eyes.

Chapter 12

Blake

MEL OPENS THE DOOR AND TAKES MY BREATH AWAY.

Her dark, glossy hair tumbles down her shoulders in sexily tousled curls that look like she just rolled out of bed. I want to take her back there and tousle her some more.

Dark liner makes her eyes dramatic, and I don't know if it's the makeup or the dress, but those unique eyes of hers—a shade I never know how to describe, even more intense tonight—are closer to golden green. She's left her naturally full lips bare except for a little gloss that shimmers in the light, looking like she's just licked them.

I want to lick them too.

"Hey." She gives a little twirl, making the bottom of the dress shoot up a couple inches. It doesn't help my caveman urges at all. "How do I look?"

"Like we'd better get to a public place very soon, or I won't be held accountable for my actions."

A blush creeps up from her cleavage and stains her cheeks. "Thank you. You're not so bad yourself."

"Now I feel really underdressed." I pluck at the black button-down I paired with dark wash jeans—the fanciest thing I packed, not expecting to take anyone out on the town.

"You look hot. If it's too much, I can change."

"No. You can't." The words come out like a growl, and I'd be embarrassed by the sound if she didn't look so damn good. This incredible woman wants to go out with me, and pride roars through my chest as if I can claim any part of that.

"Do you still want to grab a bite?"

She shakes her head. "I'm not really hungry. Is it okay if we just go dancing?"

"Hell yeah."

She grins. "Which club are we going to?" She digs through her little black purse for her keys.

"Somewhere I can see you dance in that dress."

She grins and locks the door behind us, and we get into the cab that brought me here. I ask the cabbie to take us to the hottest dance club in Miami, and we ride there in silence with the windows down to combat the heat in the car. We must have gotten the one cabbie who doesn't believe in air-conditioning.

I can't take my eyes off Mel. It's not just the dress and makeup; it's something else. A sparkle in her eyes, the way she carries herself. She's sort of…radiant.

I take her soft hand in mine, rubbing the pad of my thumb across her knuckles.

The pavement radiates warmth back up at us when we step out of the car. The line outside the club is long, but I squint at the bouncer at the door, unsure if it's really Del. Seeing someone out of context can render them nearly unrecognizable, but it's hard to forget a six-foot-four Thor look-alike you trained with for four months. He's a bruiser but had the most delicate touch when working on intraoral TMJ issues.

"Blake Wilde, who the hell let you out of New York?" he calls out, stepping down to grab my hand.

"I could ask you the same question." I return his shake, then turn to gesture at Mel. "This is Mel."

"Melanie." She smiles and shakes Del's hand. "You two know each other?"

I nod. "We went to school together. Massage therapy—until he was scouted for pro ball."

Del grins. "What are you doing in my neck of the woods?"

"Vacation. You here permanently?"

He spreads his hands in a what-can-you-do gesture. "Came down to help out my cousin, liked it enough to invest in the place as well. Now I'm co-owner, but I like to work the door from time to time. Tossing the occasional drunk out on his ass keeps me from getting soft—and it's easier on the body than massage therapy."

"I hear that."

"You still rubbing people the right way?"

I laugh. "Yeah, but I'm almost done with my practicum for PT."

"Nice. Now I know who to come to when my knee blows out again."

"Del played pro football for a few years," I explain to Mel.

"Any teams I know?" She tilts her head.

"The Vikings."

She smirks. "Playing to type there, weren't we?"

Del throws his head back and laughs, a rumbly boom that turns every head our way. "Indeed. You want in?" He jerks his thumb at the club.

How can he deal with a full beard in this weather?

"Yeah. The cabbie recommended this place as the hottest spot to go dancing."

Del grins, revealing the tiny diamond in his eyetooth. "Good news travels fast. Cool." He leads us to the door, digs in his pocket, and fishes out a business card. "Here's my number. Don't be a stranger. I'll be in New York in a couple months." He waves and tells the girl at the counter, "No cover."

"Thanks, man." I tuck his card into my wallet and hand him one of mine. "Hit me up when you're there." I take Mel's hand.

"Nice meeting you," she says. She waves at him as we head inside, and the girl slips a backstage-pass wristband on each of us.

I love the way Mel can keep up with anyone, no matter who they are.

The music is muted in the dark hallway, and the temperature drops to a more comfortable level, the swelter and humidity kept outside. The passageway is long, almost like a tunnel, and we head down it together. Amusement bubbles up as we go. I don't know why, but Mel looks at me and giggles. She feels it too. Maybe because the passageway is almost empty, so it's as though we're sneaking into someplace off-limits.

We burst through the doors, and the music swells over us as we enter the huge room, which is set up more like a concert venue. Tables and chairs sit on the graduated levels that head down to the dance floor in the middle of the room.

It's raised, set up like a large stage—the focal point for everyone at the tables. Every dancer is also a star on the stage, making it the coolest place to be.

"This is pretty awesome," Mel shouts near my ear, competing with the music.

I nod and guide her through the crowd to one of the three bars, ordering drinks for us both as the heavy pulse of sound washes over us, connecting everyone in the room through the vibrations. It's warmer in here from all the bodies. We stand and sip our drinks, taking in the dark, almost-industrial decor. Black-and-dark-purple walls, brushed-steel details on the backs of the booths and tables.

The loud music makes it impossible to carry on a real conversation, but I like the chance to drink in the sight of Mel in the darkness. Flashing lights play across her skin and eyes as she bobs to the beat, her striking features highlighted with blue, then green, then red as the lights change. I notice the stares of other men directed her way, but she seems oblivious.

How is that even possible?

She sips and I follow her gaze around the room. She frowns more with every tiny woman with long, tanned legs who passes.

Is that it? Is she so zoned in on the women she thinks are her competition that she doesn't realize her own innate, unique beauty?

Suddenly I want to show her how I see her. I want to spend all my time doing that, which should be scary, but somehow it isn't. It feels right.

"Come with me." I set my empty glass on the bar, and she puts hers beside mine.

"Where are we going?" She frowns.

I wiggle my eyebrows and lead her through the crowds, heading down the levels until we get to the stage.

Her footsteps falter a little as we approach the stairs, and I slow down and give her hand a reassuring squeeze.

Mel tucks herself closer to me when we hit the dance floor, like she's trying to become less visible rather than get closer to me.

I can't sing for shit, but I can move. Even better than that, I know the key to this kind of dancing: the best partner doesn't show off as hard as they can; they show their partner off as best they can, making them look good.

And she already looks fantastic. I just have to get her to feel as good as she looks.

I maneuver us around our little patch on the floor, sure to keep a hand on Mel at all times so she can draw comfort and confidence from our connection.

Mel's eyes—huge with surprise at first—go back to regular size as she relaxes, realizing I'm not going to show her up or embarrass her. I don't hide the attraction I feel for her, letting her see how much I want her as I lead her across the floor, around other bopping dancers. The music changes to something with a sexier bass line, an old hip-hop hit, and everyone screams around us and dances a little harder.

"I love this song!" Mel grins up at me. The tension leaves her shoulders, and the pinched skin around her eyes smooths out as she gives a shimmy, making her dress shimmer in the light like she's part of the show.

Mel sashaying, spinning, and gliding around beneath my touch is fucking magnificent. Even I'm awed when she throws her head back and laughs with abandon, finally giving in to the thrumming beat. Her hips bounce against my hands, and though I'd like nothing more than to pull her to me and grind her six ways to Sunday, I pull back so I can watch her shine.

This club is the place to be, judging by the expensive clothes and perfume on the dancers around us—a few celebs in here too. I'm pretty sure there's a Jonas brother dancing with a Victoria's Secret model…but I can't stop staring at Mel.

She tips her head back and closes her eyes for a second, sort of biting her lip. The fact that she's not trying to be sexy while she does makes it even hotter. Effortlessly sexy, unpretentious. Everyone can learn from this powerful woman.

The more she dances, the looser her movements get until she's flowing around her spot on the floor and more than one person watches her surreptitiously from nearby. I never in a million years thought I'd come here and find something like this. She steps closer and gently grinds against me, making the movements more intimate, sexier, but still flirty and fun with cheeky glances up at me.

I want her so much. I *like* her so much.

She stays on the floor while I get us another drink, and when I get back, she's so lost in the music that she no longer cares what other people think. If she actually paid attention, she'd see that she's incredible. I'm not the only one watching her move, smiling when she does, wanting to be with her.

We drink and dance and laugh.

We sweat and smile and flirt.

Her spine curls a little more, and she starts working her curves, owning her place on the floor. She throws me cheeky winks until the music slows into something heady and insistent.

I pull her close, holding her tightly against me, enjoying the way she sways. God, she feels so good in my arms. I spin her slowly around until her back is pressed against my front, and she tips her head back against my chest. For a while we live there, my arms around her, her arms around mine, gently moving together. I savor the burn of her body in my arms until I can't take it anymore.

I lean down to ask if she wants to leave, and her face is already turned to mine.

"Let's get out of here," she says.

I smile. "Sounds good to me."

The street is slightly cooler, and Del is gone when we exit the club, but it's a bright, clear night. A cab pulls up fairly quickly.

"Where to?" The cab driver makes eye contact with me in the rearview mirror.

I turn to Mel. "My place or yours?"

"I'm starving." She rubs her stomach. "It's so freaking hot." She twists her hair out of the way and fans her neck. "I definitely need food."

"Me too. What are the odds of finding some decent pizza in this town?"

She wrinkles her nose. "Compared to home? Slim to none."

"I know! Let's make a pizza."

"Out of?" She waves her hand in a way that makes me pretty sure she's had half a drink too many.

"Ingredients."

"OK." She gives the cab driver an address before turning to me. "The store by Shelby's place is open late. I made a late-night coffee run there the other night. All she had was a weird chicory-carob mixture that smelled like burned toast with wood on it."

"The hippies like carob. I do not."

"OK, but it tasted like sugary shit."

I seize Mel's hand, gripped with overwhelming affection for her. The backs of her knuckles are smooth beneath my lips, and I want to kiss my way up her arm, all the way to her shoulder and neck. But I don't want to give the cab driver a free show, and if I start, I won't be able to stop, so I give her hand a little squeeze and release it.

She turns to me, eyes bright. "Want to make it a competition?"

"How?"

"I can't see them having everything we need. How about we both grab all the things we think will make the best pizza and compare ingredients when we get home?"

She makes everything fun, which is one of the best things about her. I lean in closer. "What's the winner get?"

Her smile is slow. "Whatever they want."

A contest where there are no losers. I love it. "Deal."

Chapter 13

Melanie

I FEEL VAGUELY RIDICULOUS TRAIPSING AROUND THE convenience store dressed like this. I glance across the short shelves, searching for Blake. He's so cute with his serious expression, shopping like he's doing something fiercely important instead of scavenging for ingredients to make a passable pizza—as though that will actually happen. He busts me staring at him, and when he flashes those dimples at me, I don't care what I look like anymore.

Dancing in his arms was the best thing in the world. He looked down at me like I was the sexiest woman he'd ever seen. It felt like he really saw me—saw the woman I want to be. Confident, radiant.

OK, I can't stare at him all night and win this. I sidle down an aisle and suppress my smug grin when I find a just-add-water pizza-dough kit. It may not be the best tasting, but it's the last one on the shelf. In the small section of canned goods, I find a small, dusty can of pizza sauce and set that in my basket as well.

"What have you got in there?" Blake asks. He stands taller and cranes his neck to peer over the aisle and see in my basket, but I lower it and toss a big bag of chips on top for good measure.

"Can I help you with something, Blake?" I pout my lips to match my haughty tone.

He focuses on something behind me. "No, it's fine. I think I see someone I know near the fridge."

A shoulder check confirms what I thought—there's no one by the fridge. I grin as he saunters oh-so-casually toward the coolers. Of course! I'll stop there for some cheese after he's done. As soon as he bends over to grab something, I scurry to the counter where I noticed some pepperoni sticks on our way in. Since topping choices are slim here, it may be best to stick to the classic pepperoni and cheese pie.

I manage to snag the pepperoni sticks and get halfway down an aisle before Blake finishes in the fridge.

"Excuse me, but we're closing." A bored teenage boy sniffs affectedly and stares at me.

Blake's already at the counter, so I grab a couple cans of soda and head there too.

"No peeking," he says. He moves directly in front of me so I can't see his purchases, but I'm busy trying to hide my own.

"Never mind that. Keep your eyes off my basket."

"I'll wait for you outside, then." Blake turns to give the kid at the counter some money. "Hers too. Keep the change."

The kid bags my items, and I join Blake outside. He snags my hand in his, holding it all the way back to Shelby's. Not a word is spoken until we get inside and head to the kitchen.

"Buddy?" I wait, but he doesn't appear. I shrug. "Must be prowling around the neighborhood."

"Glad he won't be here to witness your loss?"

"Dream on." I'm not as hungry as I was—at least, not for shitty pizza—but Blake still seems excited about the game.

"Ladies first?"

I casually buff my nails on my chest. "I'd rather you go first. I'll annihilate you after."

"So cocky." He digs in his bag and sets a tube of ready-to-bake biscuits on the counter. "For the crust."

"A can of raw dough does not a crust make."

He smiles. "And for the toppings, brace yourself for this taste sensation." He slaps a package of sliced, cooked ham onto the counter. "Are you impressed yet?"

"At cooked ham? Please. Is that all you've got?"

With a triumphant flourish, he sets a can of fruit cocktail beside them.

"What's that for?"

He points at the label. "May I bring your attention to the pineapple chunks inside? With those, and my sexy ham slices, we've got the fixings for a classic Hawaiian pizza." He pulls out a few round discs of cheese.

"Hawaiian biscuits," I point out with a grin, glad I found actual dough even if I forgot the cheese. I knew I'd forgotten something in my haste to get to the counter.

"Semantics. What, you think you did better?" He crosses his arms. "Let's see what you've got."

Pepperoni is still preferable to soggy lunch ham. First, I pull out the pepperoni sticks, dragging one under my nose and holding it like a cigar. I unwrap one and bite the end. "Classic topping. Much better than cocktail fruit."

"I can't fault you for that."

My small can of pizza sauce joins the pepperoni on the counter. "Another integral part of the pizza experience."

"Damn it. I knew I was forgetting something—unless we count the syrup from my fruit…which we don't. OK, you're pulling ahead."

"Hold on for the pièce de résistance. Actual pizza dough." I thrust the box in his face. "Does it sting, baby?"

He laughs and snags the kit, setting it down on the counter. "You win with the sauce and the dough, but I'm pretty sure this counts as cheating. Fifty points from Gryffindor."

I poke him in the ribs. "You're just mad you didn't find it first. I forgot about cheese, though. Can I have some of yours?" I bat my eyelashes at him.

"Of course." He smiles. "OK, seriously, I think if we combine our efforts into a pepperoni and ham pizza, we're golden. Unless you like pineapple?"

"I loathe pineapple on pizza, so I'm more than happy to forgo that topping."

"And are we going to make biscuits or your fancy-schmancy dough?"

I raise my eyebrow. "Do you even have to ask?"

He pushes the roll of biscuit dough out of the preparation area. "You could have indulged me a little."

"Nah. You'd never have respected yourself in the morning."

He laughs and pulls me close. I relax into his arms, squirming closer and closing my eyes. I never expected to find security in Blake Wilde's arms, but it envelops me as tangibly as his strong embrace. Why can't we live here where everything's perfect and nothing hurts?

I allow myself two more deep breaths of him before

pulling back. I hand him a knife and the cutting board and let him work on the ham and pepperoni while I turn on the radio and work on the pizza dough.

A jazz song comes on, and somehow, bopping around a stranger's kitchen with Blake, making shitty, slapped-together pizza is the most adult I've ever felt. Life stretches out in front of me, and for the first time in a while, optimism bubbles up. Maybe I can do anything after all.

"What's on your mind?" he asks. "You've gone all quiet." He bumps my shoulder with his.

"I was just thinking that this is going to be terrible pizza."

He drops a slice of ham onto the dough, having opened the can of sauce and spread it around. "I find that hunger seasons things quite nicely. Also beer, but that didn't happen tonight, so that palate killer is gone."

"I notice you didn't refute my assertion about the pizza's quality."

"You caught that, huh?"

I nod. "Attention to detail is why I get paid the big bucks."

He pops a piece of pepperoni in my mouth.

<hr />

BANG.

Before I've fully woken up, Blake has shoved me to the floor and rolled on top of me. He covers my body with his while our hearts pound and we wait for another gunshot. He's steady, but my hands shake and my knees feel rubbery.

Are we under attack? Who the hell would shoot at us?

What if someone shot a window out and hurt Buddy? If anything happened to Shelby's cat, I'd never forgive myself.

We must have fallen asleep on the couch after eating our way into matching food comas and stripping to our underwear. But Blake was so warm, and the movie couldn't keep my attention.

And now we're being shot at.

I never should have left the safety of New York. I mean, yeah, we still kill each other there, but at least back home the person will look you in the eyes before shoving you in front of a train.

I try to breathe shallowly so I can hear better, but my heart thunders in my ears, covering everything else. A long moment passes, and Blake's comforting weight leaves my body as he sits up.

"You know, I don't think that was actually a gunshot," Blake says. He gives me a squeeze from behind.

"I don't know if it was or not, but should we check?" My voice shakes, and I hate it so goddamn much.

"I'll check. You get your phone ready to call 911 just in case."

I'd protest, but the way he stalks toward the kitchen is pretty hot, and at the end of the day, I'm no fighter. I'm glad he's here with me, but I need to do something permanent about this damsel-in-distress bullshit.

My fingers tremble on the phone. It's just after three a.m., so we can't have dozed for long, but I dial nine and one, waiting for a sign from Blake before proceeding.

The light flicks on in the kitchen. "Oh my God."

"What is it? Blake?"

His laughter is the last thing I expect. "Hang up the phone, Mel, and come see this."

I do, but I keep the phone on me just in case. There was a huge bang, after all.

Blake spins slowly around the kitchen, stopping to stare at the ceiling. I move beside him, taking in the weird blobs of white. "What is that? Is that biscuit dough?"

He nods. "Apparently when left unrefrigerated, the tubes turn into weak-ass percussion grenades."

Chunks of raw dough are everywhere. A blob falls from the ceiling, landing on Blake's forehead with a wet slap, and I lose it. Laughter explodes from me with the same force as the biscuits came out of the can.

He raises his eyebrows. "Oh, you think this is funny?"

Tears slip down my cheeks.

He backs me against the counter and grabs a chunk of dough.

"No! It's not funny," I gasp for air, unable to quit laughing, even while he brandishes the dough at me like it's a deadly snake curled up in his palm. "I'm sorry."

"You're such a liar."

I lean in and kiss his neck. "No, I'm sorry. Let me make it up to you."

He squishes the greasy dough against my face. "*Now* you can make it up to me."

My stomach aches from laughing. When was the last time I had fun like this? I feel more relaxed when I'm with him, like it's OK to be silly and cut loose. Like it's OK to be sexy and confident and take what I want with no regrets. Maybe I should be mad about the yeasty blob on my cheek, but all I can focus on is the way his body fits perfectly against mine—which makes me think about the perfect way he fits inside me.

And I want that right now.

Chapter 14

Blake

I PULL BACK TO HELP CLEAN UP. I DON'T KNOW HOW SO MUCH dough got everywhere. The can wasn't that big—how much did they pack in it? The bits on the cupboard come off easily enough, and I'm glad the color scheme is light, or it would look worse than it actually is.

I scoop most of what landed on the counter into my hand, using the glob to pick up more pieces that have been blasted to the cupboards.

I look up and—for fuck's sake, there's even more on the ceiling.

"This is brutal," I say, laughing.

"They should really put a warning on those things."

I toss the dough into the garbage and wash my hands. "Dangerous muffins."

She laughs. We should clean this up before it hardens, but I pull her into my arms, her back against my chest, and kiss the nape of her neck.

She tips her head to give me better access, and I take full advantage. "I believe I won our contest," I say.

She squeaks when I nip her earlobe. "I thought I was the winner."

I shake my head. "Nope. I think it was technically a tie, but I'm claiming my reward first."

"Is that so? I mean, if we had been shot at tonight, you might have saved my life. What do you want for your reward?" She rubs her ass against my erection.

I spin her around to look in her eyes. They're all pupil. "You. I want you to fuck me, Mel. I want to watch you ride me. Lights on."

She shivers. "But with the lights, you'll be able to see—"

"Everything." I press my hips against hers, and she moans. "Everything about you is incredible. Do you feel how much I want you?"

She nods and shuts her eyes.

"What's holding you back?"

"I am." Her eyes open. "Not tonight."

She grabs my hand, and we hurry to the bedroom. She whips my clothes off while I'm distracted by the taste of her neck. I don't even care that I'm standing here naked; I swing her up into my arms and head straight for the bed.

"Wait," she says. "There's something I've always wanted to try. I think I could do it with you."

Her voice is shy, but her eyes pierce every inhibition I've ever had. No matter what it is, I will do whatever she wants just to make her feel good.

I set her down but don't let go. "Anything you want. What is it?"

She smiles and kisses my chest. "I'll be right back." The look she tosses over her shoulder on the way out makes me bite my lip.

What is she doing? Maybe she's grabbing whipped cream or something she wants licked off her body—or wants to lick from mine. I'm not typically a fan of food in the bedroom, but whatever Mel wants, Mel's going to get.

Twice.

I lie back on the bed, propped on my elbows as I wait for her return. My dick is so hard it touches my stomach.

Her hand snakes inside the door, and she sets an iPod dock on the dresser. Some song I've never heard before pulses through the speakers, but it's got a sexy beat.

I can feel the giant smile on my face. She's going to strip for me.

She sidles in, every step deliberate, only now she's wearing panties, a tank top, and my black button-down. Her in my shirt does things to me and I sit up, unable to tear my gaze from her and the way she undulates her hips as she walks around the bedroom. She's stiff at first, but as she concentrates and immerses herself in the music, her motions become more languid, sexier as her confidence grows.

The buttons on my shirt take a second for her to undo, but she turns her back to me to open it and strip it off. She peeks over her shoulder and must see something steadying in my smile, because she winks and gives a little shake as it hits the floor.

Her tank top follows suit, and I swallow hard. My hands itch to touch every inch of her exposed skin— and all the bits still hidden from me beneath fabric and inhibition.

I lie back to enjoy the sight.

Mel shimmies and swivels, dancing to the beat of the song, swaying in her light-purple panties. My cock pulses in time with her movements. Her quadriceps are gorgeously defined. Her weight shifts her body from side to side while she steps out of the pants, laughing a little at her clumsiness.

"This is supposed to be sexier."

"No." My voice catches. "Trust me. You're doing perfectly."

She moves closer, reaching back to undo her bra.

I sit up, barely breathing. "You're so sexy."

Mel walks over and turns her back to me when I move to the edge of the bed. The backs of her smooth thighs rub against my legs as she grinds her way up my legs. She takes her time reaching my erection, teasing it against her ass.

I kiss her back and the nape of her neck, but I keep my hands to myself. She smiles and stands, tossing her bra at me. She covers herself with her hands, turning to the side and stripping her panties off.

"Let me see you." I swallow hard, salivating at everything I can see and tortured by what I can't.

There's a split second of hesitation, but her gaze flickers to my very hard dick. She turns to face me, dropping her hands. Even my fingertips throb with wanting. She slowly spins around, letting me drink in the sight of her.

That's it. I can't not touch her anymore.

I stand and grab the back of her neck, savaging her mouth with deep plunges of my tongue to make up for the agony of pleasure she's subjected me to with this teasing dance. She moans into my mouth when I squeeze her ass, reveling in the way it feels in my hands. It's like she's been a dream, an illusion this whole time, and I'm in a frenzy to prove to my body that she's real and I'm the lucky bastard who gets to have her.

Soon.

I nip her earlobe and pull her tighter to me, maximizing the amount of contact between us. I rub against her until she pulls at my ass too, trying to draw me closer. Her nails claw at my back, painful and gratifying.

I grab the backs of her thighs, spread her legs, and lift her against me. She's warm and wet, soaking the top of my shaft. She takes advantage of the proximity and crushes her lips to mine again, rubbing against me, killing my self-control.

I walk us backward toward the bed and pull her legs down so she's standing. I sit on the bed, shuffling over on my back so my head's on the pillow where it should be. I gesture for her to come to me. She climbs on top, kissing her way up my belly and chest, and then pauses as though unsure what comes next.

I gently grip her hips. "What's up?"

Her eyes flick down and she smirks. "Aside from the obvious? I've never really done this."

"If that dance was anything to go by, you should give your imagination a longer leash." I run my hands down, then up her thighs.

"I know, but…"

"But what?"

She hesitates.

"Close your eyes," I say. She does. I slide my fingers from her hips in toward her belly. She shivers, and her nipples pucker into tight little buds. "How's this feel?"

"Nice."

I move my hands lower, down her pubic bone, past her clit. I dip my fingers into her wetness and slick it back up, rubbing in light, slippery circles.

She moans. "So good."

"Put your hands on my chest." She does. I sit up and flick a nipple into my mouth, giving it a leisurely suck while I continue gliding my hands back and forth, using my four fingers as ridges of pleasure. When her breath turns to mewls and pants, I increase the pressure and speed until her nails dig into my chest. She sits up straight, twitching, and more honey coats my fingers.

"God, Blake."

Her lips are swollen and dark pink, the blood making her face deliciously flushed as well. When she comes, she moves so languidly it's like she's in slow motion. She forgets to be self-conscious. I can't take my eyes off her. Off that slow smile.

I palm her breasts. "What do you want now, Mel?"

"Just you."

"Which part of me?"

She bites her lip and takes me in her hands, leisurely stroking. "This part." Her gaze burns into mine, bold, sure of herself. She knows what she wants and isn't scared to take it. Coming does this to her.

I want to make her come every hour so she floats through her days exactly like this. This sure of herself, this gloriously unself-conscious.

"Get a condom," I growl.

Her lips curl into a wicked grin, and she milks me a few more times from root to tip. She tells me with her actions that this time she wants to be the one in charge, and I should lie back and take it.

No arguments from me.

She scoots back and bends, caressing the tip of my cock with her tongue. Heat lances through my belly and spreads up my torso in time with her licks. As lightly as

I'm able, I trail my fingers through her scalp and hold her hair out of the way.

I don't need to direct her movement, but the urge to thrust invades every cell of my body, screaming at me to do it. I keep my grip loose but thrust up to meet her—giving in to the impulse, but giving her the freedom to back off.

She doesn't.

She draws me deeper, sucks harder, pumps her hand faster up my shaft.

This time I firmly push her away.

"Condom. Now."

Chapter 15

Melanie

I'M SO AROUSED I CAN FEEL THE WETNESS ON MY INNER thighs, the pulsing between my legs as insistent as though my heart lies there instead of in my chest.

His body is tense, muscles ropey and flexed like he's holding back. I don't want him to hold back. *I* don't want to hold back.

That's why I danced for him—something I've pictured doing before, something to turn him on. I never could have imagined how hot it would make me as well.

I grab a condom from the nightstand and open the packet.

I want us to crash together with everything we've got. A tsunami of pleasure, forcing away everything but our bodies and this bed. He tenses when I roll the condom down his cock. His taste still lingers on my tongue. When I danced for him, I felt sexy. When he made me come, I felt free. Free from obligations and worries and doubts and indecision.

Unshackle me, Blake. Unchain me from the restrictions I use to tether myself to the person I think I should be.

He reaches out a hand to guide me. I take it and rise onto my knees to slowly move into position, spread above him. I try to keep my gaze on his when I sink down, but the way he fills me is too good, too much, and my eyes drift shut.

Blake's hands claim me more with every caress of my hips and breasts and belly. I claim him back by rocking back and forth, giving him everything I can. I open my eyes again, finding his.

I want to see in his eyes that he's mine as well. That I'm erasing everything else in the world for him like he does for me, buying us a brief time of pure bliss.

How does he connect me to a line of confidence? Is it because I want to drive him wild so badly it makes me forget all my inhibitions? Wanting to see the lust in his eyes transforms me into the sexy version of myself I've always wanted to be. With Blake, it's easy to be her.

How do I keep this feeling alive inside me when he's not?

His fingers dig into my hips, a firm pressure reminding me that we're making this together. I cover his hands with mine—laughably small compared to his—and smile down at him. "I could do this forever."

"Promise?" He thrusts up harder, nudging against a deep place inside me, and I gasp.

I want more. I want it to hurt when I sit down, want to ache inside for days knowing it was Blake who left me so deliciously sore. Secret marks only we know about.

All I want is more, and more, and more, but a dull pain in my left hip is replaced with a sharp cramp that throws off my motions. Blake sits up, wraps his arms around me, and lies me down on my back.

Still buried deep inside me, he kisses me slowly,

lingeringly, and somehow that turns me on even more. But it's nothing compared to what him pinning my hands above our heads does. My nipples ache, and my pussy convulses around him with greedy want.

He pulls back. "Mmm, Mel. I could do this forever."

"I want it forever. I want it now." The words come out husky, laced with need.

He gives it to me. God, he gives it to me. Pinned to the bed with a giant smile on my face, I feel my breasts bounce with every thrust of his skillful hips.

Blake keeps looking down at them, shaking his head and groaning as he fucks me harder, deeper. He must like how that looks almost as much as his reaction makes me feel.

I want to wrap my arms around him, hold his tight ass hard, and pull him against me like I can draw him farther inside. But his grip on my hands is unescapable—not that I want him to let go. Instead, I spread my legs wider. So much sensual friction whips me around, making me dizzy inside myself. Every nerve is lit with awareness, sizzling with the slightest touch.

I didn't know it could be like this.

I didn't know *I* could be like this.

He's breaking my expectations, smashing them with every thrust, showing me that I need more. Should *want* more—from lovers—for myself.

I tense deep inside, on the verge of coming. I want to hold off, to draw this out forever, to live on the edge of perfection with Blake.

But he already knows my body too well, and with one last thrust, I completely unravel beneath him.

"I think that's all of it." I squint critically at the kitchen, trying to find an errant blob of dough, but we seem to have gotten it all.

Blake nods and yawns. "Leaving it to dry probably made it easier to clean."

Instead of smearing, it let us just pick off the spots and sweep them along. Not that waiting was a conscious choice. After we got sidetracked, we fell back asleep. I woke him up early for our date and we were talking wistfully about coffee before remembering the kitchen disaster and got to work cleaning it. "Yeah, but I'm kind of starving. It's too bad we don't have those biscuits."

He smiles and embraces me from behind. "I could go get another tube."

I snuggle against him, enjoying the perfect fit. "No way. With our luck, we'd have a raging case of déjà vu."

"You say that like it's a bad thing."

"Spending time cleaning when we could be doing… other things? That's a waste."

He nuzzles my neck. "What other things?"

"I want to get really wet with you." I grin and pull away. "And if that clock is correct, we've got to be at the beach in twenty minutes."

"For?"

"A thing I arranged."

"What thing?" His voice goes slightly higher with excitement.

"It's a surprise." And another thing I've always wanted to do.

"Mmm. I have ways of making you talk." His lips find the sensitive spot where my neck meets my jaw, and for a dizzying moment, I forget what we were talking about.

He turns me around, moving me like I'm the clay beneath his potter's hands. His kiss can change me on fundamental levels. I think it already has.

Warmth slides up my spine an inch behind his hand, sending a parade of tingles through me. It makes me shiver even before his tongue caresses mine.

"That only works in the movies." My body is swollen with need again, but I pull away before he realizes how much I want to throw him to the floor and climb on top—and damn my plans. If they slept until noon and then cleaned and are just now getting on a charter bus for Marathon, they won't be getting there until 4:00 p.m. at the earliest. Is that okay? I tug him toward the door and lock it behind us.

"There?"

"Marathon."

He squints and doesn't ask me to elaborate, but I can tell he's intrigued.

We walk hand in hand to the beach, silent. He refuses to ask, and I refuse to offer any further information— even when we board a charter bus with a group of other tourists. His strong jaw works, but his lips stay in an amused smirk. We rumble down the road in our air-conditioned chariot, and for a while we sit in silence.

"Hey." Blake turns to me. "I thought you had motion sickness."

"No, I haven't been bothered by that since I was sixteen." Mortification hits a moment later.

The last time I had motion sickness, we'd gone on a camping trip—and Blake had been invited along as

Shawn's friend. I'd ridden in the very back of the van, the boys deciding they needed the bucket seats in the middle row. I'd been so self-conscious and distracted by the idea of sleeping next to Blake—if only through the walls of our separate tents—that I'd been unable to focus on my book. I kept looking out the window.

Big mistake. The only way I got through road trips longer than twenty minutes was by keeping my nose in a book the entire time.

I'd asked, voice as weak as my stomach, if we could stop for a minute. Shawn had turned and yelled, "Dad! Melanie's green!"

Fortunately, I'd stress eaten nearly a whole bag of chips—and then I puked them up back into their bag. Horrifyingly, I'd made eye contact with Blake just before they came up.

Now, he laughs. "I'm glad you got over it."

"Me too."

I don't know if it's a blessing or a curse, dating someone who was there to witness your most mortifying formative years while he looked like a dream. I can't rewrite history and pretend I was smoother than I was. But on the other hand, I don't have to waste energy pretending I was perfect. Pretending to *be* perfect.

Blake knows me and hasn't run screaming from the state yet. Here in Florida, I'm the most myself I've ever been, and it's because he knows everything. It's more than that, though. He knows everything but doesn't lock me into the cage of expectation.

I bite my lip, watching the foreign landscape go by.

When you've known someone forever, you expect them to behave in certain ways, even when you don't see them that often. You lock them in a static place where they keep the shape you expect them to, and you resist when they change.

A militant carnivore becomes a vegan. Someone gets the travel bug and embraces other cultures, developing worldly affectations that make you feel like they're a stranger.

But that's not fair. It's another kind of limitation, trying to force them back inside the skin of the person they used to be.

Blake knows who I was, but he accepts me for the person I am, the one I'm trying to be. That's rare. I take his hand and lay my head on his shoulder, glad he's here with me. If anyone else had shown up on the beach, who knows how things would have changed? I might have jumped back into the ill-fitting box and stayed cramped inside to meet their expectations.

It makes me glad to go on an adventure with him.

It makes me want to go on *every* adventure with him.

Chapter 16

Blake

DOLPHINS FEEL LIKE A WET, PEELED, HARD-BOILED EGG.

It's fucking awesome.

The life jacket rides up in a way that's impossible to feel cool in, but we're swimming with dolphins. The thought derails any pretenses. Mostly.

I've felt Mel's gaze on me off and on all day. Jolts of awareness slide up my spine in an electrically pleasant way to let me know when she's looking. I like knowing she's staring. I like seeing her blush when I catch her.

I like it even better that she hasn't noticed me staring in her unguarded moments.

She's especially beautiful today—sexy in an effort-less way. Maybe it's because of the way she was in bed last night. I don't know. But she's calmer. The perma-frown left her brow sometime in the last few days, and her neck has elongated since the tension eased from her shoulders, letting her relax. I wonder if she even remem-bers how her shoulder hurt just a few days ago. I guess it's been over a week.

Time flies in paradise.

The dolphin cackles at me with its squeaky voice and squirts me with a jet of water from its mouth.

Mabel is a jealous girl, apparently. I laugh and rub

her tummy, focusing on her again. "Aww, don't be jealous, Mabel. You know I love you."

She waves her left fin, and I grab a fish from the bucket on the dock and feed it to her. Happiness radiates from her bottle-nosed face. Dolphins are supposed to be one of the smartest species on the planet, and I believe it.

But I didn't know they could be so human with their quirks and personality.

Mel brought me to the Dolphin Research Center in Marathon. It was a long drive but worth it, spent talking about old times. It's funny how I never knew about Mel's crush on me. Maybe because she was young and I was focused on other things, not seeing it because I never expected to see it.

Not that she's admitting anything more than a crush then and sexual attraction now. But the way she remembers everything in vivid detail means she should either be a crime scene investigator or she was very aware of me. It could be both—she's so sharp.

Mel tips onto her side and waves, encouraging her dolphin friend Bartleby to do the same. She grins and claps when he does. "Such a smart boy, Bartleby!" She slips a fish his way, and he spins a quick spiral in the water.

Mabel clicks at me and nods as though to say, "I'm smart too!"

I give her another fish. They remind me of dogs with their expressive faces and personalities—and the way they demand as many snacks as possible.

The enclosure is huge; they really care about the dolphins' well-being here instead of making it a gaudy tourist trap. We're on either sides of a floating dock with a trainer on it, monitoring everything. He encourages shenanigans from the sidelines as the dolphins streak through the water between us and the other two people in the group.

I've always wanted to do this, and I can't believe Mel remembered that I mentioned it once, years ago.

I'm glad *Marathon* referred to a place and wasn't her sadistic decision to make us go on a running date. I have clients who mention doing that—running dates instead of coffee dates. Where's the romance in that? If I want to get a woman sweaty, I can think of four or five much more interesting alternatives than jogging up a path beside her. And if that's your first date, what are you really getting to know about her? Maybe it's an excuse to watch her tits bounce—I don't know.

I'd rather get to know someone by talking to them, spending time with them first. Maybe that's why these adventures with Mel are more fun. We already know each other, and we don't have to waste time digging into each other's histories. We don't need to get invested and then worry the person isn't who they appear to be while we wait for the other shoe to drop.

With Mel, I already know she's an amazing person. I already know where she came from.

But I'm excited as hell to discover who she is now. She's unique. She's fearless and tough, opinionated and creative, and perfectly stubborn.

I like knowing that no matter how much I push, she'd never let me run over her. If she didn't want to do something, she'd be direct and vocal. No games, no guile.

It's refreshing as hell after some of the dates I've had in the past few years.

And all of that in the sexiest package I could imagine?

I love this woman.

Shit.

I can't have fallen so hard and fast for my best friend's little sister. I practically grew up at her house. It's just affection for who she is and our shared history. Not *love*. Isn't it too soon for that?

Mel's family became my own—better than my own. My mom was a drug addict and I never knew my father, and while my foster parents weren't abusive, they were cold. Maybe they'd been attached to one too many kids before me who'd betrayed them or let them down. I don't know. But I do know this: if Mel and I were to take this back to New York and then break up, I'd lose her *and* the only family that ever mattered to me—the only people I ever mattered *to*.

It's a hell of a risk. Is it worth it?

Bartleby sprays Mel's face. Instead of squealing and fixing her hair and makeup, Mel sucks in a mouthful of seawater and sprays the dolphin right back.

Yeah, I'm a goner. It's scary as hell, but Mel *is* worth it.

"OK, guys, I think it's time for Mabel and Bartleby to go have their real lunch."

I give Mabel one last pet, staring into her eyes. They seem so gentle and playful, the best aspects of humans in one innocent creature. Carefree, but dolphins will step in and save people from sharks and danger…and I'm totally anthropomorphizing, but whatever.

"I'm starving too," Mel says, grinning at me over Bartleby's back. "But I definitely do not want to eat any fish."

Mel steals a bite of my cheeseburger, so I swipe the end from one of her chicken strips in retaliation.

"Hey," she protests around her bite. "That was mine."

"Says the woman fondling my lunch."

She takes a theatrically big bite. "Mmm, it's so good." She feeds me another bite of chicken, and I nip her fingertips.

"Thank you."

She hands my burger back and her mouth quirks like she's suppressing a smile, but she covers it by eating another fry.

"Thanks for this today, Mel."

"I give good date."

I laugh. "Yes, you do. I can't believe you remembered this was something I wanted to do."

She shrugs with one shoulder. "I think it's on everybody's bucket list at some point. I don't know anyone who hates dolphins."

"They do get a lot of love."

"Deservedly so. Though I'm a little annoyed that I won't be able to eat tuna guilt-free again." She munches on another fry.

"Funny how no one seems to care about saving the *tuna*." I take a sip of soda.

Mel tips her head. "Huh. I never thought about that. Maybe it's about personality. Dolphins are showier. Same as how we don't eat cats and dogs."

"Some cultures eat dogs."

"That's gross." She frowns. "We should do an article about that." She fires off a quick text. "Seems like it's all about perception. We attribute value to things we like

and decide to protect them just because of that attach-
ment. It seems arbitrary."

"I know. Maybe if we got to know the tuna, we'd see
they have personalities too."

She narrows her eyes. "Are you trying to put me off
my lunch?"

"Just being devil's advocate." I finish my burger. "A
hypocritical devil's advocate."

She dunks her last two fries in the ketchup. "At least
I don't have to worry about the humble potato suffering
for my enjoyment."

"It died for your sins."

"Shut up." She smiles, and we toss our garbage in the
trash can before heading inside to the aquarium.

I don't take her hand, but I want to. Instead, we sit on
the edge of the touch tank, a shallow pool where small
turtles and stingrays glide along. If you trail your fingers
in the water, you can pet them too.

"I like how hands-on this place is," Mel says. She
eases her hand into the water, patiently waiting for
something to come to her instead of chasing it around
like some of the tourists around us are doing.

A woman with flowing gray hair strides around the
pool, and a group of people follow her. They look sus-
piciously like hippies, reminding me of Fern and Ziggy.
"Stingrays represent being an expert in camouflage and
waiting for the right opportunity to act—but not hesitating to go for what you want, and not letting anything
distract you from your path once you find it."

The pack oohs and aahs and moves along, but her
words sit heavy with me. She could be talking about me
and physical therapy, or me and Mel. What if I hesitate

and lose her? What are we even doing together? Is this just a holiday fling? It sure as hell doesn't feel like "just" anything.

A turtle nudges Mel's hand, waving a gentle infinity pattern in the water.

I flick the surface of the water. "I wonder what turtles mean."

"To what?"

"Hippies. Did you hear that hippie lady about the stingrays?"

Movement in the pool kicks back a reflection, sending gentle waves of light and shadow across her face. "I was thinking about something else and missed it."

"It was about opportunities. You know. Spirit animal stuff…" I feel silly.

She smiles. "No idea what a turtle would mean then. Slow and steady wins the race? Keep pushing for what you want, even if you don't think you'll ever reach the finish line?"

Fuck it. "You know what?" I take her hand and she looks up in surprise, then smiles. "That's perfect."

Chapter 17
Melanie

I'M SO HAPPY IT'S NAUSEATING.

My breaths come out in contented sighs, and I want to spin on the spot with my arms spread wide open. This is what it would feel like to be in a musical. Everyone smiles at me when I pass, but maybe that's because I have a goofy perma-grin I can't seem to knock into submission. Every part of my body is light and relaxed.

And it's all Blake's fault.

In the four days since we went on our trip to Marathon, we've basically been together the whole time—soaking up sun, snorkeling. We even rented paddleboats one day, but that wasn't my favorite activity, despite being my idea. I'd pictured it as romantic and sedate, something relaxing you do that's active. I hadn't realized it was so much exercise and almost fainted in the heat. And while swimming in the water is enjoyable, being trapped in a pseudo-spin class with the sun blazing on you—and being reflected up from the water—was terrible.

Besides, I can think of about eighteen better ways to work up a sweat with Blake Wilde, and none of them involve clothes. He's making my life a brighter place, and I'm too smug and happy about it to properly resent it like I should. Because no matter how high a bird soars, eventually it has to come back down.

But maybe not yet.

Blake only has one day left here, and we're going to stick together like Velcro the whole time.

His good-night kiss tonight was so tender and warm, the physical representation of the feeling in my chest. As exhausted as I should be, a buzzing energy fills me to the tips of my fingers and toes at the memory of it. Who needs sleep? I'm powered by disbelief and glee that this is actually happening.

Blake wanted me to spend the night, and I want to spend as much time with him as possible, but a selfish part of me wanted time alone so I can wallow in this feeling. I can't do that when he's with me, so he went back to his hotel and I'm ambling back to Shelby's by myself. Maybe it's also to see how I feel when he's gone and reassure myself that it's all real. When he's around, all I can think about is, well, *nothing* because he eclipses everything. I'm annoyingly content right now. Even the sidewalk cracks seem charming, with plants growing through, nature bitch-slapping civilization.

Remnants of sand grit beneath my sandal-clad feet. I need a shower. I'm dry now, but there's a distinctly crunchy quality to my clothes from the salt in the water, and it pulls at my skin, making it tight.

Maybe no one's old in Florida—they're just all wrinkly from spending so much time in the water. That, or it's the insane humidity.

Staying in the water is delightful when Blake's there with me, shirtless and showing off his dimples. He was so cute with that dolphin last week. I don't know whose smile was bigger. Happiness bubbling over, I slide the key in the lock…and meet no resistance from the deadbolt.

Did I forget to lock up before I left? There's no way. I mentally retrace my steps. I clearly remember locking the door behind us before we went snorkeling today because Blake took full advantage of my hands being occupied.

Buddy shoots through my legs and out the door like he's been camped out beside it.

I trip over a few pairs of shoes, recovering my equilibrium before I fall.

Someone's in the house. My mouth waters as nauseating fear slams into me in massive waves. My gaze ricochets around, searching for details as I tense, instincts warring to freeze, confront, or get the hell out of here.

The air has a distinct rosemary tinge to it, like someone's baking.

I strain to hear sounds of smashing or rustling, noises of things being dropped into bags, stolen. Nothing.

The shoes are a mix of old sneakers and sandals—nothing like I'd expect from someone kicking their way in. Nothing in the immediate area is disturbed or broken.

A woman's musical peals of laughter cut through the deep rumbling of male voices. Iron enters my spine, straightening it. I'll be damned if I'm going to run away. It could be some stupid teenagers having a party.

I've done enough running in my life, enough being scared of the unknown and slinking away from things. I won't let someone invade Shelby's house on my watch.

I cautiously follow the voices into the living room. After all, maybe it's not teenagers. A quick peek to assess the situation. If it's a gang doing something illegal, I'll tiptoe back out and call the police.

Two pairs of twentysomething men and women have made themselves at home on the couch and floor.

I pull back out of sight again. Squatters? But they look clean and groomed. Sort of hip. What are those people who go from place to place, taking over people's houses, never paying rent…free men on the land?

Their voices become clearer, and I pause to listen.

"…an ice pick," a woman says, laughing.

"No, amputations wins," a man good-naturedly argues.

What the fuck? I stride into the room, hoping the frantic beating of my heart—and the fear coursing through me—aren't visible on my face. "What the hell?" I ask.

The young woman nestled in a blanket on the floor looks like Lupita Nyong'o but with better arms, which I didn't know was possible.

A lanky guy with black hair and ridiculously long eyelashes grins up at me from the couch. "Hey!"

Next to him, a woman with the palest skin I've ever seen, except for the freckles, turns my way. She tugs on one of her strawberry-blond, shoulder-length dreadlocks with a grin.

A bearded blond guy sitting on the floor with his back to the couch stands and holds out his hand. "Hey. I'm Andrew."

I stare at his hand, not taking it. "Hi? At the risk of sounding like a bitch, who the hell are you people and why are you here?" A couple of them look familiar, but I can't think why.

Lupita Look-Alike laughs. "We're friends of Shelby's. I'm Ariella." She points at the woman with dreads. "That's Lindsay."

The pictures on Shelby's wall! That's where I've seen these people before. So their story checks out, at least. My spine marginally relaxes, and I take a deeper breath.

Eyelashes on the couch nods. "I'm Gaz." And Australian, judging by the accent. "Want to join us?"

The talk of ice picks and amputations comes back to me. "Doing what?"

Ariella holds up some small black cards. "We're playing Cards Against Humanity."

"Oh." Belatedly, I notice the cards on the coffee table and in their hands. So they are. I've heard of it—never got around to playing it, but it sounds like fun. I'm still unable to wrap my mind around the fact that they just let themselves into Shelby's house, though. Who does that? "Well, Shelby's not here, you know."

"No, we realized that," Andrew says, settling back onto the floor. "But we figured we may as well hang and play a game until she gets back."

I frown. "She won't be back for a while. She's in New York."

Gaz grins. "That's what she said when we called her. Shelby in the Big Apple. I can't even imagine."

Andrew nods. "Remember that time in Denver with the tattoo artist and the chef?"

"Classic Shelby." Gaz takes a sip from his can of beer. He's not using a coaster.

"So you're from New York?" Lindsay asks. "How did you and Shelby meet?"

I shuffle my feet. "We've never actually met. We connected online through a website where people switch apartments for specific amounts of time. Sort of a way to experience someone else's life."

"That's wild," Andrew says, shaking his head. "I could never do something like that. What if the person you switched with was a total psycho?"

Lindsay pokes him none too gently in the ribs.

"Ouch, what was that?" He follows her gaze to me. "No, I'm not saying *you're* a psycho."

"Says the strange guy and his friends who let themselves into my temporary place?" I smile, letting them know I'm not offended. "I was worried about the same thing, to be honest. I don't typically do things like this."

"Shelby does." Ariella sets her cards on the table. "She's always doing strange things, getting caught up in things that would freak most people out. She thinks they're exciting. Somehow, she always ends up OK."

She sounds too good to be real, and yet I'm in her house with her too-hip friends.

"You attract what you expect," Lindsay declares. "She puts out nothing but positivity, and that's why she only gets that back."

Sounds like hippie bullshit to me, but I smile politely while they nod among themselves. Is that why things don't always work out for me? Because I expect them to fall apart? Whatever. Things are obviously turning around—look at Blake and me.

"So, do you want to join us?" Andrew asks.

Suddenly, I'm hyperaware that I've been snorkeling with marine life all day. I probably smell a little ripe. "I really need to grab a shower first."

"Cool. I've got some fries in the oven, so they should be done by the time you get out, if you're hungry." Lindsay's blue eyes crinkle at the edges with her disarming smile.

"That sounds awesome." I smile back and head to the bedroom first to grab a change of clothes.

It's odd, but I don't feel weird having a shower while strangers sit in the living room playing a subversive card game.

Maybe because they're only my strangers, not Shelby's. And they obviously do this all the time. Still, I double-check the photo collage, making sure I remembered them correctly. If the sheer number of photos of them is any indication, they're a huge part of Shelby's life.

There's a shot of Ariella and Shelby, arms around each other at the top of a rock-climbing wall, which explains Ariella's arms. She's as sporty as Shelby seems to be. Another is a candid of Ariella in a kayak—which always makes me feel claustrophobic because it's like a boat you wear. Your legs aren't really trapped in them, but I've had bad experiences with too-small shirts in department store changing rooms that made me panic when I thought I'd be stuck. I can't imagine being in a kayak that's flipped over. I don't have to do it to know it's not for me.

Ariella is in more pictures than anyone, other than Shelby herself. She must be her best friend.

The others are sprinkled through many of the pictures with Shelby, alone or in groups.

I shake my head and hop in the shower.

Getting to know them—and getting to know Shelby through them—is too tempting an opportunity to pass up.

This carefree woman so unlike myself has an open life filled with friends and adventures. I want to taste that a little, to know what it's like. And I want to know if playing Cards Against Humanity is as much fun with strangers as it looks.

Wallowing in what I may or may not be feeling for Blake can wait.

Chapter 18

Blake

I DON'T KNOW IF IT'S THE ENDORPHINS OR IF I'M JUST REALLY excited to see her, but I wake up early the next morning, bright-eyed and bushy-tailed like someone's flipped a switch.

Maybe having spent the whole night sleeping instead of making love to Mel has something to do with it. It was good for us to take a break for a night. My muscles feel better after a full night's sleep. But maybe it's like the saying, and absence makes the heart grow fonder. Either way, my batteries are fully charged—and I can't wait to see her again. I was disappointed that she wanted some alone time last night, but that will make it all the better when we're together again.

It's my last full day in Miami, and I want to spend as much time with Mel as possible.

I shower and dress, but it's still only nine thirty-seven when I finish. Screw it. She can't be mad if I show up with coffee and something sweet for breakfast—or a good-morning snuggle. Or a *really* good-morning snuggle-fuck. I get turned on just picturing sliding into bed with her, her sleep-warmed body nestling against me. Her eyes will flutter open with surprise and then happiness that I'm there. Her lips will part, and I'll kiss her as she spreads her legs and wordlessly encourages me to climb on top.

And after, we'll talk about what happens when we get back home. I'm ready to dive in face-first, hands first with Mel, despite how it might turn out. I can't think about bad things that might not happen. What we have could be forever.

I hurry down to the lobby and grab a couple coffees from a place the guy at the front desk recommended. They also sell pastries, and unsure of her favorites, I grab half a dozen different ones before hopping into the first cab I find and heading for Mel's.

We're not out in the wilderness, but there's something so open and wild about seeing this much blue sky at once. It's almost oppressive, but I'm growing to really love it—not that I don't miss the way the crush of buildings in New York feels private, blocking all but your little corner from the skyline.

You can see forever here.

She doesn't answer when I knock. I laugh. Being spontaneous with Mel is something I should choreograph. Where did she go?

On impulse, I wiggle the doorknob. The door's unlocked when I try it, which isn't like Mel. Safety conscious and anal retentive, she wouldn't leave it open. I lock the door behind me and set the coffees and breakfast on the counter, swiftly checking the living room and bathroom for signs of trouble. Nothing. Did she fall asleep with the door unlocked?

The bedroom door is open a crack, but no light shines through the opening. She must have drawn the curtains to sleep in. I push the door open and stride into the bedroom. She's under the blanket, curled into a tight ball with her back to me, nestling in just like I pictured.

I toe my shoes off, ease the blanket up enough to slip under, and spoon her. "Morning, gorgeous." I pull the covers down to give her a kiss and come face-to-face with a bearded twentysomething blond man. *What the fuck?*

He blinks and yawns. "Sorry, bro. I'm taken."

What the fuck is a strange guy doing in Mel's bed? "Jesus." I sit up, stunned, just as the lights go on and two feminine voices giggle by the door.

Mel and a pretty, athletic black woman clutch each other with the hands not holding coffees.

I stand and put my shoes on. "It's really not that funny."

Mel clears her throat. "I mean, we can come back later, if you and Andrew need a minute to yourselves."

I don't even care about the strangers in the room. Mel's presence fills me, and I walk to her and wrap her in a hug. "Maybe he and I *will* take a minute to ourselves. He's pretty cute."

"Beards are very in," Andrew says, voice still husky with sleep. "Aww, is that coffee for me, Ari?"

The other woman hands him his coffee before turning and offering her hand. "I'm Ariella, Shelby's friend. That bearded ego-patch is Andrew, also friends with Shelby."

I shake her hand. "Nice to meet you. I brought coffees over for Mel—only the two, but it looks like you got some already."

Mel nods. "We grabbed some. We were going to deal with breakfast later."

"I brought some pastries too."

Ariella grins at Mel. "Your boyfriend's pretty awesome."

Mel blushes. "He is."

The fact she doesn't correct Ariella makes me want to grin like an idiot. "Maybe we should give Andrew a second," I say. I'm pretty sure he was naked under that blanket.

"Appreciate it," Andrew says. "I don't want to be the only one wearing a toga."

The women and I head to the kitchen and paw through the bag. We select a pastry each and dig in; a fully dressed Andrew joins us a moment later.

"Thanks for breakfast, man," he says. "These hit the spot."

"You're welcome. You're Shelby's friends?"

Ariella wipes some icing from her lips. "Yeah, we sort of crashed the place before realizing Shelby wasn't here. But Mel was gracious enough to let us stay over."

"It was certainly a surprise to come home to strangers in the living room." Mel smiles and licks glaze from the pad of her thumb.

She's so cool with it. Another layer of tension has peeled away from her—but maybe it's not parts peeling away. Maybe she was this gorgeous flower that was scared to bloom and tried to hide its beauty by staying as tightly closed as it could. Now she's letting herself relax and unfold. She's blossoming.

She's radiant.

"Did you guys have plans? We can get out of your hair if we're intruding." Ariella stands from her casual lean against the counter. "We did just show up out of nowhere, and—"

"I'm crashing this morning too," I say, waving my hand dismissively.

"Hey, do you see me kicking anyone out?" Mel smiles. "The others had reservations for diving or you could have met them too, Blake. Why don't we all go to the beach? Soak up as much of that vitamin D as we can?"

Andrew and Ariella share a glance and nod at the same time.

"I didn't bring a suit, but I can borrow one from Shelby." Ariella finishes her coffee.

"Or, you could go without a suit. Clothing optional beach, babe." Andrew winks at her and she slaps his chest.

"You know I could never do that! What about you, big guy?"

Andrew grimaces. "Nude beaches are sexier for women. When your parts get cold, they tighten up, get more interesting. When our parts get cold, they try to crawl up our asses to keep warm and we look like Ken dolls."

My gaze cuts to Mel, who's trying to suppress her surprise by chewing on the inside of her cheek the way she always does. She's thinking about how she did it, and she's shocked someone as outgoing as Ariella obviously hasn't. Mel constantly underestimates herself. Or, she used to. The image of her that first day I saw her on the beach pops into my mind.

Mel's skin, glowing in the sun, water glistening off every plane and curve. The way she confidently strode out of the water, not worrying about who was looking.

A dip in some cold water would be great for me right about now.

"I think the beach sounds awesome." And I'm already wearing shorts.

Mel turns to Ariella. "I'll grab some towels, if you want to pack some drinks. You know where everything is better than I do."

"I'll take care of the drinks. You go get a bathing suit," Andrew says to Ariella.

Later, we make our way to the beach, which is quieter this time of day. "Does it always rain in the afternoon?" I ask.

Ariella nods. "Pretty much. They're our summer rainstorms. Clouds roll in for about twenty minutes, shake everything up, and then disappear. It's good, really, or it would be sweltering. Isn't New York hot in the summer too?"

Mel makes a face. "You'd think the buildings would give shade and at least trick you into thinking it's cooler. But they trap the air between them like an oven. Haven't you ever been to New York?"

Ariella sighs. "My travels have taken me mostly to Australia—and that obligatory backpacking trip around Europe when I was nineteen."

"Any highlights?"

Andrew laughs. "Bulgaria was way too much fun."

I find that surprising. "Really? You don't hear about it being a barrel of laughs."

Mel nods. "I would have thought Amsterdam or Ibiza—the usual suspects, but not Bulgaria."

Ariella wags her eyebrows. "Sunny Beach. More debauchery than you can shake your tits at."

Andrew laughs. "It's like the G8, if the G8 were made up of spring breakers from all over Europe. Lots of people from the UK."

"Huh." Mel whips out her phone and sends off a text.

"That would make a good article too—unexpectedly sexy vacation hot spots."

"Who are you texting?" Ariella asks.

"My boss," Mel replies.

"You're a writer?"

Mel shakes her head. "I think I'd like to become one, but no. I'm in HR."

Ariella scrunches her nose. "I never would have guessed that. You're too much fun. Ever think of switching to writing as well?"

Mel huffs out a small laugh but looks pleased. "It's never really come up." She bites her lip. "But I don't think I'd total hate it. I get a lot of ideas for things... and there are more people to interact with in Editorial. And I feel like I've gone as far as I can go in my current area—there's nothing left to strive for. If I were in Editorial, there would be more to do."

"Why don't you go for it when you get back?" I ask.

She smiles. "Maybe I will."

We pick a prime place and spread out our towels. The heat and sun have been beating out the clouds, kicking the temperature up a few notches. I peel off my shirt and lie back, ready to soak up some rays.

Mel clears her throat. "Uh, forgetting something?"

I squint up at Mel. "What?"

She wiggles a bottle of sunscreen at me, and I sit up and hold out a hand. She squirts the piña colada–scented lotion into my hands, and I spread it on my arms and shoulders and down my chest and torso.

"I'll get your back," she says.

I lean forward and accept her offer, feeling way

too content about the way her hands move across my skin—even in that innocuous way. "Thanks." I squint at Andrew and Ariella, wishing I'd brought sunglasses. "So, was Shelby with you in Europe?"

"Yup." Ariella opens the oversize umbrella, angling it so we're all partially shaded. "It was her idea. She works in the surf shop here and meets a lot of people— not that she needs an excuse. If Shelby wants to meet you, you're going to be shaking her hand at some point." She sits on the towel Andrew spread for her and settles beside Mel. "She met a tattoo artist who'd just gotten back from Sunny Beach and was raving about the amazing time he had. He's her go-to tattoo guy, now."

"She has tattoos?" Mel asks. "I didn't see any in the pictures on her wall. She must have a lot if she's got a regular artist."

"Yup. She has some work on her feet and a dolphin on the back of her neck."

Mel squints out at the ocean. "Yeah, her pics didn't show her back." She laughs. "That makes me sound like a stalker. I swear I'm not. But you know the mural in her room, and I was dying of curiosity about the person whose house I'm staying in."

"*Suuuure,*" Andrew drawls, obviously kidding. Then he switches gears. "You don't have any tattoos?"

Mel shakes her head. "Not yet."

Not *yet*? Interesting. Maybe Mel's loosening up even more than I thought.

Chapter 19

Melanie

I LIE BACK AND FOLD MY ARMS BEHIND MY HEAD, sandwiched between Ari and Blake and feeling lazier by the second in the heat. "I'd love to travel more. You guys traveled around Europe a lot together? Which place was your favorite?

Blake lies back beside me. Ariella slathers sunscreen on her legs. "Berlin. It's beautiful—there's artwork everywhere, and the people are so edgy and cool without even trying. If you had access to their closets and a month to put something together, you still couldn't look as effortlessly hip as them."

"And the food…" Andrew groans. "A little of everything, and it's all done so well. We need to go back there so I can violate my diet. I gained twelve pounds last time, and I think I can double that with a little effort."

"Definitely," Ariella affirms. "The food, the music, the art… It's a place where diversities crash together into something bright and bold and way different than here. It's unique. I stayed there for two months, and then Andrew and I went back for a three-week vacation two years ago."

"I needed two years to recover." Andrew rolls onto his elbow and grins down at Ari. "Remember that reggae bar on Oranienburger?"

Ariella lifts her sunglasses, revealing serious eyes
that she fixes on Blake and me. "That bar was amazing.
The street's kind of touristy but worth it. Covered with
hookers—it's legal there—but the club scene is second
to none. We danced on a rooftop bar until pink streaked
through the sky. We only stopped dancing because we
needed breakfast."

"Did Shelby go there with you?"

Ariella flips onto her stomach. "No, but we want to
go there together at some point. The coolest thing about
her is that she's the least pretentious person I know. She
comes from money, but she doesn't act like anything's
beneath her. You've seen her apartment—it's lush.
There's no way someone scraping by on minimum wage
could afford that. But she *could* afford nicer. She just
doesn't give a shit about that. Where you come from
doesn't matter as much to her as who you are. People
are drawn to that. Hell, I'm drawn to that. I see a little
of that in you, Mel."

Having Ariella compare me to her best friend in such
a positive way warms my heart. "I don't think so. I wish
I were more like Shelby. She seems so adventurous and
free—my total opposite."

Ariella snorts. "Says the woman doing the same thing
Shelby is. You're just as adventurous as she is. Maybe
you haven't had as much of a chance to explore that, but
the fact is, the similarities are there. Birds of a feather,
Mel. They find each other and flock out—"

"With their cocks out," I finish with a throaty laugh.
"We are on a nude beach, after all."

"No one's getting their cocks out," Andrew says.

I look at Blake out the corner of my eye. It's probably

a good thing since I already have trouble with self-control where he's concerned.

He slips his palm against mine and laces our fingers together.

How can holding someone's hand reduce your awareness to only the places where your skin touches theirs—and all the jealous places on your body where they aren't touching? My world throbs with Blake for a moment, and I like it.

My words dry up with the contact and the sun. It's nice. Sweltering and muggy, but nice.

Ariella's breathing evens out, and I sigh, contented. For a while we doze, soaking in the rays without talking much. But soon the tension coiling through me like a flattened spring gets to be too much and I need to expend that energy, so we all go for a walk.

One by one, everyone breaks off from the group until I'm alone but can still see them, content to dip my toes in the ocean for a little coolness. Andrew decided to go surfing. Ariella and Blake are tossing a football back and forth, a free show of athleticism. Ariella has a killer spiral, but no matter how she tries to trip Blake up, he catches everything easily and returns it.

I'd give it the old college try, but football isn't in my wheelhouse. Besides, I'd rather watch Blake while he's not watching me.

More people mill about, but it's slower, maybe because it's midafternoon on a Wednesday, and now I get what oppressive heat really is. Fan yourself all you want, but you're still going to be covered with a thin sheen of sweat. The heat also slows your thoughts to a syrupy pace so everything seems suspended. You can't quite focus, but you also can't move very quickly from one thought to another. Right now, I'm dwelling on the fact that it's Blake's last day—and I'll be following him home soon.

I'm not quite ready to leave this place. Things will change when we get back. It's strange to think of people living daily lives in paradise, but I guess everywhere is a paradise to someone. It's all about perspective. Some people would give anything to live in my tiny apartment and work in publishing like I do. Kids dream of packing up their things and heading for the Big Apple.

If you can make it there…

The grass is always greener on the other side of the fence, but honestly, I love New York and I can't imagine living anywhere else. I think this much blue sky would crush me. The people are friendly, but everything moves at a slower pace. Maybe it's the heat. Maybe it's the retirees. Maybe it's just that there's concrete in my blood and I miss the bustle and speed of NYC.

How many restaurants have opened and closed since I've been gone? How many plays and art installations haven't I seen? If you blink, you miss a hundred things—and I miss it all. Living here wouldn't feel like life; it would feel like a vacation. It's not enough, no matter how awesome Shelby's friends are. It's not my life—not my real life.

And I'm not a fan of grass being greener on the other side. That seems like trying to escape responsibility for your life turning out a certain way. Water your own grass and see what happens…but that's easier said than done. Sometimes you don't realize how to fix something and nurture it into what you want it to be because what's already there is so deeply rooted.

The warm water splashes over my feet and I want to swim, but the squishy softness of the wet sand is strangely relaxing. I'd rather enjoy it for a minute instead of getting back to the others. Ariella and Andrew are so cool. They've seen so much, done so much. They have the best stories. I've got nothing in common with them, and yet we get along so well.

I want to be more like them, but it feels too late. If I tore off on a world tour, trying to soak in the culture and experiences, I'd feel like a raging impostor. That mom at her teen's party trying desperately to be hip while her kids cringe and wince. She doesn't realize how lame she is until later, when self-awareness hits and she cries herself to sleep.

Water pools in the small pit I dig with my toes, and I move back a little closer to the group.

Fitting in with Shelby's friends is surprising and pleasant, but it makes me wonder what else I've missed because of the rigidity of my life. I take a step deeper into the ocean. How do you shake up a life that still has really good parts?

If I start picking parts of it away, who's to say the whole thing won't fall apart, crumbling into the empty spots left behind?

Unless I fill them with something else.

My gaze flits to Blake, and I grin at how filthy that sounds. There's no guarantee that we can be anything once we get home. He hasn't offered or made me any promises.

It's ridiculous that I want him to. Completely, utterly ridiculous.

He laughs and tosses the ball again, muscles rippling

in his arm, chest, and abs. A flash of heat ripples through my core. It makes me blush, but I don't regret a thing.

OK, maybe it's not completely ridiculous to want him, but what happens when we get home? He goes to his place, I go to mine, and we both pretend this never happened?

Or do we make it work, mashing our lives into something amazing? It wouldn't be that big of an integration. He's got no family for me to meet, and he already knows mine.

The transition would be smooth…unless we couldn't make it work back in the real world. Then what? He's best friends with my brother. Would it come between them if we broke up? Shawn would be pissed if Blake hurt me. He'd be pissed if I hurt Blake too. They've been best friends forever. Blake's been there for my brother when no one else was. They're more like siblings than friends.

If Blake and I dated and broke up, my brother would be put between us. Even if we didn't make him choose a side—assuming there were sides—he'd be in an awkward position. Family dinners would be so strange if we were both there, freshly after having decided not to be together. It would be even worse if the split was acrimonious. If this isn't forever, I could cost Blake my family.

Blake catches me staring and grins, unleashing the full force of those dimples on me.

When he smiles at me like that, there's only the present.

Ariella runs over to me. "So, there's this thing tonight you should come with us to."

"What is it? Can Blake come? It's his last night and—"

"Of course! I assumed that was a given since he's your boyfriend."

"We're not quite there yet," I admit.

She tips her head. "Really? It seems like you two have been together forever."

"We've known each other forever, but nothing happened until we came here."

"Why not? With the chemistry you two have… I mean, the way you two look at each other?" Ariella fans herself with a grin.

"I was too shy to go for it."

"Yeah, right." She nods, looking completely unconvinced.

"Seriously. I'm trying really hard to get out of my comfort zones and be more adventurous."

"I have trouble believing this isn't exactly who you are all the time."

I smile at her incorrect estimation. "Like I said, I'm a work in progress." At least, I hope the progress continues when I get home. What if it doesn't? What would it mean for Blake and me if I reverted as soon as I got back to New York?

She gives me a viciously skeptical look but lets it go. "So the thing tonight…it's a midnight beach party with some of our friends from the Islands."

"Hawaii?"

She nods. "They're bummed Shelby isn't here, but I think they'll be happy to meet you. Say yes." She shimmies her hips. "Andrew's a terrible dancer. You wouldn't make me shake my ass alone, would you?"

Ariella gives the biggest, brownest puppy dog eyes I've ever seen, and I laugh. I do want to hang out more with her before I leave.

She thinks I'm fun and a suitable substitution for Shelby.

I nod at Ariella. "How can I resist?"

....

Ariella and Andrew leave us on the beach, and Blake goes back to his hotel to get a change of clothes.

I shower at Shelby's place and slather on extra lotion to make up for the sun I got today. An unsettled feeling crawls through my joints, making me twitchy.

Dressed, I wander through the house, unable to sit still. The peace I felt on the beach has been chased away by my doubts about the future.

Can I only relax and be the newer Mel when I'm living Shelby's life? If so, what does that mean for Blake and me when I go back to being myself at home?

I paw through the cupboards, looking for a snack even though I'm not really hungry.

This vacation was the best thing I could have done, but what's the takeaway? What can I really bring home from this experience to enrich my life? The thought of going home and having the vividness of Florida fade more each day until it becomes just another holiday is intolerable. But already the relaxation, the certainty I felt, is slipping through my fingers like a handful of sand.

Ariella thinks I'm a fun girl who wouldn't be out of place dancing around a bonfire on a beach with hip, worldly, effortlessly cool people. But I'm not. And I'm not going to magically transform my job into the one I really want. Instead, I'm going to have to go back to my lonely apartment and back to my job where no one really knows me. Where I no longer know myself.

I sigh and focus on the cupboard.

I've arranged the cans according to food group and type and have alphabetized them.

My stomach swoops. I did this Switch for a reason—switched lives with a stranger because of one shitty day—but I can't go back and be the same rigid person. How do I stop being who I've always been?

If I can't hold on to these changes, I won't be able to keep Blake either—or be the person he deserves. Tears prickle my eyes, but hell if I'm going to slip back without a fight. This calls for something drastic.

I text Ariella. She responds right away, and I call the number she forwards with about eleven smileys and thumbs-up emojis.

When I've booked an appointment, I text Blake, letting him know we've got a pit stop before the bonfire. I'm going to make his last night here count.

I've got to.

Chapter 20

Blake

I READ HER TEXT THREE TIMES, MY MIND TAKING ME TO A dirtier place every time.

> Plans have changed. Want to do something
> wild before the party?

I smile and reply. With you? Yes. No matter what it is, you bet your sweet ass I do.

Lying beside her on that beach was exquisite torture that seeped into my skin where we touched and has burned my flesh all day. But it's not just about sex with her. I want to make her smile so I can see the way her nose crinkles. She makes everything newer and brighter, and I want to do everything in my life again with her at my side, so I can see it from her perspective and hear her thoughts.

How do people focus on their day-to-day lives feeling like this? It's such a distraction—not that I'd trade it for anything. It's like realizing I was only breathing with one lung, only seeing the world with half the colors. Now it makes me wonder if this is how the world has been all along. Fuller, richer, more vibrant. But I know that's not it. The world hasn't changed, but the way I see it has.

And I have Mel to thank for this.

I plan on using as few words as possible. Instead, I'll show my appreciation in other, more interesting ways.

Ones that make her moan and shake.

I shower, shave, and change, hopping in a cab as quickly as possible. It's only been hours, but I miss her presence already.

I jog up to the door and knock. Mel must have been waiting because she throws it open immediately and shines a blinding smile at me.

The restraint in her body when I hug her shows she doesn't want this to lead to the bedroom—interesting—so I keep it flirty instead. I give her a squeeze and a quick kiss before moving out of her personal space. "So, what's this wild thing you want to do?"

She bites her bottom lip and toys with the hem of her turquoise tank top. "I don't want to tell you. I'm scared I'll talk myself out of it if we do."

"We're not skydiving, are we?"

"Nope."

"Because I'll do that, but I'm not bungee jumping. I saw this gnarly video where the cord got wrapped around the guy's neck, and then—"

"We're not doing that either." She laughs and locks the door behind us, and we head down the sidewalk. "Quit fishing for information. You'll see when we get there."

"It's nothing with alligators, is it?"

"Gee, what a lovely night." She strolls along, hands in her jean pockets, and I half expect her to start whistling.

"Did you eat already?" I ask.

"Yeah, I made a sandwich after the beach. You hungry? We could grab something before we—" She glares both ways down the street to check for cars before we cross. "Nice try. I'm not talking."

I laugh. "I always could distract you with food." We stop on the corner and wait for the light to change.

"Hangry is a thing. But if we're being honest, I just liked when my cool older brother's cooler friends paid attention to me."

"Friends?"

She smirks. "Not jealous, are you?"

Yes. "No."

But the feeling goes away when she grabs my hand and laughs, leaning her head on my shoulder for a second before pulling me up the next street.

"Back-alley high-stakes poker?"

She shakes her head. "Nope."

"Hey, are we going to reenact the restaurant scene from *Lady and the Tramp*?"

"You, sir, are no lady."

I press my lips together prudishly. "I think I should feel insulted."

"Leave the feeling to me." Her eyes widen at my raised eyebrow. "No, I didn't mean it that way!"

I kiss the top of her head. "I'm OK with whatever types of feelings you have."

I realize what I've said a second after the words leave my mouth, and she takes a step away. It's the most I've said about a future between us, and her reaction isn't good.

But she smiles a few paces later and leads us up the next street. "Here we are."

I relax and follow her gaze to the sign above the shop. The shop with the big, neon sign flashing the word *Tattoos*. The windows sparkle, clean and shiny, and the rest of the building front is well kept—a good sign. "Really?" I ask.

She chews the inside of her cheek. "Yes."

"So, this is what you've been trying not to talk yourself out of all night?"

Her deep breath is audible. "I really want to do this."

Part of me wonders if she's only referring to the tattoos, or if what I said in the alley has sunk in. "Do you know what you want?"

Her brow scrunches into a frown. "No. I just know I want to do this with you."

I pull her close so she can't see my face—and realize how uncool I've been since I realized the depth of my feelings for her. "Then let's go do something permanent and painful."

She leans back and takes another deep breath. "You only live once, right?"

Mel pushes the door open ahead of me. It knocks into an old-fashioned bell instead of an electronic chime, unleashing a pleasant, low-pitched tone.

"Be right there," a guy calls from somewhere out of sight.

The walls are a deep red. A black-and-white tile floor and decor make the place feel classic. Everything's clean and taken care of, which is reassuring. I'd have grabbed Mel's hand and hauled us out of here if it was dingy or dusty, but it's tasteful and I can tell it's diligently maintained. The artwork on the walls—likely done by the artists—is all amazing and incredibly detailed work. "Not to question your due diligence, Mel, because this place looks good, but what made you choose it?"

She leans against the counter and inspects her nails. "It's where Shelby goes. Stephen is her guy. Ariella recommended him."

Something about her too-casual tone suggests this isn't just about a tattoo recommendation, but I let it go.

"OK, I'm ready." A stocky guy with short hair and a beard strolls up to the counter and looks at Mel. "You're Mel and Blake?"

Mel nods.

"Awesome. I'm Stephen." He grabs a dark-green binder and sets it on the counter. "Here's my book, if you want to take a peek at my style."

Mel waves her hand. "I already know I like your style."

"Ah, right. You know Shel. Hey, Shel and Mel!" He grins and so does Mel.

"Yup." She turns to me. "Do you know what you're getting?"

"Wait, me? I thought I was just here for moral support."

She bites her lip. "You don't want a tattoo? I mean, you don't have to get one."

I flip through the book, stalling for time. Do I want to do this? I think we all debate getting a tattoo at some point, and I like the idea of body art as snapshots of moments in our lives. Right now is an amazing time, and I do want to remember this. If I got something, I'd need it to be someplace I could easily cover for work. Not that ink is a big deal anymore, but I like having the option of keeping it to myself. I smile at her. "I guess I do."

Stephen works in bold colors, but he has a lot of black and gray with dashes of red and words that really pull my attention. The tattoos are interesting, some more abstract than others, but I flip the page and fall more in love with the style with every tattoo I see. It draws me in more than any other. But what would I get? What represents this trip, this adventure of going for something and not hesitating? The aquarium comes back to mind.

I know exactly what I want.

Mel smiles when I tell Stephen my idea, and he leaves to go sketch it up. Mel's still biting her lip ten minutes later when we're settled on the couch in the waiting area.

"What are you going to get, Mel?"

"I'm not sure yet. I don't think I want something realistic, but some of these are too out there for me."

"Where will you put it?"

"I've heard that ankles or anywhere the skin is thin hurts worse, so none there. I like the idea of having it just for me, so somewhere I can cover it. I was debating my wrist, but I think I'd get sick of it if I had to look at it every day—even if it was amazing." Her phone buzzes inside her purse, and she takes it out and rolls her eyes.

"I guess it would be like wearing your favorite T-shirt every day."

She nods, stuffs her cell back in her bag, and flips another page.

"Blake?" Stephen calls. "I'm ready for you to come back."

I leave Mel bouncing her foot and check out the sketch Stephen made. "Looks awesome."

"You sure?"

"Yeah." I smile. "It's even better than I expected."

"Then let's get cracking." He applies the stencil to my right shoulder, and I check it out in the mirror for placement.

It looks badass. I may have been the tagalong on this adventure, but now I'm legitimately excited.

I keep up a steady stream of chatter with Stephen as he gets ready, but I'm worried it will hurt more than I expect. I don't want to freak Mel out—she's already looking twitchy.

But when the first line is done and it just feels like a hot knife against my skin, I relax. Mel wanders back and pulls up a chair after a bit, smiling at the design appearing one high-speed needle poke at a time.

Just over an hour and a half later, Stephen cleans it up and proclaims me done. Mel's been pacing by the window for the last twenty minutes, probably too excited about her turn to sit still.

I get up and look in the mirror, smiling at the black-and-gray stingray that now adorns my shoulder. "Mel, come see this."

Her phone buzzes again, and she frowns as she fires off a rapid text. "Hang on."

The tail trails down my arm, almost touching my elbow. In the background he's worked a pattern that complements the stingray, and he's got the Latin words *Citius*, *Altius*, and *Fortius*—*Faster*, *Higher*, *Stronger*—in blue and black, with the same bold turquoise touches. A reminder to be the best version of myself I can be—and a reminder of Florida with that shade of blue.

Mel grimaces at her phone, then shoves it in her bag. "That looks amazing," she murmurs. "You did such a good job, Stephen! What's that style called?"

"Thanks. It's realistic Trash Polka. What do you think, Blake?"

"I think the name of the style sucks, but I love the tattoo." I shake his hand.

"That's what I love to hear. Give me fifteen minutes, and I'll get going on yours, Mel."

Her lips quirk to the side. "Actually, I, uh…" She wrings her hands. Mel's nervous? Now I've seen it all.

"Mel, if you don't want to get a tattoo, don't get one. It's OK."

"You're not pissed? I'm sorry. I really thought I could do it. I wanted one, but I can't."

I grab her into a hug with my left arm. "I'm not mad at all. I didn't get a tattoo for you. I got it for me. I wanted to get one with you, though."

"I'm sorry," she mumbles against my chest.

Stephen clears his throat. "It's not something to rush into if you're not sure about it."

I nod. "Stephen's absolutely right. You don't have to feel bad about anything. I'm glad I got mine done." I tip her chin up so she looks me in the eyes. "I'm still glad we did this. Even though you're a totally bad influence on me."

She smiles, and I kiss the tip of her nose. "I'll pay Stephen, and we can go do something else to celebrate my last night here," I add.

"I already had one idea."

"OK. As long as it doesn't involve alligators, skydiving, or the water. One thing's for sure—I won't miss the sand that creeps…everywhere."

"Neither will I. And no, no swimming in my plans." She glances to make sure Stephen's not paying attention. "But they do involve a bed and you touching the parts of me that are very white."

"I can't wait to greet those white bits."

Her smile is so dirty it could use a glass and an olive.

"Then let's get out of here."

Chapter 21

Melanie

GUILT GNAWS AT MY GUTS ALL THE WAY BACK TO THE BEACH where we're meeting everyone, but worse than that squirmy, murky feeling is the regret. I should have gotten a tattoo. I wanted one. I've thought about getting one for a while, and I wanted something tangible to show myself I can change. So why didn't I bite the bullet and choose something?

Thaddeus sent a barrage of ridiculous texts that tore me from the fun of the moment with Blake. Thaddeus actually questioned my professionalism and commitment to my job—and he cc'd my boss on another email, basically calling me a negligent party girl, like he knows exactly what's been happening in Miami. It made me want to throw up.

So, overwhelmed and unable to focus on what to choose, I chickened out.

Blake strokes the back of my hand with his thumb, but my heart pounds for another reason. Does turning down the tattoo mean I haven't really changed? Is my nature more powerful than my desire to change? Was it all just a fun getaway? Has Florida only been a break from my life instead of a new beginning?

"Hey." Blake gently pulls me closer, and I lean into

his warmth, tucked beneath his arm. "I can practically hear your thoughts working overtime. Knock it off."

"I can't help it. I've gotten a lot better." At least, I thought I had.

"You really have. But there wasn't anything wrong with you to begin with, Mel. Not everyone is the same. If changing things makes you happier, then fine. But don't change just for the sake of it. I like you as you are."

Yeah, but you only like Florida me—and I don't even know if she's permanent.

It's ridiculous. Ink has zero to do with anything other than personal expression, but Thaddeus managed to seep under my skin. Ugh, that's ironic. I sigh and nestle closer to Blake. "Thank you."

"And"—he lowers his voice, brushing his lips against my earlobe—"if you're still upset when we get back to Shelby's after, I'll have to work that much harder to make you forget about it. Especially since we have the place to ourselves again."

Heat chases the shiver that ripples through my body. "Yeah?" I like Ariella and Andrew, but at this moment, I'm ridiculously happy they'll be gone.

"Yeah." His teeth graze my earlobe, and I struggle to keep my moans to myself, lest the cabbie hear and kick us out.

"What are you going to do?" I narrowly manage to keep my voice a whisper, closing my eyes to block out everything but the sound of Blake's voice and the vibrations of the car beneath us. I shouldn't ask. We're not going to be able to do anything about it until later…but that's part of the fun.

"I'm going to take your panties off with my teeth, for starters."

I gasp. *Yeah, that's a good start.*

He traces a gentle line down my collarbone. "I'm going to kiss you everywhere. I'm going to lay you on the bed, spread your legs, bury my face in your pussy, and lick and suck at you until you can't take it anymore."

A high-pitched whine fills the air, and it's an embarrassingly long minute before I realize *I'm* making that sound.

Blake chuckles. "Then I'm going to fuck you. Hard. Hard enough that you feel it for days. And every time the turbulence jostles you in your seat on your flight home, I want you to think of me and remember why you're sore. I want you worn out. Exhausted. Your throat raw from screaming my name."

I'm so wet I'm a little worried I might leave a spot on the seat, but I'll be damned if I'm going to go down without a fight. I want Blake to remember me too, the way I am when I'm with him here, with his hand on my thigh and my inhibitions unlocked. I turn so my lips are near his ear. "I'm so wet right now, Blake. You wouldn't even believe it, but you're going to feel it. You want to take my panties off with your teeth? That makes me wish I were wearing some right now."

His chest expands, and his head tips down like he'd be able to see beneath my calf-length skirt.

I smile. "What's the matter, baby? Wondering if I'm telling the truth?"

His hand reflexively grips my thigh just above my knee. "Christ."

"One stiff breeze could have blown my skirt up.

Anyone could have seen if I wanted them to." I set my hand on his upper thigh, wanting to brazenly run my hand up to feel his cock straining against the crotch of his jeans—but even in my wildest flirting, I've never dreamed of taking things so far in the back of a cab.

Yet my hand creeps steadily up, fingers trailing over the rough denim. My mouth practically waters with the desire to take him in my mouth, but I'll settle for feeling that hard bulge under my palm until we're behind closed, locked doors. Unfortunately, we're not heading for a private place but a party. I can't resist, though.

His grip is like steel, fingers locking around my wrist. He stops my hand before I can feel if he's as hard as I hope he is.

"Mel."

"Yeah?"

The tremble in his fingers says it all. I smile in the darkness, power coating my skin. It's heady and I love it.

I'm still grinning when we pull up to the beach and get out of the cab.

We're immediately swept up in a flurry of introductions and handshakes, cold beers and warm buns covering juicy pulled-pork sliders. A couple of the guys roasted a pig in a pit, and while looking at it grosses me out the tiniest bit, I have to admit that the end result is pretty fabulous.

A few drinks later, an impromptu dance party's begun on one side of the fire. Little by little, the stress of the texts with Thaddeus melts away, and I leave them in the sand beneath the feet I stomp on the ground.

Shelby's friends are amazingly warm and open and

welcoming, and I realize with a start that they've become my friends too. Maybe we all just need to borrow some-one else's life for a bit and dance around a fire like they did back in the day.

There's an article in there somewhere—parallels between stress relief and outdoor music festivals that take us back to more primal roots where we express things with sound and movement and energy, but I'm thirsty and wander back by the fire, snuggling against Blake.

Ariella flops beside me in the sand. Someone's busted out a drum, accompanying a woman who's play-ing something soulful on an acoustic guitar. Blake's shoulder is pressed against mine, and the smoke from the fire mingles with the salty tang of the ocean in a way that makes me want to bottle it up and keep it forever. Blake and Andrew are debating the finer points of some-thing to do with some old rock band when Ariella grabs my hand. "Where is it, then?"

"Oh. I didn't end up getting a tattoo."

She frowns despite my casual tone, not missing a thing. "Do we need to talk about it?"

I shake my head. "It's been a crazy trip, Ari. Blake got one. I still might, but I don't know what to get and didn't want to choose something just to have one." It's technically the truth but not the whole truth.

Ariella's friend leans over. "I don't blame you one bit," Ka'aina says. "Come to Hawaii. My brother does traditional tattoos, and he can really hook you up with something cool."

That's an interesting thought. "So, how do you feel about the whole 'Free Hawaii' movement?"

Ka'aina shrugs. "Mostly, we just want to be left

alone. We're not like the mainland and couldn't care less about what you guys get up to."

I nod, pondering another article. "I can see why. You're basically like your own country anyway, far enough away and so different. Do you guys hate the tourists?"

He shakes his head. "We don't hate them—well, we don't hate all of them." He smiles, white teeth sparkling in his brown skin. "We hate the ones who are disrespectful or try to play local."

"The ones who show up and start aloha-ing? And yet, you're willing to help me with a traditional tattoo."

Ka'aina laughs. "But you're cool, and that makes all the difference. A little respect goes a long way. You don't know our culture or history, or how it feels to be invaded and taken over, then exploited years later as a means of making money for the people who tried to stamp out our culture."

"That's brutal," Blake says.

"It is," I agree.

"Way to kill the party, Kai," Ariella chides, punching him in the shoulder.

He laughs. "Then let's get it going with a little midnight surfing!"

We stand and brush ourselves off and head toward the water. Blake can't go in the water because of his fresh tattoo, and I can't quite bring myself to go too far away from him right now, so we give the surfing and swimming a pass. I'm secretly glad because, well, sharks. They didn't bite my ass off before, but that doesn't mean the odds have gotten more favorable. Instead, we decide to go on a little walk down the beach.

It's completely breathtaking. The sand is so soft

between my toes that I don't even mind when it gets between my soles and the sandals. Instead, the sensation makes me more acutely aware of everything—and everything I'm going to miss when I have to go back home.

The scent of the breeze, the warm, radiant heat, the music. It feels like there's thrumming music everywhere, trying to seduce you into dancing in the street. Some people do. A rhythm lives just beneath the surface of Miami, waiting for you to stop everything and listen to it. Maybe it takes the heat to open your pores so you can let that pulse inside you. I'm going to miss it.

A little uneasiness enters my stomach at the thought of this coming to an end. We created this relationship while on vacation, but that doesn't mean it's going to fade with my tan.

We walk a little farther up the shore, and I try not to think about what comes next.

Chapter 22

Blake

SOMEWHERE ALONG THE WAY, I MISSED WHEN THE SAND turned into a sidewalk leading to some docks, and we pass a bunch of yachts lined up in big, white rows with the dark ocean sparkling between them. Maybe because I can't stop sneaking glances at Mel.

"This must be the yacht club Ariella told us about," Mel says.

"Have you ever wanted to sail or boat or whatever they call cruising around on a yacht?"

Mel shakes her head. "Not really. I feel like it's more of a lifestyle, and beaches aren't typically my thing."

"And you need water with a yacht, which limits the places you can go on one."

"Exactly. And the places I want to see aren't along the U.S. coasts. Where do you want to travel?"

"All over Europe. I'd also love to see the pyramids, maybe do a safari to see what animals are like when they're not in cages in zoos."

She grins. "Faster and more dangerous, I imagine."

I bump my shoulder into hers. "Smart-ass."

"It is strange seeing animals out of their natural habitats, though. Like, most zoos have lions, even ones where it snows a lot. Are the lions like 'What the hell is this cold, white crap?' or are they used to it? Maybe most were born in captivity and they don't know any differently. That's kind of sad. I mean, we've saved some species from extinction, but I don't think that counts as a coup when we're the ones who wiped them out to begin with. We're so destructive, and it's brutal."

I think of the dolphins in Marathon. "It is," I agree. "I had a client who was an environmental engineer, and she said that the only way earth could be saved would be to wipe humans off the face of it."

"Wow, that's cheerful."

"Yeah, she carried a lot of tension." I laugh. "I don't think we're that bad, but at the same time, I want to see the things in the world before we destroy them and they're gone forever. Spend a night in a jungle, see the North Pole."

She smiles. "You lost me with those last two. I hate bugs, so staying in a jungle does not sound appealing, and I hate cold weather, so the North Pole is out for me."

"Aww, you're not going to make me go to the jungle all alone, are you? I could get eaten by a man-eating tiger."

"A big, strong man like you? You'll be fine."

I grin.

"You're definitely more adventurous than me."

I take her hand. "Oh, I've seen you get a little wild, Mel. It's a beautiful thing to behold." Warmth spreads through my body, and I never want this night to end.

A buzz of activity draws my attention to the right, behind a low iron fence. Through the palms and foliage, I catch the low strains of jazz and glimpse people milling around a pool.

Mel squeezes my hand. "Want to check it out?"

Two women exit through a gate, champagne flutes—and shoes—in hand, giving me matching, very thorough head-to-toe once-overs. "Are you on the list?" the tall brunette sneers at Mel.

Her spine stiffens, and fire enters her gaze. *Uh-oh, I've seen that look before.* "Cute. But I'm surprised they let you in, Becky."

"It's Kirsten."

"Whatever." She turns to me and winks so only I see it. "Come along, Rufus. I'm thirsty." She snaps her fingers, and I follow her past the girls inside the gate like a dutiful dog. Surprisingly, they don't stop us.

"What was that?" I ask when we're out of earshot.

Mel grins. "We don't look enough alike to be siblings, so obviously we're dating. And if I am the entitled rich girl in this scenario, that means you're my boy toy—and I've seen how the glitterati in New York treat their boy toys."

"I'm not sure if I should be impressed at your bravado or insulted that I've been demoted to your boy toy. I prefer the term *man candy*."

She lightly taps my cheek. "Still waiting on that champagne, MC."

I laugh and hand her a glass that I snag from a waiter's tray, appreciating the crispness of the perfectly chilled bubbly as we find a semi-empty spot by the food where we can stand and assess the party.

The crowd's a little older—and a lot wealthier—than the party we left behind. Chanel logos wink at me from purses, red soles flash from women's heels, and the only thing more plentiful than the bubbles in my glass are the diamonds dripping from earrings, fingers, and necklaces.

We're surrounded by serious wealth, and judging from the men in suits with suspicious shoulder bulges, this party doesn't look like an open-invitation affair. Maybe coming in here was a bad idea—I'm in cargo shorts and flip-flops. "Think we're a tad underdressed?" I murmur.

Mel tilts her head. "Maybe. That just means we have to pretend we're wearing this stuff ironically." Her eyes sparkle, and she winks at me. "We are the cutting edge of fashion, darling. These people don't know that we're not elite trendsetters whose clothing choices are *so* ten minutes from now."

That makes a certain amount of sense, but I try not to cringe as one of the men zeros in on me and Mel standing by the buffet table no one else has come near.

"Oh shit. I think the jig is up." Mel leans toward me. "Follow my lead."

The tuxedoed security guard comes toward us with narrowed eyes. They say the best defense is a good offense. He opens his mouth, and Mel puts on a falsely bright smile and interrupts. "Hi, it's probably not your department, but can you find out if this caviar is non-GMO? Thanks so much." She then promptly turns her back on the guard and smiles up at me. I cover my discomfort with a sip of champagne while Mel prattles on in a voice unlike her own.

"So, of course Oprah had to bring Gayle along, and then we had uneven numbers for tennis, and Mummy was pissed but couldn't say anything, because you know how Oprah gets. I thought Mummy's head was going to explode." She pauses to stare pointedly at the guard, who still hasn't moved, this time pooching out her lips into a bitchy little moue. "Hi, the caviar? Thanks, that's *super* helpful of you."

I take her lead and raise my eyebrows at the man, gesturing at him with my champagne flute. "Sometime soon would be nice. She's hypoglycemic and needs to eat, like, five minutes ago."

The guard's jaw tightens, but he walks away.

"He thinks we're some rich asshole's entitled kids," I murmur.

"Yup. Making a scene is the best way to fit into places like this. Bailey did an article about it once to see how outrageous she could behave before someone finally called her out on her behavior."

"That's awesome."

"Yup."

I take another sip of champagne. Mel's bluff seems to have worked, but a tiny part of me has the urge to duck my head and flee before we get in shit. I've been around wealth the last few years and am doing fairly well for myself, but the poor kid in me who was dumped from one home to another with his meager possessions held in a garbage bag still gets a little bit of impostor syndrome—especially considering we technically gate-crashed looking like street urchins…and I never really thought about that turn of phrase until being on the beach with actual sea urchins.

No one knows the truth, but still. I focus on Mel, which makes me feel better. Her cheeks are flushed and her eyes sparkle. She's actually having fun with this charade, and I'm glad to see her tension's completely burned off.

"Do you want to try some of this?" I wave my hand at the buffet.

She nods. "You'd have thought that eating those pork sliders would have filled me up, but I'm starving." She grabs something floppy and green and leans closer. "Do you think these are food or garnish?"

"I have no idea." I look at the people around us for a cue, but no one else is consuming anything other than alcohol. "But it doesn't really look that good."

She gives it a shake and sets it back down. "You're right, it doesn't." Her eyes light up. "Have you tried sea urchins?"

Ha, I was just thinking about sea urchins. "Nope, but from the excited look on your face, I'm assuming I'm about to?"

"We're about to," she corrects, handing me one of the tiny plates with the top of the urchin cut off, revealing something custardy inside.

I take the crostini laid over the top and dunk an end inside the goop. "This really doesn't look amazing." Taking a subtle whiff of it reveals that the pinkish bits are crumbled pancetta, so that perks me up a bit. Even the weirdest things can be made better with a little bacon on top.

She knocks her bread against mine. "Cheers!"

We take bites at the same time and make the same grossed-out faces. The texture is off-putting. I know I shouldn't have expected something buttery or custard-like, but I guess I did, and now that the real flavor is rolling over my tongue, I gnaw off another piece of bread to force the whole works down.

Mel looks around like she's contemplating spitting

the offending mouthful onto the ground. "I thought it was going to be more…buttery. This is awful." She spits it into a napkin and tosses it into a nearby trash can. "I can cross that off the bucket list, but that was bad."

A petite brunette strolls up just then and scrunches her face. "Isn't the food here atrocious? You're braver than I am to try it."

Mel nods emphatically. "So disappointing."

I lean in, unable to stop myself from playing along. "And the security guards? So unhelpful. We asked them, like, twenty minutes ago about the caviar."

The stranger rolls her eyes. "*So* unhelpful. I haven't seen you guys around here before."

"I'm from New York," I say, splaying a hand over my chest.

Mel smiles. "I live here, though. Shelby Kellerman."

"And I'm Blake. Blake"—I try to think of a last name, but the only one that pops into my mind is from *Star Wars*—"Solo."

It's ridiculous, but the stranger nods and smiles at us. "I think my cousin mentioned a Blake Solo. I'm Monica Norberry, and I definitely know you, Shelby! It's been ages, though." She leans in and gives Mel an air kiss.

"Really?" I take a sip of champagne. "How do you know Monica, Shelby?"

Mel shoots me daggers from her eyes, sets down the rest of her urchin, and waves her hand dismissively. "Oh, who even remembers things like that anymore? The important part is that we're finally catching up. How's your brother?"

Monica pokes at a canapé. "Chip is still in Provence. I only came back because Tay asked me to."

"Of course." Mel nods sagely. She's actually a pretty good actress. "This party is pretty—"

"Stiff, I know," Monica finishes. "And your outfits are genius. Screw these people. I get so tired of wasting outfits at these parties filled with nobodies. I wish I were brave enough to do it too, but Daddy would kill me."

"Right? We were at another one earlier. Way better, with actual people there." Mel sips more champagne as she looks at me. "We never even found out if the caviar is non-GMO."

Monica nods. "I'm on that kick too, and only organics. Fruit, nuts, and sea salt included."

The whole situation is ridiculous, and as I watch Mel simper along with Monica's first-world problems, I can't help but smile at my date. She's the least pretentious person I've ever met, and I want to spend as much time with her as possible. She makes everything feel like an adventure.

She makes me feel comfortable no matter what we're doing. Even here, surrounded by people who sneer at the buffet table I'd have killed for as a kid—hell, anything's better than nothing when you're a growing boy—and instead of cringing into myself, I'm enjoying this experience on the other side of the fence.

All because of her.

I want her so damn bad.

Chapter 23

Melanie

His eyes.

I want to push him down onto one of the fancy chaise longues and show him just how much I need him. Surrounded by strangers in public, surrounded by high freaking society—I definitely spotted a senator over by the bar—the only one I want to pay attention to is him.

The only party I care about is a party of two. A very private party with very private parts, and oh my God, I'm wet again just picturing it.

I smile at Monica and interrupt whatever inane thing she's prattling on about. "It was great seeing you again, Mon, but Blake and I have to take off. We have somewhere else to be."

Monica smiles. "Room for one more?"

"Not where we're going." I wink at her and she smiles.

"I don't blame you one bit." She air-kisses me. "Keep in touch."

I seize Blake's hand and practically run from the party, passing the guard we were dicks to. "I'm sorry you take so much shit from people." The words rush out on our way past, and I feel instantly better. Even faking it, I didn't like being a jerk to someone who was only doing his job.

But I don't stop to hear his response, if there even was one. I'm too busy rushing to get us home.

The cab ride takes forever, but we arrive at Shelby's in silence, keyed up from the ride over, from the whole evening, from the fact that this is Blake's last night— and we both know it and feel it hanging over us like a thick fog we can't see through. I don't know what's going to happen when we get back home. All I know is that I have to put it all out there tonight and give him everything of myself that I can.

I need him to see the real me, to know the person I want to be.

And that person is the Mel who lives inside his eyes and arms and life. The relaxed person I am when I'm with him.

I lock the door behind us.

The coolness of the wall seeps into my chest before I realize he's spun me around. And the air is kissing my thighs as he slowly drags my skirt up, up, all the way. He groans at the sight of nothing but my bare flesh.

OK, so maybe the tattoo wasn't the only wild thing I'd chickened out of doing in public tonight, but I'm starting to think the yacht club and this make up for it.

Blake's warm hand cups me from behind. His palm brushes against me enough to coat his skin with my arousal, but it's not enough pressure to please me.

I push against his touch, hungry for more. "Please."

"Please what?" His breath hits the back of my neck.

"More."

"Oh, the woman who couldn't keep her sexy hands to herself in the cab, who drove me fucking crazy, wants more now?" He presses against my ass. Even through the jeans, his arousal is apparent.

I push back against it. "Yeah."

He rams two fingers inside me and my knees go weak, but I spread wider for him. A loud moan tears from my throat, and he kisses the back of my neck. "You got me hard in the cab to the party, and I've barely thought about anything else since. Because of you, Mel, I got a tattoo—I had a needle going in and out of me for hours tonight. I can't wait to return the favor in a slightly different way. In and out. For hours." His hand works me with a steady rhythm that curls my toes, and I sag against the wall.

God, it feels so good right there that I can't move—

He slips his fingers out and I whirl around, furious over the loss. I'm unable to speak, but his lips claim mine with such brutal sensuality that all I want is more of this kiss. More of his hands threading through my hair, more of his body pressing me against the wall and grinding against me.

His tongue turns teasing, barely touching mine. He makes me chase his mouth to get what I want, but when I do, he pulls back and kisses his way down my neck. When he reaches my collarbone, he does something with his tongue that short-circuits my brain.

God, I love what this man does to me.

I love what this man does.

I love this man.

"I love you, Blake." The words slip out like a thief in the night, and I hold my breath.

He takes an unsteady breath of his own. "You do?"

"You're pretty amazing."

He rests his forehead against mine for a second. "I love you, Mel."

I smile. "Melanie."

"No. You're my Mel. You've always been there, and you're the first woman I've ever wanted to always be there. I never want this to end."

I wrap my arms around him, and he lifts me like I'm weightless. He carries me to the bedroom steadily but not hurrying.

I want him to hurry.

At least, until we're naked.

He sets me on my feet just inside the bedroom door and flicks on the light. "I want to see every second of this," he explains.

"I want it too." Careful of his freshly tattooed shoulder, I slide his T-shirt up to his chest, where he takes it the rest of the way off. I kiss his pecs and trail my tongue between the center ridges of his abs until I reach his belly button and kneel.

His gaze sears itself into my memory. I'll never forget the way he's looking at me right now, even if I live to be a thousand years old. It's tangible, this awe-filled, hungry stare. He's holding himself back from devouring me because he wants me to get everything I want.

And what I want is for him to devour me.

One by one, I pop the buttons of his jeans. I keep my gaze on his, staring so deeply into his eyes that I feel like they could suck me in.

His jeans brush against my nipples on the way to the floor, and then his boxers do the same. He hisses in a breath when I take him in my mouth. Using my other hand, I stroke the base of his cock while lavishing the head with my tongue until his breathing becomes uneven and I can taste him even more.

He pulls out of my mouth, urging me to stand and walk with him to the bed.

He lies down on his back. "I want you to fuck my mouth, Mel."

"What?" Uncertainty swirls though the desire, but I like the idea. I just want to hear him tell me what he wants.

"I want you to sit on my face and ride my tongue."

My stomach tightens at the thought, but from arousal, not fear. Blake unlocks things inside me. He undoes me in a way that leads to freedom, not regret. With him, things that are taboo become…interesting. I straddle his belly and shimmy up until I'm on my knees, spread over his mouth. His breaths wash across the most sensitive parts of my body. He blows on my clit, the coldness making me shiver, but when I lower myself more, his mouth feels hot against me. I shudder with pleasure.

A dirty thrill courses through me as my hips start rolling of their own accord. Doing this feels like using him for my own pleasure. Normally oral sex makes me feel vulnerable, at the mercy of him and his mouth, but now that talented tongue is at *my* mercy. Now I'm the one on top, grinding around, taking his mouth in the way I need it, want it. I move forward more, pressing my hands to the mattress above his head. He reaches around and penetrates me with his fingers with one hand, using the other to play with my breasts.

I spread wider, moving my hips in an infinity pattern— which is fitting because, fuck, I want this forever.

Spread this far, he's got access to everything, and soon it's all I can do to brace myself and try not to collapse on his face when an orgasm crests through my core with waves of warmth and darkness. It brings my awareness to a few inches of flesh between my legs, aching, still pulsing around his fingers as he strokes me with his tongue and suckles with his lips.

Shakily, I lift one leg and move to his side. He wastes no time rolling on a condom.

"Stand and brace your hands on the bed, baby. I'm going to fuck you like I promised."

Chapter 24

Blake

HER RELEASE STILL SHIVERS THROUGH MY CHEST. EVERY moment with her makes me want two more.

She loves me.

I want to live inside her. I'd reduce the world to our bodies making each other feel as good as we can, as often as we can.

It would be a hell of a way to live.

I can still taste her on my lips, and I lick them, waiting for her to stand and present that gorgeous ass to me. Even knowing how sexy she is, I still bite my lip when she bends and spreads. Fuck me. Everything this woman is makes me want to be better for her so I can be worthy. Smart, strong, passionate, capable, fun, beautiful. She's so damn perfect that I don't deserve her. But I'm not going to question my luck too much. I just thank God while positioning myself behind her.

I'm lost. One hard, long thrust, and I'm buried deep in the only woman in my world.

I give a few steady strokes to let her get used to my size in this position. She's already tight, but a woman tightens more when she's come, and I don't want to accidentally hurt her by not giving her a second to adjust.

Her lower back relaxes a little, and soon her hips move in a counterpart rhythm to my thrusts.

Now I don't hold back. I go hard and slow, matching my rhythm to the cues she gives with her body. For a while, we live only inside the movements of our bodies, the beating of our hearts. Her "I love you" is inside my veins, pounding inside my chest with every thrust of my hips, and I might explode from the memory of her eyes when she said it, so I focus on her body. On the way she moves. On the way I move with her. Skin on skin.

My fingers dig into her hips, using them to pull her back into me when I penetrate her again.

She moves from her hands to her forearms, squeaking out little *yes*'s and *oh God*'s. I go faster, the increased friction heating us both. I want to come, but I also want to stay inside her, making her feel like this forever. I release her hips and trail my hands over the globes of her ass, running my thumbs up and down her crack. She tenses.

"Relax. I'll never do anything you don't want," I reassure her, but keep running my thumbs up and down, slick with her wetness, intent only on giving her more pleasure. I stimulate her in places she probably didn't even know could feel good.

"I think I want it," she moans.

"You think?"

She looks over her shoulder at me, eyes dark and wild with lust. "Just make me feel good, Blake. I know you know how to do it. Do whatever you want. I trust you completely. I'm yours."

Christ.

I reach around and start rubbing her clit with one hand. I slow my hips to a sensual grind. She's mine? How the hell did I get so lucky? I need to live up to the trust she's showing me by making this amazing for her. My hand's soaked from her, making it easy to stimulate her clit as fast and light as I want.

When her body relaxes again, I coat my thumb with her wetness. As I pull out, I push my thumb gently into the tight ring, just an inch or so. Then I push all the way back inside her until my hips hit her thighs and wait, letting her relax and get used to the unfamiliar feeling.

"You OK, baby?" I ease my thumb in another inch, keeping the hand on her clit moving, giving her something to focus on.

"I… That feels…" She pushes back against my hand, moaning when my thumb's all the way inside too. "I feel so full."

"Good?" I give a few slow thrusts of my cock while barely wiggling my thumb inside her.

She groans. "Yeah."

Encouraged, I alternate slowly, pulling out my thumb while pushing into her pussy, taking my cock nearly all the way out while putting my thumb back inside. I don't stopping rubbing her clit with my other hand until her hands fist the sheets and she collapses farther, chest on the mattress, unable to hold herself up.

"Don't stop. More. So good." Her voice is low, so damn low-pitched and earthy.

I push everything inside her at once and she moans loud and long.

I do it again.

And again.

Soon she's back up on her hands, pushing into me with everything she's got. Her arms shake from the exertion.

So I give her everything I've got too, rutting into her tense body with every ounce of finesse my hips can give her. I try to hit that sweet spot inside her, gently pressing down with my thumb, increasing the power of the friction. Her cries fill the air, and I press everything deep, once, hard.

That's all it takes. With one giant inhale, everything clamps down on me at once, squeezing my cock like a fist, seizing my thumb, the muscles trying to draw everything deeper inside. Two more pumps and the tightness makes it impossible for me to hold on any longer. I spill into the condom with hot spurts of pleasure that stab through my belly and balls.

We collapse onto the bed together. Still inside her, I roll us to our sides so I don't crush her, because I'm pretty sure my legs can't take the way Mel's pussy still milks my cock.

Mel shifts beside me. "You're trying to kill me, aren't you? Admit it."

"I was going to ask you the same thing. I think my heart almost burst inside my chest." Warmth overtakes me. "Not just from the sex, either." I kiss her shoulder and give her a squeeze. "I meant what I said earlier. I love you." This time I feel less vulnerable when I say it.

"I meant it too." Her voice is gentle. "And I love being in your arms like this, Blake."

My heart stutters in my chest. "But?"

"I can't relax until you wash your hands."

I burst out laughing, relieved I wasn't getting the "It's not you, it's me" speech. "What, you're saying you don't want me to hand-feed you some fresh strawberries right now?" I pull out of her and sit up.

She giggles and sits. "Definitely not. I can't believe I did that."

"I was there too."

"Mmm, you were." She grins and kisses my shoulder. "I've never done anything like that before. You make it easy to do whatever I want."

"Glad to hear it." I stand. "I'm going to clean up. How about we get something to eat, and then do whatever you want again?"

"That can be arranged." She winks.

"Do you want to join me in the shower?"

Her pupils dilate. "Showers with you are probably one of my favorite things." Her stomach growls and we laugh. "But food needs to be the next thing getting inside me. I'll fix us a snack while you clean up."

She uses the washroom first, and then I hop into the shower, lathering and rinsing as quickly as I can to get back to her as fast as possible.

What a weird trip.

A weird, amazing, life-changing, fucking epic trip.

I thought I was coming here to poke my nose in and check on her. Maybe I'd hook up with someone and then go back home. I never thought I'd find something lasting, never mind with Melanie.

I stand and brace my hands on the tile, letting the water drip down my body. I turn so the spray pounds some of the tension from my back. The hotel's nice, but their beds are too firm for me to sleep well, and when I'm not in them, I'm not getting sleep with Mel.

You're getting old, Blake. Next you'll be monitoring

your fiber intake and yelling at the kids to get off your lawn.

If knowing a great thing when you see it means you're getting older, then old age, I embrace you! I am older and smarter, and there's no way I'm letting go of Mel. Florida's been amazing, and I could stay here forever, but I want to get back to my real life in New York so Mel and I can move on together.

I turn the shower off and grab a towel.

It's going to take some time to adjust to the shift between us—in more than a few ways.

Her family is going to be the biggest shift. I hope her brother understands that I truly love her and want the best for her, because I can't pass up this chance at happiness with her. I've been part of the family for so long that I hope they don't think this is weird or that I somehow took advantage. Then again, when has Mel ever let someone take advantage of her?

But I've been alone for so long that I've gotten used to it. Not that I've liked the prospect, but I hadn't thought it would be fair to get serious with anyone with my tight schedule the last couple years.

That's almost finished, though, and with a little work, I'll be opening my own practice in the next few years. I can't think of anyone I'd rather have by my side as my partner in crime than Mel. She's everything I've ever wanted and more, inside the bedroom and out of it. Just having her there by my side back in real life is going to be amazing.

Dried off, I hang the towel over the rack and realize I don't have any clothes in here.

I head back to the empty bedroom, inhaling deeply to

hold the mingled scents of our lovemaking in my lungs. We even smell good together. She's probably still in the kitchen, or in the living room. I grin and step into my boxers, shaking my head at the way my dick's already at half-mast thinking about her again.

I can't believe how unrestrained she was. We've only been together for a couple weeks. What will she be like in a year or two, when we're completely comfortable with each other?

I can't wait to find out more about her. She's wild, passionate, caring, strong. Fierce.

No one could get tired of making love to Mel. *I* could never get tired of talking to her, listening to her thoughts. I've got it bad, but she's analytical. I can't rush her into anything or try to extract promises tonight. No, tonight's about enjoying each other, wallowing in this amazing feeling of trust, lust, and love. Friendship turned to more.

So much more.

She's bending over the oven when I walk into the kitchen.

Hot damn.

I don't know if it's better with her on top of me or the other way around, feeling her undulate beneath me. It doesn't matter who's where as long as it's her and me. We'll make this work because we're perfect for each other. Nothing else matters.

Mel and me.

Chapter 25
Melanie

BLAKE LEFT YESTERDAY. THAT WAS EASIER THAN TODAY. I had laundry and cleaning to do to keep me busy, keep my mind occupied. But waking up alone today was harder than it should have been. It reeked of neediness.

For crying out loud, you've slept with him for a couple weeks, not a couple years. It's ridiculous to miss him already.

But I do. Bailey picks up on the first ring. "The blood's gone back to your fingers enough to call me! Excellent."

"Shut up. Blake left yesterday."

"Awww, the debauchery has come to an end."

I bite my lip. "Yeah."

"I'm hearing a sad trombone tone. What's wrong?" Her tone sharpens. "Did he turn into a jerk? Because if he did, so help me, I will stab him in the—"

"No, he's amazing. I'm just feeling a little blah, I guess."

"I feel like that when vacations end too, and I have to come back home to laundry and work. Is that all it is?"

No, but it's nothing I want to think about. "Yeah. I'm a little worried about meeting Shelby too. I've scoured her house, practically erasing my entire presence. I washed her sheets twice and flipped her mattress—though I still feel guilty—and I replaced some of the fresh produce that was in her fridge so she's not coming home to an empty pantry."

"That would make me sad too. It's like you're erasing your vacation in a way."

"Yeah, that's probably it." More than she knows. "Anyway, I should probably get going. She'll be here soon, and I'm dying to meet her."

"She's probably just as nervous to meet you."

Somehow, I doubt it. "Love you, Bails."

"Love you too, and I will see you soon!"

Shelby being nervous to meet me seems unlikely. I want to cultivate a sense of cool like she has—or at least, as I've heard through her friends. I've been texting Ariella and Andrew. They're in Tampa today so I can't say a proper good-bye, but they've promised to keep in touch.

I intend to, so I hope they weren't blowing smoke up my ass.

I've been to the dry cleaners to pick up the dress I borrowed, and I'm pulling fresh cookies from the oven (fine, reheated store-bought cookies) when there's a knock at the door, followed immediately by a woman's deep voice. "Hello?"

I startle but hold on to the tray. "Hi."

Shelby strides into the kitchen, pulling a wheeled suitcase almost as big as she is behind her. She shoves her shades onto the top of her head. "Holy crap, you made cookies? Are you sure you have to leave me?"

I smile and set the tray on the top of the stove. "Don't tempt me." I hold my hand out. "I'm Mel."

"Nice to actually meet you." She eschews my handshake

and grabs me in a tight hug. "It's been so strange living in your house—not that your house is strange, but it's a different world in New York, you know?"

"Definitely a different world."

She lets me go and snags a cookie, wincing and blowing on her fingers. "They're better when you get burned just a little."

I grab one as well. "The meltiness is worth it."

"It is. So, how was your Switch? Did you like Florida?"

"I really did. We went down to Marathon one day but mostly hung out here or at the beach."

"Did you go surfing? I should have said you could use my board!" She grins, huge and charming. It's easy to see why Ariella said everyone wants to hang with Shel.

"No, it's cool. I've never been into surfing, but we tried flyboarding."

"Holy crap, that's awesome! I've always wanted to, but it looks scary. I don't think I have the coordination for that."

Is she serious or trying to make me feel better? "Hey, if I can do it, anyone can do it. You should try it."

She grins again. "Maybe I will. You up for some wine?"

"Sure."

She pulls a bottle of sparkling white from her bag and gets us each a glass.

I grab another cookie, hand her one, and we head into the living room.

"Holy shit," Shelby says.

I follow her gaze to the shelves, cringing a little at how different it looks. My cheeks heat up as I blush. Maybe I overstepped my boundaries when I organized it the day I fled the nude beach. "Look, I have a little bit of a cleaning thing, but if I went too far, I'm sorry. I didn't throw anything out. It's just—"

"No, it's awesome. I've been meaning to get around to it, but organization's not my strong suit. I get overwhelmed pretty easily with stuff like that. But you made a whole freaking system—I can find everything so easily!" She walks over and picks up a ring with a tiny tree frog on it. She holds it up and smiles at me. "I've been looking for this for two years."

"It was behind a stack of movies."

She tilts her head. "Are you sure you can't stay? I've got an office that looks like a bomb hit it."

I laugh. "I noticed but didn't touch it."

"Aww, nuts." She snaps her fingers, and we sit on the couch. "I can't believe how quickly the Switch flew by."

"Did you like New York?"

She tips her head back, resting it against the cushion. "It was more than I thought it would be. Bigger, faster, bolder. Everything moves so fast there. It's like the world's trying to cram every exciting thing into one tiny area to bombard you with options. You'll never have time to see it all, but damned if you're not going to try your best."

Affection warms my heart. "That's exactly it."

"I'm definitely going back. Did you like my stomping grounds?"

"I did. I can't believe how big your place is. Mine must have felt like a Hobbit hole in comparison. I can't imagine being this close to the beach every day, though. I'd never feel like I was in real life. Every day would feel like a vacation."

"But isn't that the point of life? Living like you're free and always having fun?"

I take a sip of wine, letting the bubbles pop against my palate. "I could use a little more of that philosophy in my life."

"Will you be coming down here again soon?"

"Probably not as soon as I'd like." I wrinkle my nose. "All this fresh air and space is bad for my constitution."

"You're hilarious, just like Shawn."

My eyebrows fly up, and I almost spit out my mouthful of wine. "*My* Shawn? My big brother Shawn? How exactly do you know him?"

Her hesitation says it all.

I squeal. "Oh my God, spill! I mean, spill the situation, not the nitty-gritty details because he's my brother and that's gross and I'd have to bleach my brain. But what happened?"

She nibbles her cookie and sighs. "He came over on my first night to read me the riot act and make sure I wasn't some psycho taking up residence in his sister's house. I managed to convince him I wasn't a thief. He was also concerned that you'd been tricked into being sold into slavery, so that was charming."

"Shawn's such a dick sometimes."

"He is. And after he ran out of steam and realized I wasn't a criminal mastermind, we got to talking. He was intense, but he's fun and funny too, and I know he only came in with guns blazing because he cares. He has a goofy sense of humor that you don't see anywhere. It made me want to hang out with him. I asked if he'd point me to a good restaurant in the area, and he offered to be my date for the night. We talked for hours. He's had some crazy adventures."

"Coming from you, that's saying something." I qualify my statement when she frowns. "I met a few of your friends. I came back from snorkeling, and they were in your living room playing a card game."

"Oh shit, that must have been weird."

"It was, but they're pretty awesome."

"So, did you and any of them…"

I shake my head. "I've, um…I've sort of been seeing someone while I'm down here."

She squints and then flaps her hand. "Oh my God, please tell me it's your brother's friend he sent down here."

I choke on my wine. "What the hell? How do you know about that? Yes, his name's Blake."

"I'm right? Yes! Shawn was with me when Blake called to reassure him you were OK. I knew something was up. No guy is that thorough in seeing to a woman's well-being unless he's really interested in her."

"Wow."

"I love being right." She smugly nestles into the couch. "So, you guys hooked up? Where is he? Can I meet him? Is he cute?"

"He's amazing." I pull up a selfie I took of us at Marathon.

"He *is* cute. Look at those dimples."

"And he's great with his hands." I waggle my eyebrows and laugh, telling her about our history, including the painful crush I had on him growing up. She makes all the right sympathetic sounds and winces along with me. She has refilled our glasses once by the time I get to the day on the nude beach, when he saw way more of me than even *I* would have wanted.

"No wonder he suddenly didn't see you like his best friend's kid sister anymore. Not with those dangerous curves."

"You should talk. Victoria's Secret called; you're late for the runway."

"Please, I bought my boobs when I was twenty-three. Have you seen your eyes?"

"Anyone could have them with contact lenses." Mine are real, though. I roll them but glow from her compliments. Or the wine. Probably both. "Thank you. I really needed this girl time. I got a little of that with your Ariella, but it wasn't the same as with my best friend, Bailey, at home—and even if Ari and I had had the time, the guys were right there most of the time. Plus we'd just met. I realize you and I just met too, but I've been living in your house. Somehow, it feels—"

"Different." She smiles. "It really does. You think your house was cramped, but to me it felt safe. Secure. Sleeping in your room was like sleeping in a warm hug."

"Thanks for saying that."

"I mean it. So tell me." She leans forward. "Do you think you'll see Blake again?"

"Oh, I know I'll see him again. He and my brother have been best friends forever."

She quirks one perfectly arched brow. "You know that's not what I'm talking about. You're glowing in that picture with him, and you light up whenever you mention his name. You can't glow like that and not be with the guy."

I sigh. "I'm worried that it's all just a dream. That

I'm making more of it than what it is. And we're so not ourselves right now. Well, I'm not. Florida has made me a different person."

"And you can take those changes back to New York. Don't put limits on things, and you won't be limited."

"That sounds like an affirmation."

She shrugs. "One of the guys I work with is kind of a hippie. Sometimes he comes up with good things."

"All I know is that I love him and I don't want what we had here to end."

"So keep it going." Shelby clinks her glass against mine. "Do you think you'll do a Switch again?"

"Probably not. There's no way it would be as positive as this. Will you?"

She tucks her legs under her. "Probably not. I'm not about trying to chase a positive experience. It doesn't usually work. That's why I like trying new things. Anyway, I didn't mean to pry about you and Blake. It's just that I heard so much about both of you from your brother. He's worried about you, you know."

"I know. To say this was outside my realm of personality is the biggest understatement ever."

"I wonder what his reaction will be when he finds out about you two."

Panic splashes through my stomach. "You can't tell him! Please, promise me you won't say a word to my brother. I don't know what we're going to say or when we're going to say it. How we're going to say it. I want to enjoy things with Blake as they are before we label things and tell my family."

"Whoa there." Shelby's eyes widen and she leans forward. "Save some oxygen for the rest of us."

Shocked at her candor, I bark out a laugh and notice I'm hyperventilating all the air from the room. "Sorry. Ugh, this is exactly what I'm talking about. I'm not a relaxed person. Ever. I have a thousand thoughts in my head all day, every day and they all lead to—"

"Stress. I don't know who made that speech a second ago, but she is headed for a stroke. Hold on to the way you feel here. Hold on to the relationship you had here. All of that good stuff doesn't disappear because you change locations. I promise."

I take a breath, relaxing. "You're right. I need to keep that in mind."

She puckers her lips. "I'm not normally so bossy."

"Must be the New York seeping from your pores."

She laughs. "Maybe. I'm glad you had a good time here. It sounds like you needed a vacation."

"I did. The day from hell sparked this whole thing for me." I feel stressed just thinking about it, and before Shelby can respond, I add, "Don't ask."

"Fair enough."

"I do have one question for you that's been weighing on me since I got here."

"What's that?"

I set my empty glass on the table. "What is your cat's name? I've been calling him Buddy the whole time, and he's gone along with it...but..." The look on Shelby's face dries up my words. "What? Oh God, what? I fed him, mostly tuna—I hope that was OK. I looked for dry food and couldn't find any."

She bursts out laughing.

"What?" I ask. "Is Buddy really a girl cat, and I've been confusing her the whole time?"

"Melanie."

"Your cat's name is Melanie?" That's a coincidence.

"No." Her eyes sparkle with mirth. "I don't have a cat."

"What?"

"I have no pets. At all. I'm allergic to everything with fur—not that I knew you had a cat in here with how thoroughly you cleaned the place!"

My face heats with mortification. "Have I been feeding your neighbor's cat?"

She shakes her head. "We're a pet-free building. There are a lot of strays in the area, though. Maybe one of them took a shine to you and kept coming around."

Buddy wasn't Shelby's cat. Come to think of it, he only came when I was alone, and I never thought to ask her friends about him. "But he was so friendly."

"I bet he was, if you were petting him and feeding him tuna."

"My tuna brings all the strays to the yard?"

Shelby throws her arms up and shimmies. "You're darn right it does! Come on—the boys are waiting."

Chapter 26

Blake

"SUMMER'S ALMOST OVER, AND MY BACK IS A MESS. NOW that I'm an adult, I feel like I should have the power to make every summer an adventure, but it always slips away from me somehow." Denise shifts under the sheet while I work on her lower back. "I think it's because when I was a kid, I always had high expectations about how epic summer would be, and it rarely measured up."

"It's not too late, Denise. We're still only in July. There's plenty of time to turn things around if you really want to."

"I guess."

I laugh. "Look, what's something you really want to do?"

She takes a few deep breaths. "It sounds stupid, but I've always wanted to go horseback riding. I never do it, though I probably would be able to now that you've fixed me up."

Denise was in a car accident seven years ago that left her almost as mangled as the car in which she was a passenger. She came to me eight months ago, after five surgeries and six years of physio. She still has some issues with the traumatic brain injury, but at least now when she walks, you can't tell that a world of scar tissue lies beneath her clothes.

"You're not limited by this." I run my hands over the scar running up her spine. "Not anymore. Fear is worse than any physical limitation. Our bodies automatically heal a lot of damage. Fear takes work to get rid of."

"I hear that. I just don't know how to do it."

I think through my roster of clients and smile. "I'm going to give you someone's phone number. She's been breeding horses for a decade, and her daughter's a show jumper. They run camps for people healing from traumas."

"What, like therapy horses?"

I move up to her shoulders. "Sort of. I can hook you up with them. Their horses are used to nervous people, and you'll be in the best hands."

"Second best," she quips.

"Second best." She tenses as I work through a particularly vicious knot in her bicep. "You've been slacking on your stretches."

"It would be annoying that you can tell, but it also means you know your shit. I can't even hate you for busting me."

I shake my head and grin, pleased at her assessment. It's true. Bodies speak more than clients most of the time. There's no point in telling me you're doing the work when you're not. All that does is show me who I'm wasting time on.

Maybe not wasting time on, but I'm not going to go out of my way to help someone heal if they're not willing to put in the effort as well. I make detailed notes, and I look up the best stretches and activities for clients to do when they're at home. But I look up that information in my free time. If my clients aren't doing their exercises, it's a waste of my breath.

Some people just want a massage and a place to lie still and not have to think for an hour, and that's fine. I'll save my extra time for the clients who are doing their best and meet me halfway.

"I think you're going to like Rachel and Emily," I say.

"Either way, I need to not be scared anymore. Or be scared, but not let that fear cheat me out of cool experiences."

I wipe my hands off on a towel, agreeing with her completely. "Denise, that's exactly it. I'll see you outside in a minute."

I take her file with me and sneak a look at my cell. I check my voice mail, but there's nothing from Mel. I'm disappointed but not surprised. She'd texted to say she was staying for a couple days to hang out with Shelby, then coming back tonight, so I probably won't hear from her until tomorrow.

I'm glad she's made a new friend and done something spontaneous, but man, I miss her. My body's going through withdrawal from the soft, silky feel of her flesh curled up next to mine. I miss her smile, her frown, and that glint in her eyes when she teases me. I'm going to have to work hard not to pounce on her the second I see her again.

And bite her lower lip. Suck her tongue into my mouth while I cup her ass and pull her close. Hear her moan the way she does when I slide inside her—

The pencil in my hand snaps, and I open my eyes, glad no one was around to catch that little display.

Real smooth. I definitely need to get myself under control before I see her again. I want her to know I've missed her, but I don't want to hump her fucking leg. I don't just miss her body; I miss her. All of her. My bed suddenly feels massive and cold now that she's not lying beside me at night anymore.

Denise exits the room, smoothing her hair.

"Hey, so I'd like you to do those stretches we talked about." I show her the stretches I mean, using the doorjamb so she gets a visual and enjoying the way my shoulder gets a nice stretch in the process. I hand her a slip of paper with Rachel's number. "Here's the number to those women with the horses. You can do it. You're ready."

She smiles. Her eyes get a little misty, but she blinks the emotion away. "Thank you."

"And I'd like to see you again in three weeks or so, if possible."

"I'll book an appointment now." She heads to reception.

Her shoulder tension reminds me of Mel's on our first day in Florida together. What's she doing right now? Does she miss me like I miss her?

For our first date in New York, I think I want to take her dancing again. She was so sexy in that little dress… Hell, she's sexy all the damn time, but the way her smiles lit up her eyes when we were dancing…

I shake my head free of the images bombarding my mind and focus on my one voice mail.

Not Mel, but my now second-favorite member of her family. Shawn has left me a message, inviting me to our favorite pub in an hour. I scrub the oil from my forearms and write up my notes before hurrying to the subway. What the hell am I going to say to him? Mel and I never discussed telling her family, and I'm not comfortable outing us as a couple before talking to her—though I'd cartwheel down Broadway with her name painted on my chest if I could.

It's probably best to say nothing for the time being—at least until Mel and I discuss things. My friends with the horses remind me that family is whatever we make for ourselves. The people we choose to have around us are more important than the ones we share genetics with. Mel and her family are already family, but that feels like skipping a step because of our history. I want her so damn badly, but I don't want her to feel any pressure because I already know her parents. Just because we won't have that awkward meet-the-family introduction in our future doesn't mean I assume we're further along than we are. This is still new territory for us, no matter how comfortable it feels.

And she already knows my painful, lonely history. I won't have to ease her into a conversation about my past because she already knows. It's liberating even while it solidifies our ties in my mind and heart. Our histories connect us.

I make it there only five minutes late, but Shawn is already at our regular spot by the corner. I wave to him and grab a draft from the bar before heading to our table. It's a pub, but people are overdressed as they usually are, wearing clothes to impress.

That's one thing I'll miss about Florida. It's not as trendy and doesn't take its fashionable appearance as seriously. Not that I'd roll out in cargo shorts all the time, but I'd forgotten how much black clothing people wear. It seems a little dingier, despite all the expensive lines and impossibly high heels making women's legs look good. Heels are bad anyway.

Mel's bare foot covered in sand was infinitely sexier. Mel in a life jacket playing with a dolphin was even better.

"Hey, man, how are you?" I ask, sliding into the booth.

"Not bad!" Shawn takes a deep pull from his beer and wipes the foam from his stubbled upper lip. "You've got a spring in your step. Did you get some down there?"

I roll my eyes. "Wow, jump right into the important things."

He shrugs. "It was a vacation. I pictured you on a beach with a bunch of babes in bikinis. Miami's hot, right? Rappers sing songs about it. So?"

Christ, this is awkward. I rub the back of my neck, unsure of what to say. We've always shared everything, and hiding this from him—even with good reason— feels bad.

He slaps the table. "Oh, you did! Was she hot? Where'd you meet her? I bet she wasn't as hot as Shelby."

If I give him some of the facts without going into details about Mel and me, maybe I can ease him into this. "I saw her on the beach." If he realizes I don't just see Mel as a quick fuck and chuck, there's a smaller chance he'll freak the fuck out. "She's just my type. We did a bunch of stuff while I was there."

"Kinky stuff?" He waggles his eyebrows.

I shrug. "Dates. We went dancing, did water sports, saw some dolphins." God, Mel was cute that day. The day I realized I love her.

"Geez. You're acting like you fell for this chick after, what, a couple weeks? You know you don't have to wax poetic about the pussy to get your dick wet."

No, I can't tell him about Mel and me yet. "Real charming, Shawn. Anyway, weren't you playing tour guide for Shelby?"

The smug expression leaves his face like wind being sucked from a boat's sails. "I wasn't her guide, man. We had a fantastic time, but I wasn't her puppet or anything like that."

Interesting how defensive he is. Shawn is normally as laid-back as it gets. "I believe you, but thousands wouldn't."

"Shut up. I've got to admit, Shelby's pretty amazing. I haven't met anyone like her for ages. Maybe not ever. I told you about our trip, right?"

"You did." Private jets, multiple casinos, something about an ex-NFL player and a stuffed duck.

Shawn runs his fingers through his hair. "Yeah. There's something about her, man. She's hot, but it's more than that. She's fun too. Smart. Down to earth. I'll be thinking about her for a while."

"That's how I feel about M…my Florida chick." *Nice one, asshole.* "She was different, but it feels like I've known her forever."

Shawn nods. "Isn't it funny how someone can just walk into your life and take over your thoughts like they've always been there?"

This is too weird. I can't talk about Mel without talking about Mel, so I focus on him and what he's just said. "Seriously, though, do you think you'll pursue anything with Shelby?"

He takes another sip of beer, eyes growing solemn.
"I'd like to. I can't get her out of my head. I don't know
if it's her or the timing, or some combination of both,
but I don't want her to ride off into the sunset with some
other asshole."

I clink my glass against his. "I hear that. So what are
we going to do about it?"

"Drink?" He laughs.

"And then?"

He taps his coaster against the table. "Shelby did
invite me to go down to Florida with her."

"So why are you still here? If you can't get her out of
your head and she invited you to spend more time with
her, why are you here?"

He crosses his arms, rocking the same stubborn look
Mel gets. "Why are *you* here? It's cool and all to give
me shit, but I don't see your girl here on your arm. You
didn't extend your stay in Florida to be with her." He
picks up his drink and takes a sip like he just dropped
the mic on me.

"Shawn, you're absolutely right." I grin. "And I'm
going to do something about that."

Chapter 27

Melanie

AFTER GETTING ALONG SO WELL WITH SHELBY, I DECIDED to extend my stay for a couple days. Not just to spend more time with her, but to make certain arrangements—including driving back to JFK Airport instead of flying, which took almost nineteen hours broken up over two days.

I splurged on a cab from the airport car-rental place, nearly dozing off twice on the way home.

Now, I walk up the steps to my building, my butt sore from all the sitting I've done over the last two days. I drape a sweater over my new carrier bag and try not to jostle it too much when I grab my keys and stride in, choosing to take the rickety elevator instead of the stairs. If anyone sees what's in my bag, I'll get into so much trouble.

The tiles in the lobby seem smaller, dingier. Everything's dark compared to Shelby's place. She said she didn't see my building as less than hers or foreboding, but it feels that way. Even so, the smell of spicy Thai food that wafts through the lobby makes my mouth water in a good way.

The residual bad feelings could be the long trip talking, and I relax once the elevator doors close and carry me to my floor. The hall's abandoned at 11:37, my floor occupied by mostly older residents. That's good—means my neighbors don't cause a disturbance, other than when they crank *Wheel of Fortune* to insane decibels.

A thin sheen of sweat covers my face, and I blot my top lip before sliding my key into the lock and letting myself into my apartment.

No one saw what I smuggled from Florida in my bag. Am I doing the right thing?

I lock the door behind me and flick on the light, wincing at how cluttered my apartment feels. Sure, it's organized to the nth degree, but there are so many things crammed into the tiny square footage. It's like an episode of *Hoarders* compared to Shelby's minimalistic space.

Of course, she has about four times the space I do, so that probably has something to do with it.

This place has been my home for years, and it's suited me just fine—but now that I'm back, it feels off. It's been three weeks, not three years, and yet the place feels cold and impersonal. There aren't any touches that reflect *me*. Nothing screams *Melanie*; nothing marks this place as uniquely mine.

I felt more comfortable in Shelby's place than I do here.

The day after tomorrow I'll go back to work, back to the job I'm great at. I'll slip back into my work clothes, feeling like they're a costume, and be the person I've always been. But I don't know what I'd rather do, who I'd rather be. Where I'd rather be.

I think of calling Blake just to hear his rich, warm voice, but being with him swallows the world. I miss him, but I'm floundering a bit and wouldn't be much fun as a date. Right now, I need to find my place.

Tomorrow. I'll call him tomorrow.

I head to the dark-red velvet couch and ease my bag to the cushion, finally unzipping it.

A fuzzy orange head pokes out as Buddy emerges from the carrying case.

Smuggling him in here has made me a criminal, since no pets are allowed in my building. A small criminal, but still.

He took the drive surprisingly well, but his fur is raised a little on his neck, so I don't try to pet him in case he takes a disgruntled swipe at me.

"This is your new home, Buddy. I'm sorry it's tiny, and technically you're not supposed to be here, but it's our place now."

I couldn't bear the thought of leaving him behind, knowing he had no home to go back to. What if a hurricane hit? He'd be forced to crouch beneath some cardboard box or hole up somewhere cold and dark to stay safe. Beneath a Dumpster with rats or whatever they have in Florida. Alligators.

What if he got hurt? What if no one fed him tuna again? Maybe making him an indoor cat wasn't the best plan, but I made the choice to take care of him.

He sniffs the air and climbs out of the bag, immediately prancing across my legs and curling up on my lap. He looks around the room, kneading my thighs. I wince at the pointy jabs of his claws, but I stroke his back, pleased when he purrs. We'd gone to a vet friend of Shelby's who confirmed Buddy was healthy and male, as well as a stray, judging by his condition and the lack of a chip.

Shelby told me I should bring him home with me, and I did.

Maybe I was trying to cling to something from Florida, like bringing him here would help me hold on to the positive things that happened there. Something good to come home to after another shitty day at the office.

Guilt singes my skin, making it prickle, and my eyes fill with tears. "I'm sorry, Buddy. You deserve better than that, but I'm going to be the best owner you've ever had."

The thought that he's always been alone is almost too sad to bear.

I head to the kitchen and pour him a bowl of water, setting it on the floor. He ignores it until I open a can of tuna, and then he comes running.

Not really hungry but feeling peckish, I grab a granola bar from the cupboard and munch it on the couch while Buddy eats his dinner. He finishes before me and jumps on my legs, purring when I scratch his back right above his tail.

I get a text.

Bailey: You back yet?

Me: Just got in. I may have smuggled a cat
         home and into my building. Meet Buddy.

I send a pic of Buddy.

Bailey: OMG he's so cute! Permission to tell every-
        one you got some pussy while in Florida?

I snort.

Me: Permission DENIED.

Bailey: Fine. OK, the best Disney prince and why.

Me: Hmm. Eric?

Bailey: Weak.

Me: What, who's the best, then?

Bailey: The Beast, obviously.

I grin.

Me: He doesn't even have a first name.

Bailey: How dare you?! He does so! It's...um...
         damn it. Adam? Evan? Jeff? Dallas? What-
         ever, he doesn't need a name. Belle can
         call him Baby in the important moments.
         #giggity

Me: OK, but the Beast before or after the trans-
         formation?

Bailey: Hmm...that's a good question. We don't
         really know the guy after, and before he
         was so big and savage and intense...

Me: I feel like we're about three conversations
         away from you telling me you're into furries.

Bailey: !! That's a fabulous idea for an article:
         Cartoon characters after dark. I mean, I'm
         pretty sure the fox from Robin Hood was
         directly responsible for my sexual awaken-
         ing. GTG! You're in tomorrow, right?

Me: The day after. See you then.

I chuckle. Buddy hops off my lap and starts making
a slow circle of the living room, poking his face into
all the crevices between the furniture. He doesn't seem
that upset to be away from the only world he knows,
but we'll see what happens when he wants to go outside
and can't.

Shit. I hurry over to the window to make sure it's
closed and get a whiff of something faint and chemical,
but not completely unpleasant… Paint?

My gaze ricochets around the apartment, searching
for anything out of place, but it's all just as I left it.
Shelby had more self-control than I did—at least in this
room. Everything looks exactly the same.

I head to the bathroom, but it's the same as I left it,
which leaves the bedroom as the source of the difference.

The closer I get, the stronger the smell is.

It's definitely paint.

What did Shelby do? She didn't say a word about
anything like this while I was there.

Movement near my right foot startles me, and I jump,
clutching my chest. Buddy meows up at me.

"You're going to give me a frigging heart attack, cat."

He looks toward the bedroom, in the direction I'm
heading, then back at me.

Not wanting to seem like more of a pussy than my cat, I confidently stride the last few feet. Buddy trots at my side, keeping pace as if to say "I've got your back."

Not bad for a wingman. Tiny and fuzzy, but full of spunk.

I flip on the light switch, blinking against the bright light, but it's not the only thing my eyes are trying to blink against.

Holy shit.

My boring, slate-gray walls are gone, replaced by a shade of turquoise that is fresh and clean and vibrant without feeling harsh on the eyes.

It's like being back at Shelby's. The walls match the bits around her house that were this exact shade. The umbrella on her patio, some knickknacks, the blanket on her bed...

And on the wall at the foot of my bed, she's made a giant photo collage, just like the one on her bedroom wall.

I rush forward to see a note pinned to the board.

Melanie,

I couldn't match the amazing woman your brother told me about with the personality of your room. It was so BLAH. No offense. I hope you take this in the spirit it was given. I just wanted to give your bedroom a little fresh air. Don't worry, the photos I made the collage with are copies. The originals are safe and sound, tucked into the albums where I found them. And

don't worry about Mimi. I got her permission
to paint in here. She was tickled at the idea.

Shelby

Shelby talked to my landlord about painting? I don't even know what to say. It's the most invasive but perfectly personal gift I've ever received. This room is suddenly the only one that feels like home in my apartment.

My eyes blur with tears, and this time they slip down my cheeks.

A stranger knows me more than I do. She came into my life on the periphery and shook things up, made me want more. Made a gorgeous collage of my life in pictures. It's something I'd never have done, but it fills me with warm, affectionate memories.

I text her right away, thanking her for the amazing gift before heading into the bathroom to shower the return trip off my body.

I don't know if my life will be different now, but I know that I want it to be. Water streams down my body, the scent of my own body wash enveloping me in brown sugar, but it no longer smells like…me. I've gotten used to Shelby's honey mango. I'll have to go get some.

People can change. Hell, I smuggled a cat into my no-pets apartment. Maybe there's hope for me yet.

I get out of the shower and slather myself with lotion, noticing the light tan I picked up while gone. Will anyone else notice the difference in me?

Still wrapped in a towel, I head out of the bathroom and crawl onto the bed. I notice the matching turquoise chenille blanket and pull it over my head, letting the light filter through it and paint everything a bright, beautiful shade.

The bed shifts slightly beside me, and Buddy's head pokes beneath the blanket. I stroke his forehead between his eyes with my thumb, and he settles beside me and purrs.

I fall asleep like that, basking in the smell of new paint and a new beginning.

Chapter 28

Blake

I SNAG A SOFT DINNER ROLL AND SPREAD BUTTER ON IT. I'VE been starving lately. I grin at Mel's mom. "These rolls are awesome. Thanks for inviting me to dinner."

"Don't be silly, Blake. You're part of the family. It's been too long since you've been over."

I take a sip of wine to battle the sudden dryness in my throat. Shawn had invited me to Sunday dinner, and I came, hoping Mel would be here and I could surprise her. They still didn't know about Mel and me, and it feels wrong to tell them by myself, so I'm waiting for her. "Is Mel coming tonight?"

"Melanie said she'd be a little late. She got a cat. Can you believe it? But she'll be here. It's been a while since you've seen her, hasn't it?"

Not knowing what to say, I smile. "She never seemed like the type to want a pet, but that's cool." Mel's mom clearly doesn't know about Shawn sending me to Florida.

"Hello?" Speak of the devil… Her voice rings out from the living room.

I lick my lips to catch any errant crumbs and set the roll back on the plate just as she strides into the dining room. Surprise flashes over her features when she sees me, but she grins before she looks away. "How is everyone?"

Her mom gives her a quick squeeze. "Good. Look at you, all tanned from your trip! How was it?"

Mel's dad gets to the table with the pot roast and grins at Mel as she takes a seat across from me. Shawn messes up her hair when he returns from the bathroom.

"Hey, Sis."

"Jerk." She blushes and fixes her hair, glancing at me. "Yeah, I hung out on the beach a lot, Mom."

"Well, I hope you used plenty of sunscreen. Tans fade but—"

"I did."

Mel must have spent more time on the beach after I left, because her tan's even deeper. Are her white bits even starker in comparison? I want to see.

I try not to rake her body with my gaze. I'd really like to hold her close and tell her I love her and missed her, but we should tell her parents about us before jumping straight to PDA.

"Mel, you haven't said hi to Blake," her mom chastises.

"Hey, Blake. How are you?"

I stroke her foot with mine. "Fine, thanks. Did you have a good time in Florida?"

"I did," she says primly, dishing up some green beans.

I spoon some mashed potatoes onto my plate. "Did you do anything exciting down there?"

She presses her lips together like she's trying not to smile. "I did."

"Don't overwhelm us with details there, Melanie." Mel's dad pours gravy over his roast, and I try not to choke on my bite.

"Some attractions were bigger than others," she says, lips twitching.

I squint at her.

Her mom tops up our wine. "Looks like you mostly lay around on the beach."

"Yeah, there was a lot of lying around."

I bite the inside of my cheeks, giddiness rising inside me like we're a couple of teenagers flaunting that we didn't get caught screwing on the couch.

Talk shifts to Shawn and his recent exploits with Shelby, and I zone out when Mel trails her toe up my shin. The edges of my vision go dark.

It's been too long since we were together.

I manage to choke down my meal, not tasting a bite. I remember Mel's taste instead, and I want it on my tongue again. It takes a few minutes for me to realize we're all finished, and everyone is discussing dessert but Mel and me.

I know what I'd like for dessert.

"I'll take the dishes away and grab the pie." Mel stands.

"I'll help you clear the table." I stand and smile at her, but she's already turned away and started carrying plates to the kitchen.

I grab a few things and take them into the kitchen, trying not to make it look like I'm rushing to follow her.

"Hey, stranger." I keep my voice low so it won't carry into the dining room.

She flashes a quick smile at me but continues loading the dishwasher.

"Mel?"

"What?"

I laugh once. "What do you mean, what? This is the first time we've seen each other since Florida."

"We're at my family's dinner," she answers quickly, then sighs and scrapes a plate's scraps into the garbage. "It's so good to see you." But she doesn't look at me while she does it.

"Look at me."

That gets her attention, and she finally meets my gaze. "I don't want to do this here, if you don't mind."

"You didn't call me back last night."

"I didn't realize it was a competition." She turns from me and rinses her plate in the sink.

My jaw is tight with tension, but I move behind her, embracing her from behind. It's not sexual—we're at her parents' house—but I don't know why she's suddenly being weird, and I need to feel her in my arms. She melts into me with a barely audible sigh.

I kiss her temple. "I don't care if you never dial my number again, as long as we still talk."

"I've missed you." Her damp hands grip my forearms, pressing them tighter to her belly. "I've missed you so much, you don't even know."

"I've dreamed of you every night." I close my eyes and breathe her in, relaxing more in this warm moment than I have the whole week I've been home, knowing I shouldn't be touching her right now but unable to stop myself. "I don't want you to feel pressured if you think we jumped a step by hanging with your family."

"Speaking of which, they could walk in at any second."

They could, and yet her hands grip my forearms even tighter.

I pull my hips back to avoid grinding against her ass. "I don't care. I love you, and I miss holding you."

"I love you, and I miss more than that," she whispers, pushing back against me before jerking forward.

"Mel," I warn her with my tone, and she turns in my arms, smirking up at me. I ease my lips closer to hers, but pause, wanting her to make the first move.

"I missed your words, but I missed the mouth that speaks them more."

Laughter floats to us from the dining room. "You're going to get us in trouble with your parents." The worst part is I literally can't force myself away from her.

"Oh. I thought you liked it when I was bad." She closes the inches between us, pressing her lips to mine. My entire body tenses at the electricity shooting between us. *Fuck, this woman.*

I want to.

I shouldn't.

Her tongue slides across mine.

I wind my hand in her hair and caress the nape of her neck, deepening the kiss, losing myself in her soft lips and eager tongue.

"What the hell is this?" Shawn demands.

I take a step back, and Mel and I both turn toward his shocked voice.

Mel clears her throat and hastily finger-combs her messy hair. "We were just—"

"Making out in the kitchen. What the fuck? Are you drunk?" Shawn's voice rises.

Mel sighs and takes my hand. "Let's go talk at the table. Mom and Dad need to hear this too. Might as well tell everyone at the same time so we're not repeating ourselves."

We ease past Shawn, whose posture is rigid. I hope it's from surprise and not because he hates the idea of me dating his little sister. No matter what they think—if they think I'm not good enough for her, if they think it's weird that we've fallen in love after all this time knowing each other—I am not going to stop seeing her. Even if it means losing them all, because losing Mel would be infinitely worse.

"What's going on?" Mel's mom asks. Her gaze narrows on our joined hands, and then Shawn flopping to his seat. He folds his arms across his chest.

"Mel?" Mel's dad frowns. "Shawn? What's going on?"

"Why don't you ask Mel and Blake?"

Mel rolls her eyes. "Shawn's being dramatic. Blake and I are seeing each other."

"What? You're dating?" Mel's dad frowns.

"I think it's wonderful," Mel's mom says, beaming at us. "We've known you forever, and you're a good man."

I nod. "I promise, my intentions—"

"You said you were seeing someone," Shawn interrupts.

"I am. I'm seeing Mel."

"Yeah, but you said—"

"I didn't want to lie to you or pretend anything. Everything I said about the woman I'm dating was about Mel."

Mel's brows knit together and her lips pinch shut, and I hastily clarify. "I never went into details, and I wasn't bragging about anything. I promise."

"He didn't, thank God." Shawn shudders. "Hindsight on that would have made me vomit."

"Why didn't you tell us right away?" Mel's mom asks her.

Mel shrugs. "It's new, and we're still figuring things out. I didn't want it to be awkward for any of us if…" She trails off, but I catch the unspoken meaning behind her words.

She didn't want things to be awkward if we break up.

She's already thinking of breaking up? My gut tightens.

Well, of course she is. This is Mel we're talking about. The woman who plans and visualizes every eventuality. If she wanted out, she wouldn't be sitting here holding your hand. Mel's not the type to go along with something she's not into.

I relax and give her hand a squeeze, chest loosening when she smiles at me.

Mel's dad doesn't smile, but he shrugs the way he does when he's pleased with something. Man, I really have known these people forever. I won't lose any of them. I won't fuck things up.

Shawn narrows his eyes at Mel. "I can't believe you've poached my best friend. What happens if you break up? I can't believe this."

She raises her eyebrows at him, rearing up in her chair. "I can't believe *you* sent him there to spy on me like I'm some sort of helpless little princess."

"I'm glad he did." I kiss her knuckles.

Her expression softens.

"Whatever." Shawn scowls at me. "But if you break her heart, I'll break your jaw."

Chapter 29
Melanie

WE DON'T STICK AROUND LONG AFTER DESSERT—IT'S TOO weird. The air is heavy with expectation, like they want us to regale them with the Adventures of Melanie and Blake, but I just feel awkward and tired.

Seeing Blake made my heart jump into my throat, and my belly fluttered like I'd swallowed a rainstorm. Memory doesn't do the man justice. He's sexier, brighter, and even more appealing than my memories. I don't know how that's possible.

I might have been OK, might have been able to play it cool if he hadn't touched my feet under the table. OK, fine, maybe I touched his first. Seriously. A game of footsy made me horny as hell. The week I took trying to get some perspective didn't help. Fine, he arrived back in New York a few days before I did, and it's only technically been possible to see each other for two days, but I did try to take a minute to think about the future. But as soon as I saw him, time slipped away, and all I wanted to figure out was how I could lure him to my old bedroom and fuck his brains out.

Not exactly subtle or sane with my parents there.

And that was hard too. Seeing the easy way they interact with Blake… They love him. It threw me off completely and made me feel like I should push him away when he approached me in the kitchen.

We know the same stories. He knows all the punch lines to Dad's weird jokes. I could be the reason Blake loses that. For all my determination not to cost him anything, there's no guarantee we'll work out. If Shawn hadn't busted us, I don't think I'd have told anyone yet. Blake makes me lose myself, and I like it. As far outside the realm of who I am as that is, it felt right when I saw him again. It felt good for everything else to burn away beneath laser-like certainty about something.

But it's scary too, and I tried to keep my cool by not reacting to him. Maybe I should have pushed him away. Part of me wanted to, but when he touched me…

I can't say no to him because not a single part of me wants to say no to him. My heart and body scream YES when his hands touch me.

When his mouth touches mine.

When he said he loves me and missed me.

That's not fair to him either—because when you love someone, you want the best for them. Right now, I'm not a complete person. I'm so conflicted I don't know if I'm coming or going or who I'll be when I figure this all out.

What if I'm never going to be the person Blake needs?

These are the thoughts that whir through my mind as we head to the station. My hand grows colder in his on the train to my place. I invited him over, but more and more I wonder if I should break things off until I get my head on right.

But his hand strokes mine and his thigh bumps against me, and I can barely see straight for wanting Blake on me. In me. Chancing one glance makes it worse. His eyes simmer with dark promises I want him to pour over my body.

His hand tightens around mine. "I know. But you can't look at me like that when we're in public."

"Like what?" I whisper.

His lips brush against my earlobe. "Like if I'm not inside you in three seconds, you're going to scream. It's not fair to look at me that way when I can't do anything about it."

"Do you want to know a secret?" I move so my lips are on his jaw, burning his flesh with need. "I'm not even a little bit sorry. You made me wet at Sunday dinner, Blake. I wanted you to take me to my old bedroom. Do you have any idea how goddamn inappropriate that is?"

He turns his groan into a cough just a second too late, and I smile when people nearby glare at him.

The whole train ride and walk to my place is fore-play. By the time we stumble out of the elevator, I'm lit up with hot need. It takes a few tries to unlock my door because my hands shake too much to get the key in the hole.

I fling the door open, and a disgruntled meow rings out. "Hurry, get in!" I urge Blake.

He laughs. "I mean, I'm all about being inside you, but—"

I slap his chest and lock the door behind us before turning on the light. "That's so not what I'm talking about. Meet my new roommate." Blinking, I search for my fluffy companion, bending and crooning to him when I see him lying on the couch. "Come here, nice kitty."

Blake strides over and holds his hand out for Buddy to sniff. Apparently Buddy finds him acceptable, as he allows Blake to pet him. "Who's this guy? Your mom said you got a cat, but I wasn't sure I heard right."

"He's Buddy, and the reason I extended my trip a few days. I had to make arrangements to drive back so he could come home with me." I forgot that Blake hadn't met Buddy. Then again, anytime anyone other than me showed up, Buddy made himself pretty scarce. He's skittish around strangers, like the stray I should have realized he is.

But he seems to like Blake, which is oddly pleasing.

"He was hanging around Shelby's place. I actually thought he was her cat, so I fed him. Turns out he's a stray. No family."

"You're such a softy."

"Shut up."

"Make me."

I bite my lip and take a couple steps toward the bedroom, glancing back at him over my shoulder. He rises and follows right away, and we reach my bedroom as one. His front heats my chest, but he doesn't press against me like I want him to.

I turn on the light to better see the look in his eyes. I'm going to suck him off and keep my gaze on his the whole time. If it's anything like how it was on the train…

He steps away and walks around the room, looking at the walls. "Wow, this is gorgeous." He sniffs and frowns. "Did you just do this? Paint? It was years ago when we helped you move, but I don't remember the walls being this bright."

I tap my fingernails together, a little annoyed that the paint job pulls his focus from the looming blow job. "No, Shelby did it as a welcome-home surprise."

"That was nice of her. Especially since you guys hadn't even met and become friends yet."

I'd told him about Shelby—and how well we got along—on one of our calls. "Yeah, and she made the photo collage as well."

"Maybe we can add to it." He grins. "It doesn't really match the rest of your apartment. The new color."

He noticed that too. "No, it doesn't," I agree. The rest of the apartment is dingy little me. This one room Shelby changed is an oasis of vibrant freshness. It's got personality. It shouldn't make me feel sad, but it does. I'd never have painted in here, and I don't know if it's because of apathy or lack of imagination. Things need to change, and I can't wait for Shelby to come back and transform my place and life one area at a time. I need to do it myself, yet I have no idea what else I'd do to change things up and make them different. I just know I'm not content with the way they are now. It's easier to reinvent yourself when you're a thousand miles from home and can start from scratch. Tweaking things that have always been a certain way, re-forming the grooves of your life is infinitely harder.

Blake squints. "How did you feel about a stranger painting your room?"

I smile. "It was a bit of a shock at first, but she cleared it with the landlord and I really like the color."

He nods. "It's nice. It reminds me of—"

"Shelby's. Yeah, I know." Annoyance pulls my face into a bitchy expression I can feel. Perfect, breezy

Shelby. She didn't do anything bad. She's one of the most genuinely nice people I've met lately, and I can't let my jealous issues turn her into a villain. "It's almost exactly like the umbrella and blanket on her bed."

He frowns. "No, it reminds me of Marathon. I guess it's close to Shelby's stuff too, but my first thought was of Marathon. The walls are the same color as the tables in the cafeteria. Remember?"

"Oh yeah. I guess they are." I like that the shade reminds him of a memory with me instead of another woman's house.

"God, that day, Mel." He strides over, pausing close enough that he bathes me in the warmth of his body. "I realized how much I'm into you. The way you were in the water. You were so fun and playful. So sexy."

Yeah right. "I wasn't sexy. I had no makeup on, and my hair was a mess. I reeked like the ocean."

"You. Were. Sexy." He tucks a lock of hair behind my ear. "You are sexy. Without even trying, you're the sexiest fucking woman I've ever seen."

I want to be. I want so badly to be who he deserves. I want to be the woman I've been for the past couple weeks because she would make her own happy ending. I don't want to be the woman who blows his life apart because she's a coward and retreats back into who she used to be. "Take me," I whisper. "Now."

He tugs my top over my head, leaving me standing in a pearl-gray bra and jeans. I shiver but don't move. I need him to do this, need to feel how much he wants me.

I have to see every ounce of desire in his eyes.

My jeans are next. They slide down my legs in a

fluid movement, and while I haven't shaved in a few days, it doesn't matter when he trails his fingertips over my skin.

My heart pounds in my chest. "How do you make me feel so beautiful?"

His eyes almost turn angry. "Because you are."

Kneeling in front of me, he tugs my panties down as well. Then there's just a bra.

He reaches up to get the clasp open and eases it down my arms, dropping it once it's free of my body.

Naked. Standing in full light. Everything out in the open, everything visible in unforgiving 150-watt illumination, and yet he looks at me like he can't believe this is happening. Like there's nowhere else he'd rather be than in my personal space. Like I'm the most beautiful woman he's seen.

How is this even possible?

His hands whisper down my belly and reach around to stroke my flank. They finally land on my butt as he brings his face between my legs. I tense, locking my knees and trying not to let them buckle.

He wouldn't be too mad if I just collapsed directly on his face, would he?

The vibrations from his groans draw me closer to release, but it's so soon, so fast, so goddamn good. I want this forever.

Feeling this good forever…

It's not possible. Nothing this good lasts.

Shut up, brain.

There's a reason they write ballads about men that seem this good. Because they're myths.

I grit my teeth. Blake's as real as the tongue on my clit.

*And how long are you going to last in the real world
once he realizes you're not that relaxed, adventurous
woman he met in Florida?*

Chapter 30

Blake

HER BODY IS FULL OF THE WRONG KIND OF TENSION. THE RIDE over here got her out of the weird funk she was in, but it's come back hard.

I take my mouth away from her and stand, putting my hands on her shoulders. "What's wrong?"

She bites her lip and stares at the floor, shaking her head like she doesn't know what to say.

"Mel?" When she doesn't clarify, I shrug and scoop her up in my arms.

She squeals. "What are you doing?"

I set her on the bed and flip her over onto her belly. "You're tense. I don't know why, but I'm pretty sure it's because you're overthinking something in that massive brain of yours. So I'm going to sit here beside you and give you a massage. That's it. And when you feel better, we'll reassess. But right now, no pressure." I start on her shoulders, digging my thumbs in and holding them, doing a trigger-point release. "I'm great with my tongue, but even better with my hands."

She sighs and folds her arms under her head.

"Lie there and work through your thoughts while I work through your tension." Her spine relaxes bit by bit below my fingers. It's not ideal, and I can't go as deeply as I'd like without oil, but after a while her sighs become happy.

It's funny how we started in Florida with a massage.

Maybe we didn't. She'd already invited me back to Shelby's, so I can't imagine Mel only realized she was interested in me when I was massaging her body. Her arms are next, then her legs. By the time I reach her feet, she's practically purring.

"That feels so good."

I work back up her calves. "Think I should look into it as a career?"

"That or male prostitution. I know four women at the office who would rent your hands by the hour for nefarious purposes."

I laugh and then notice her hips shifting, moving more languidly than before. Her ass cheeks clench ever so slightly in time with my touch. I dip my fingertips to her inner thighs and draw them up the silky skin. "I'll do anything you want me to, Mel. For as long as you want me to."

She spins over onto her back. "Stand up. Take off your shirt."

I stand and pull it over my head. My pants are practically crushing my cock, but I'll keep them on all night if it keeps that gleam in her eyes.

She traces a line between her breasts, from her chest to her belly button.

Well, maybe I won't keep my pants on *all* night.

I lick my lips. "Now what?"

"Stroke yourself. Pants on."

I make a slight adjustment and rub my cock up and down through my pants, growing harder as I do so. The tip peeks over the top of the waistband.

"Take them off." Her voice trembles.

So do my fingers when I drop the jeans to the floor.

"You were commando at my parents' house?" She sits up. "Such a naughty boy."

"Oh no, I'm wearing boxers. They're invisible. Go ahead, feel them."

Her lips curl into a smirk. "Well, you should bring that invisible boxer–covered ass over here."

I move closer. She swings her feet off the bed and grabs the base of my shaft with a firm grip. "There's no fabric at all. Liars get ten lashes."

A growl forms in my throat as her hot tongue circles the bottom with firm motions that turn my hands to fists.

"I think your punishment is backfiring. I like it." I like it too much. I'm going to come in her mouth if she keeps doing that, *looking* like that.

She stops as abruptly as she started, shimmying back out of reach and staring at me expectantly. "Well?" She adjusts the pillow beneath her head.

It takes a minute to pry my tongue from the roof of my mouth. "What do you want now, baby?"

"Oh, we're still playing Simon Says? Simon says get on the bed."

I ease onto the mattress by her calves, devouring her with my eyes.

"Simon says suck my nipples."

A soft sigh escapes her lips when mine lock around her tight little bud and suckle. I move to the other nipple, swirling my tongue around it until it hardens in my mouth. Fuck me, that's sexy.

Her fingers wind through my hair. "Simon says kiss me."

I release her breast with one last suck and kiss my way up her chest and neck. I take my time over her chin and plant gentle kisses on each corner of her mouth. Her body gently writhes beneath me until she wraps her legs around my hips, encouraging me to put my weight on her.

When I bring my lips to hers, it's slowly, gently, a delicate kiss to draw her out even more. I want her to lose control. I want her to remember the way she felt in my arms in Florida, to remember how fucking wild she can be.

"Simon says put this on." She hands me a condom, and I obey.

She sucks my tongue into her mouth and drags her teeth down it. Even more blood surges to my cock.

She wants my tongue in her mouth? Very well.

I kiss her with everything I've got, until I'm the one in control again. Her thighs squeeze me closer, and it's not long before her wetness spreads over me.

I pull back with a groan. "Fuck, Mel."

She nips my lip. "That sounds perfect. Right now. Fuck Mel."

I circle the tip of her nose with mine. "You forgot to say 'Simon says.'"

Her lips part, but I push the tip of my cock inside her, and she forgets what she was going to say.

I pause. "Does this mean I win or lose?"

"We both win." She grabs my ass, and I let her pull me all the way inside, both of us sagging for a second and releasing identical moans. Being inside her feels like home.

"You have no idea how fucking good you feel," I say.

Her one bark of laughter makes her pussy convulse around my cock. "I'm right here too. I know exactly how good this feels."

For a while, we speak only in silken thrusts and soft moans. Gasps are road maps to pleasing her. Shivers tell me when she really likes what I'm doing.

I reposition her leg, pulling her knee out to plunge deeper and hit that spot that gives her a languid grin and makes her teeth pinch her lower lip.

Her tits shake with every thrust, and the beauty of her curves is mesmerizing. I go harder to watch the ripples move through her body. Lust for her crawls along the inside of my skin, clawing to get out.

It shouldn't be possible, but the more I have her, the more I want her. Being inside her doesn't ease the aching need. It stokes the want, increases the frenzy, until I'm almost desperate for her to come, come again, and keep coming. I want her to unravel underneath me like I unravel when I'm inside her.

I need to please her, to make her feel good. It's the best kind of revenge, and it brings a smile to my lips just as her eyes widen and she gasps, rhythmically clenching me as she comes.

I slow down, but I'm not stopping.

Her hands squeeze mine when I raise them above her head and pin them to the mattress. "I felt how hard you just came, baby."

"You make me come so good."

"But I'm not stopping until you come again. See, feeling you come on my cock is addictive. It's been too long. I need it again." I thrust. "And again." I grind to rub against her clit and she cries out. "And again."

"Fuck yes," she says breathlessly.

....

Half an hour and some sexual gymnastics later, I collapse to the bed beside her, mission accomplished. When I cool off and my breathing slows down, I pull her close, nestling behind her. "I missed you. Let's not go that long apart again."

She sighs happily and kisses my hand. "That was good. Are you thirsty?"

"My throat's a little dry."

She sits up. "Time for pants, I guess. Not to chase you out of here right after that, but I have to work in the morning."

"And you'd rather sleep alone?"

"It's my first full workday back from vacation, and my desk is going to be paper-bombed with memos—not to mention my inbox. I need a clear head to deal with everything." She frowns.

"It's cool. I'll get out of your hair. Is everything OK at work? I know it's work, but you're not looking as eager to get back to it as everyone says you are."

"Everyone says?" She clutches the sheets to her chest. "What do they say?"

"Just that you love your job and you're amazing at it. But you got a look just now while talking about it."

"No one likes getting back to the grind after an amazing vacation, Blake."

I smile and kiss her shoulder. "It was pretty amazing, wasn't it?"

Her gaze softens. "It was the best time I've ever had."

Chapter 31

Melanie

MY HEART POUNDS AND MY PALMS SWEAT WHEN I ENTER THE building and flash my pass at the security guards.

I can do this.

My stilettos punctuate my steps down the long hallway. After so many days in flats, I'm surprised how good it feels to slide my feet into heels. I'll have to mention that to one of the writers. Jerry, perhaps. Though, if I moved into Editorial, I wouldn't have to pass along my ideas and see someone else execute them. They'd still be mine. Sure, people give me unofficial credit around the office, but how good would it feel to see my name in the byline?

I'm not the first at work, but whoever is here is out of sight.

At eight in the morning, the office is quiet. Sienna is not yet at reception, but I wanted it this way. I'm likely to be buried under a mountain of paperwork, and if I get in later, people will keep stopping me to ask how my vacation was. Before I know it, it'll be lunchtime.

My vacation was spectacular, but I don't have time to chat about it. But I'm feeling more than a little conflicted about Blake, and how I can still see him now that the fantasy is over and I've got to go back to being the real me.

Note to self: Avoid Bailey today. She'll want to talk about why I'm not glowing.

Coming in early is partly psychological too. Being hard at work in my office when people come in shows my dedication, and it's a subtle discouragement from talking. People will snag you into chitchat if you're on your way to your office, but they hesitate to interrupt you if you're already there.

It's hard, but I've tried to cultivate aloof professionalism in the office. I'm not against getting to know my colleagues, but as head of HR, I can't be seen to have any kind of bias. I have to treat issues impartially. Even when the person complaining is a raging pain in my ass and I want to dump scalding coffee down their throat so I don't have to hear another lie come out of their mouth.

I pry my hands open from the fists they've turned into, noting the crescent indentations in the palms.

Three minutes in the office, and I'm wound tighter than a coiled spring. Florida unwound me, Blake untangled me, and I can't let go of the positive things that happened there—despite the way those good feelings slip away with each shallow breath I take in New York.

But I do love this place, with its polished granite floors and brushed-chrome details. It's modern, chic, and tasteful, while still having personality.

One rotten asshole can't spoil the barrel for me. I just have to keep that in mind when I see Thaddeus Mitchell's smirking, weasely little face.

My favorite thing about the kitchen is the fancy coffee machine the boss bought a year ago. It chugs pleasantly while I pour in the milk, wait for it to steam and froth, and then add a generous heap of raw sugar to the bottom of my mug. I could do with the extra energy this morning. The journey from *power on* to *Ah, that's a damn good cup of coffee* takes about four minutes, and while the coffee isn't quite as fancy as a Starbucks, it's free and delicious.

"Hello, Melanie. Did you have a nice vacation?" Reese asks as he enters the kitchen.

"I did, thanks." I stir my coffee, thinking of something else to say. Reese has never acted like I intimidate him the way the rest of the staff do, which makes it easier to relax around him. Then again, his background is…interesting, to say the least. It's no wonder he's not intimidated by anyone, growing up a diplomat's son.

His expensive suit is impeccably tailored and shows off his trim build and broad shoulders. He adds a splash of hazelnut syrup to his cup. "Florida, correct?"

"Yes, Miami."

"Any wild stories?"

"Oh, you know. Identity theft, nude beaches, and cat smuggling. You know how it is."

Where the hell did that come from?

"For sure." He laughs, and I smile, unsure if he realizes I'm not lying, but I take a careful sip to avoid being scalded and head back down the hall, encouraged at my bravado. Maybe it won't be impossible to open up and let these people in a bit more. The light's on in Nick's office, but that's not a surprise. He's incredibly talented—and cripplingly shy—so he tends to come in early to avoid the rush.

My office is as neat as I left it, except that my inbox has hit maximum capacity and vomited the excess across my desk and onto the floor. At least the cleaners didn't throw away the papers on the floor like they did during the last vacation I took. Even I knew I'd crossed the line with my haranguing after that episode, but I'd been so flustered that I couldn't stop myself.

What would I do in the same situation now? I'd have to do the same amount of work, but I can't seem to access the same feelings of panic and outrage. If I'd walked into the same thing, I think I would have shrugged and sprung to work.

Huh.

I scoop up the pile from the floor and toss it onto the desk, sipping my coffee while my computer boots up.

Maybe I should pull in one of the interns to sort through my mail, alphabetically or chronologically, but I prefer doing it myself. I'm the one who needs to know what's going on, and besides, the information I receive in emails isn't appropriate for an entry-level employee's eyes. The biggest annoyance is when people send multiple emails and paper memos about the same thing, clogging both of my inboxes for something that never ends up being the emergency they think it is.

No, the worst are the emails sent to apologize for sending so many emails. It's like those people cannot stop word vomiting.

I'll deal with the emails first and then comb through the paper mess, cross-referencing duplicates I've dealt with via email and shredding when necessary.

I underestimated.

Inbox: 438 Unread Messages

There are only sixty-three employees at the magazine. What the flaming fuck happened while I was gone?

My cell dings with a text.

Shawn: I don't think I want you and Blake dating.

The words hit me like a punch to the gut, and it takes a full three minutes of clutching my phone staring at that text before I can reply. If my own brother doesn't think his best friend is good for me…

Me: Why not?

Shawn: I don't know. It's weird. He's basically family.

Me: It's not weird. We love each other.

Shawn: Maybe you had fun in Florida, but it can't be more than that or you'd have gotten together sooner. I'm worried he's taking advantage of you.

Me: He isn't! Stop it, Shawn. What's he said about this?

Shawn: I'm not talking to that fucking guy. What a weasel.

Me: You're going to shut him out? You've been best friends forever.

Shawn: Whatever. What happens when you break up? I lose my best friend because he can't come over anymore in case he runs into you. Is it worth it?

Me: Stop being selfish.

But the words apply to me as well. Isn't that what I'm doing? If Blake and I don't make it, then Shawn loses the guy who's been like his brother and Blake loses all of us, not just me.

Blake's worth it, but am I just prolonging the inevitable and arrogantly thinking I'm worth ruining his life over?

I stuff my phone back into my purse and focus on my computer. I forward a few emails mistakenly sent to me to the appropriate places. Some people nag me with problems about their paychecks, but that's not my department. Nor is it my responsibility to get the burned-out light in the stairwell fixed. I forward eight emotionally escalating messages about that to Maintenance, cc'ing the offended party so they'll realize I'm not the appropriate channel.

Unfortunately, that also includes an email to Thaddeus Mitchell, who sent quite a few himself regarding the lightbulb.

From: tmitchell@H2T.com
Subject: Can we deal with this please?

Miss Walker,

The lightbulb is still burned out. Please address this.

And another two days later:

> **From: tmitchell@H2T.com**
> **Subject: safety**
>
> ---
>
> Ms. Walker, I've been reaching out to you regarding the burned-out bulb. This is a health and safety issue that requires your immediate attention. If anything happens, you are directly responsible.
>
> Thaddeus

One day later:

> **From: tmitchell@H2T.com**
> **cc: VDawson@H2T.com**
> **Subject: Immediate action required**
>
> ---
>
> I don't think it's unreasonable for you to monitor your email in case of emergencies like this one. A month is a long time to be on vacation, and it's irresponsible to leave without filling in your position. It's basically a leave of absence.
>
> Thaddeus Mitchell

Old money, same old assholes.

The fact that he's cc'd our boss, Valerie, is maddening. She's the owner of the company, not a referee or a mom we need to run to about this stupid crap and tattle on each other about.

Yeah, I need a minute to decompress.

Deep breathing doesn't help, but I remember the poster I'd carefully folded and placed in my purse. I grab it and the tape.

The shot of the beach during a vivid sunset—no people in sight—makes me relax, remembering the heat on my skin, the sand between my toes. I cross my arms over my chest and sigh happily at the little window it provides into my vacation.

"I'd have thought your time would be better spent catching up on business correspondence than redecorating your office, Melanie."

My spinal cord quivers against the inside of my vertebrae.

Thaddeus.

He smirks at me from my open door.

"I've been answering emails. I was just taking a breather." *Stop justifying yourself to him.*

"Oh? Coming back from a vacation can be tough, but if the job's too hard for you…"

"I love my job."

His watery blue eyes blink incessantly. "Funny way of showing it. I know why you got this job."

"I got my job because I was qualified to do it."

His eyebrows raise. "If you want to keep your job, you need to be a professional. None of this redecorating the office on a whim." He walks out my door, closing it behind him.

I should be relieved, but a moment later, my email dings, and I know he's sent something else. Seething too much to type, I stand and pace around my office. I'm glad for the lock on the door and the blinds that block prying eyes when I start punching at the air, imagining it's his royal asshole's face.

Times like this, I wish I'd become serious about a martial art somewhere along the way. Even boxing. Something gritty, and raw, and physical. I could head to the gym on my lunch break and take out my frustrations on a punching bag. I'd get fitter in the process, and I could return to work feeling Zen and looking dewy with a healthy glow.

More likely, I'd come back sore and blotchy. Still, it's a good idea for stress relief, something that could help morale. The office has a small gym, and we have a small entertainment lounge with a pool table for wooing potential clients or informal brainstorming sessions. Maybe I could look into adding some boxing equipment to the gym.

I suspect taping a photo of Thaddeus's face to the bag would be a step too far.

My inbox dings with another new email, and I head back behind the desk and viciously click the notifications off. I don't need an audible reminder of my workload growing while I flail around the office wasting energy on an asshole.

Time to switch things up.

Plunking back into my chair, I take about twenty minutes to sort the mountain of papers chronologically into two large piles, the most recent on top. Working backward is the way to go. If an issue's been dealt with, the employee will have sent me a notice, and I'll be able to disregard earlier emails, saving myself some time. I hate trying to solve a problem that's already been taken care of.

Satisfied at the appearance of progress, I take a sip of coffee—and gag on the cold, milky liquid.

Why is it that I love coffee, love iced coffee, but can't deal with hot coffee that's grown cold? I swallow it with a grimace and head to the kitchen to make a fresh cup.

The happy chatter dies down when I stride into the room and rinse the dregs from my cup.

"Hi, Melanie. How was your vacation?" Katka asks in her shy but sincere way.

I start the coffee machine. "It was fine, thanks. I got a lot of sun—Florida, you know."

"I can tell. Your skin is glowing."

The other two smile politely, but it's clear they're uncomfortable around me. They think I'm stiff and judgmental, probably someone who's never done an uninhibited thing in her life. "Thanks."

What would they say if they knew about the Switch, or the nude beach, or Blake? Any of it. I almost got a tattoo. Would they be surprised and reluctantly admire me if I suddenly opened up, or would they be mildly horrified, like I was a stiff aunt suddenly trying too hard to fit in? It's not like I can drag them all into the boardroom and pull up vacation slides. "Here's me on a nude beach. Here's me doing a water sport. Here's me fucking my old crush! Aren't we a cute couple?"

I want to bridge the gap between myself and these people. They're cool, interesting people, and I know all about them. I'm head of HR—it's my business to know about them. Yet, what I know are just facts and figures. Salary, ages, family situations, benefits, sick leaves.

I don't really *know* them—and they know even less

about me—but even if we were work friends, it's not like I could bitch about anyone to them. I'm in a position of power that the majority of them don't have, and I'm tired of it. I want to be one of them.

It's harder this way, more isolating, but maybe it's better if I want to keep my job as it is. I wouldn't even know how to start bridging this gap anyway.

I give them another polite smile when my coffee's done and head back to my office.

Chapter 32
Blake

I'VE NEVER ACTUALLY BEEN HERE, BUT I BROUGHT FOOD for Mel. A woman's got to eat, right? The guards check my bag carefully and take my details from a photo ID before signing me in, which seems like overkill. It's a women's magazine, not a controversial political paper. Then again, feminism has become a polarizing topic, and some of the articles published here are quite provocative.

I know because I've spent the last few hours reading back issues on my phone. They're an online-only publication. I liked a few articles by Bailey Monroe, who I'm pretty sure I've heard Mel mention as her best friend. It's weird to think we've never hung out with any of each other's friends. We'll have to remedy that. If we're going to be part of each other's lives, we need to merge them a little, have them bleed into each other—or an analogy that doesn't include bodily fluids.

I turn left off the elevator and stare for a second at the serious wealth of the place. Whoever designed it had taste—and a shit ton of money. Pride fills me that my girlfriend works in a place like this. Not just works here—she's in charge of a lot of things here.

The walls are a light sage that stops the low-ceilinged

halls from feeling like tunnels. The main desk has a higher ceiling that opens up the place, drawing you toward it. A leggy Chinese woman with a side-shave hairdo strides up to me when I stroll past reception. "Hey. You look a little lost." Her Marilyn piercing glints when she smiles.

"Yeah, I'm looking for Mel." At her blank look, I clarify. "Melanie Walker's office. It's on this floor, right?"

"Is she expecting you?"

"Not exactly."

She toys with the lace at the cuffs of her fitted jacket. The ensemble reminds me of a pirate, but I know jack and shit about fashion. Her glance drops to my bag. "You're a delivery guy?"

"Today I am. We're dating, and I'm surprising her with lunch."

Her slow head-to-toe appraisal is blatant but quick, and she ends it with a small smirk. "Wow. Well, *Mel's* office is the last door on your right." She points in the opposite direction. I turned the wrong way getting off the elevator.

"Thanks. What's your name?"

"Sienna."

"Thanks, Sienna." I turn and head to Mel's office, feeling a little nervous, which is ridiculous. It's Mel—the woman I've spent an insane amount of quality time with the past few weeks. Hopefully, she's not too annoyed that I'm interrupting her on her first day back.

But the nerves are excitement too, and even though I just saw her last night, I can't wait to see her again.

The doorknob doesn't budge when I try it—locked—so I knock instead.

"Just a minute." Her voice is muffled by the door.

The door whooshes open, and her frown turns to a look of surprise.

"Blake."

"Hey, Mel."

She fiddles with her earring. "What are you doing here?"

"I needed to make sure you're not neglecting those curves while hard at work. I hate to think of you wasting away." I hold up the bag. "I brought you some lunch." I pause. "Are you going to let me in your office, or should I spread out the food here in the hallway?"

"Uh, sorry." She steps back and shuts the door behind me when I walk in. "It's been a crazy day. I didn't realize it was this late already."

I glance at the clock on her wall. "It's only 12:13."

"I came in early to get a head start. If I'd known it was this bad, I'd have come in last night. I probably should have, anyway." She gestures toward the small, round table in the corner of her office, and I set the bag there.

"Burning out isn't going to help anyone."

"I'm not going to burn out. I can handle things, Blake. I'm good at my job."

"I know that. I didn't mean for it to come out like I don't think you're competent."

"Sorry, I'm hangry. Where you go past hungry to angry." Her posture relaxes. "You brought me food?"

"Any guesses?"

She sits on one of the chairs. "Sandwiches?"

I raise an eyebrow. "Give me more credit than that." I set paper plates on the table for both of us and hand her a napkin. I open the bag and set a slice of pizza in front of her before taking one for myself and sitting down.

"Pizza. Real New York pizza." She bites her lip. "I'm sorry I'm being a jerk. It's been a long day, and it's barely half over."

I take a bite and swallow before answering. "It's fine. I'm used to dealing with Shawn."

That earns me a genuine laugh. She folds her slice in half and takes a big bite, closing her eyes and savoring the pie. "Now, *this* is pizza."

"Unlike the crap we had in Florida."

She dabs her lips with a napkin. "Unlike the crap we *made* in Florida. That was your idea. I take no responsibility for the results of that edible experiment."

"Barely edible experiment." I hand her a soda can and open one for myself. "This place is gorgeous. I've never been here before."

She nods. "The owners care about appearances, but I think it's because they also genuinely care about this place. They're proud of the business they've built."

She's nearing the crust of her slice, so I set another on her paper plate.

"So, should I stop by tomorrow and take you out for a bite to eat? There's this amazing Mongolian barbecue place that opened up. Well, I've heard it's amazing. I was saving it for when you were free, but I got reservations. It's quieter there at lunchtime. One of my clients said I should try the—"

Her phone rings and she glances at it. "I can't."

"Do you need to get that?"

"It's probably not an emergency."

"Oh. Maybe tomorrow night? I can see if they can move the reservation." Unlikely, but I'll call.

She sets her crust on the plate and tears open a wet nap, cleaning her hands before moving back behind her desk. She sits and pulls a stack of papers toward her. "Tomorrow's really not good. In fact, I probably should stop at one slice or I'll spend the rest of the afternoon fighting off a food coma."

The paper stack is pretty big. No wonder she's tense. I clean my hands as well, moving behind her and laying my hands on her shoulders. "Holy shit. Your shoulders are like rocks."

The door flings open. "Melanie, you need to deal with the... Oh." A fortysomething guy with a put-out expression stops when he sees me standing behind Mel. "I'll come back later, since you're obviously...taking a long lunch."

Who the hell is this asshole?

"Thaddeus, wait!"

But he's already closed the door.

"That's the prick who's been giving you a hard time?"

"That's Thaddeus, yes. Ugh, this is a disaster."

I'm glad he's gone. Her shoulders tightened even more the second he arrived, if that's possible.

She shrugs away from me when I start kneading them. "Stop. I can't do this right now."

"Sorry." I step back around the desk and sit in the seat facing her. "Now we've got a big, professional desk between us in case the chaperones come to check up on us. Why do you care what that asshole thinks anyway?"

"I've worked really hard to be seen as a professional around here. I want to be taken seriously."

I hold up my hands. "I get it. You're right. I shouldn't have surprised you at your workplace like this, but screw that guy. He's the unprofessional one who was hassling you on your vacation."

She picks up her pen and scans the paper on top of the pile. "This job's everything to me."

Maybe plans will bring some levity back. "Well, if the Mongolian grill doesn't tempt you, I also made reservations on Friday night for this edgy little wine bar—"

"You can't just go making plans for me without asking. It's presumptuous and oppressive." Her jaw tightens so much that part of me worries about her teeth.

"Hey, they're not set in stone." Clearly Thaddeus has rattled her. Swear to Christ, if I see that guy in the hallway… "If you want to do something else, I'm all ears. The point wasn't what we were doing. The point was that we were doing something together."

"Maybe we shouldn't."

"Shouldn't what?"

"Do anything together anymore." Her voice is mild, like she hasn't just kicked my legs out from under me.

I stare hard at her, but she doesn't return my gaze. She just shuffles papers around, sorting them like I'm not here. "Are you fucking kidding me, Mel?"

"Please keep your voice down," she hisses, closing her eyes. "The picnic was bad enough, and then *he* came in and saw you behind my desk."

"You're focusing on some asshole getting the wrong idea? Who gives a fuck what he thinks. This is more important than a misunderstanding."

She signs the bottom of a form with a flourish. "Have you talked to Shawn today?"

"He hasn't returned my texts since we told everyone. He'll cool off. What does that have to do with anything?"

She finally looks me in the eyes. "I am not that person in Florida, but I faked it so hard you believe that's who I am. The only person I didn't fool was myself." She grabs another sheet of paper and signs the bottom. "Now, you'll have to excuse me. I've got a lot of work to catch up on, and people are going to think I've been slacking off all day."

Is it really this easy for her? Did she never give a shit, or is she too scared? "Are you kidding me?"

"Don't make this harder than it already is." Her voice is bland. "We should have ended this in Florida instead of pretending it's something it was never meant to be. I'm sorry." The woman in front of me is a stranger, a weak shell of the woman I know her to be. An uncaring, all-business version of the woman I fell in love with.

"What the hell is this? Yesterday we had dinner with your family. Last night I was inside you. Christ, not even twelve hours ago you were ordering me to fuck you."

She cringes and her eyes close. "That's just it, Blake. When I'm with you, everything else disappears. But seeing you with my family? They're your family too. I mean, Christ, Shawn's already freaked out and stopped talking to you. He's sent me some texts about you. You're his best friend, and because of me, you guys aren't talking. My family is already yours. And I can't take them away from you."

"By doing this, you are."

She shakes her head, emotion finally cracking her veneer of composure. "No. You need them."

Anger tightens my stomach. "Because I'm the poor

little orphan? Thanks, but I've had enough people deciding my life for me. This isn't your decision to make. I can't believe you actually think you're breaking up with me for my own good."

"I'm sorry."

"Not as sorry as I am. Maybe that's not even it, but if you didn't want to be with me as anything other than a fling, you should have just said it. I'm a big boy."

"Blake—"

"I hope you and your spreadsheets are happy together."

It takes every ounce of self-restraint I have not to slam the door on my way out.

Chapter 33

Melanie

I HAVE NO IDEA WHAT I SIGNED. I HAVEN'T SEEN A WORD, blinded by the tears I refuse to let fall. I manage to hold them back until Blake closes the door softly behind him.

Then hot bitterness pours over my heart and leaks down my cheeks.

What the fuck are you doing? Go after him!

I force my ass to remain in the chair and reason with my stupid heart. It's pounding in my chest so hard and fast it hurts.

I'm doing the right thing for both of us. Ending it before it gets messy and he loses the one good family he's ever had.

It's already messy.

He needed to see what I'm really like.

This may be who you were, but it's not who you are—or who you want to be.

What the fuck is wrong with me?

I pull my cell out, but my work phone rings.

For the first time in my career, I let it go to voice mail.

I heard the words coming out of my mouth, the hurtful bullshit I said to push Blake away, but I didn't mean any of it. All I wanted was for him not to lose anything. From the moment I walked in here this morning, I've been hardening back into the rigid person I was before I left. Blake doesn't deserve that—hell, that's not who he fell for in Florida—so I know things are doomed between us. His relationship with Shawn has already suffered.

He looked so hurt. Is he right? Am I just another asshole trying to dictate his life? Growing up, he never had a say over whose house he'd be moved to, stay at, or get taken from and moved again.

I've already tainted things by thinking I know what's best for him.

I want to call him, but what the hell would I say?

I snivel into a tissue, trying to pull myself together enough to leave my office. I can't let people see me like this. I can't let my coworkers see me like this. It's completely unprofessional.

Chatting about my vacation is one thing, but running after a guy while sobbing my heart out? No way. My job is all I have.

It is now.

The job I don't even really want. I focus on a memo, thoroughly hating myself, and grab for my phone instead. I need to get him back, need to talk to him. But what do I say? I don't trust myself not to freak out when I hear his voice. I snivel and cough. Freak out *more* when I hear his voice—no, I can't call him.

I try to text Blake instead, but my thumbs hover over the keyboard, and I'm unsure what to type. I close the window and absentmindedly scroll through my texts, stopping when I see one from Bailey.

Hope you're not busy, because I'm coming up.

It was sent five minutes ago. Shit. I sniff hard, a snotty sound that makes me gag, and frantically type a response telling her now's not a good time. But it's too late. The door swings open.

I forgot to lock it behind Blake. At least it's not Thaddeus.

I scrub a hand down my face to blot the tears and try to give a smile to my best friend.

Bailey's smile dies on her lips. "What's happening? You're *crying*? You never cry. Oh God, who died?"

"Shut the door."

She locks it behind her and rushes forward. "Well?"

"Blake just left." My voice cracks, making the admonition come out weak.

She sits in the chair Blake vacated a few moments ago. "I haven't pushed, but what's happening with you?"

"In what area?"

"Melanie, you swapped houses with a complete stranger out of nowhere. You don't even lend your shoes to me, never mind letting a stranger sleep in your bed or touch all your things."

"I get it. I'm a control freak!"

Bailey doesn't even blink. "No. I think you were, but it's not fitting anymore. Otherwise you'd have gone nuts on this Switch."

"I might as well have. I did all kinds of weird shit."

"Good! You were due to let your hair down. Now tell me the truth. What made you go?"

I trace meaningless patterns on the desktop with one of my tears. "I had a day from hell just before leaving. It's what made me want to go."

She uncrosses her legs and sits forward. "Go on."

"You know Thaddeus and I haven't been best friends since he started here."

Bailey wrinkles her nose. "He's such a bastard. The other day he was ranting about food banks, saying they shouldn't exist because people need to help themselves instead of getting a handout. I wanted to wave a hand in front of his face and congratulate him on the magnificent privilege of never needing to use one."

Bailey grew up extremely poor, but she's proud of her family. "And you didn't punch him in the throat?" I ask.

"Nah. I've got a venomous cartoon series brewing, though, planted the idea with Paulina. He won't ever read it, but I'll know it's there burning people like him."

Paulina does a cartoon series as well as illustrations for some of the articles. "Smart. Don't give him an excuse to come after you."

Her smug expression fades. "What's he doing to you? Melanie, if he's touched you—"

"No, he hasn't. He's too smart for that, and it isn't sexual. It's like he knows I'm not impressed with his wealth or connections, and it gets under his skin. He does things to try to intimidate me."

"You need to report him."

"To HR?" I wave at her. "Yeah, the thing is, he hasn't technically crossed the line from obnoxious to harassing. He's—"

"Too smart for that. Shit. We need to do something. No wonder you wanted to get the hell out of this place for a break."

"Yeah. He'd been shadowing me nearly all day and did enough tiny awful things that I'd had enough." I bite my lip hard, bracing myself against the truth I haven't even allowed myself to think while I've been gone. "And then on my way home, I got mugged."

"What? That's awful!"

"Obviously I'm OK. I convinced them to only take the cash from my wallet, not my wallet itself or any of the cards." She snorts, and I look up, shocked. "Bailey, it's not funny. I was scared out of my mind. He had a knife."

"Are you listening to yourself? You argued with a mugger. You're such a stubborn asshole! You could have been stabbed, and you told him no because it would have inconvenienced you to have to get new cards and identification."

My lips twitch. She's absolutely right. "I'm worse than I thought. The mugger didn't even argue. He was probably rolling his eyes under his mask, eager to get the hell away from me."

She laughs. "But you're OK, and that's the main thing. Did you tell the police?"

"I filed a report, but there wasn't much for a description."

"And that made you leave?" She narrows her eyes. "You don't think Thaddeus had something to do with the mugging, do you? Maybe he wants your job, or you're stopping him from getting what he wants, so he hired one of his goons to take you out."

I laugh. Bailey's always had a vivid imagination. "Bailey, come on. It's not a bad TV movie. He's not a villain. He's just an asshole. Besides, he's not that imaginative. He just hates that I'm not throwing myself at his feet."

"But you've stayed quiet about his treatment—and

the freaking mugging. I'd have called you right after—maybe during—to snivel about being robbed! I think you should say something about Thaddeus."

"To Valerie? Who hired him? Yeah right. Their families have probably summered in the Hamptons together for three generations. And today he came in during lunch and saw Blake giving me a massage."

Bailey twists her tawny hair into a rope and trails it over her top lip, unaware that it makes her look like she has a fabulous mustache. "Were you naked?"

"No!"

"Darn. I mean that's good, but darn. I wish there was something we could do."

"Until Thaddeus steps over the line, my hands are tied. Being a dick isn't a fireable offense."

"Unfortunately." Bailey sighs. "You still haven't explained the whole Blake situation."

"I fired myself from that relationship for being a dick."

"What?"

"He brought me a picnic lunch."

She grins. "Awww. That's so... What's with your face? It wasn't romantic?"

I blow my nose and toss the tissue into the trash. "No, it was. Everything he does is fucking perfect. But it was more what it meant."

"It didn't mean he thought you would want something to eat at lunchtime?"

"No. It's like he's copying and pasting what we were in Florida to here, and he expects me to be able to roll with that as though nothing's different."

"What's wrong with that?"

"I'm not that person."

"Aren't you?" Bailey crosses her arms. "Seems to me that you're whoever the hell you want to be. You're the strongest woman I know, Melanie. If you want to be with Blake, be with Blake. The only thing stopping you is yourself."

It's not quite that simple. "Maybe. But I don't know how to change back into that person I was on vacation."

"Who says you have to? Change is a process, not an instantaneous reveal like some reality TV makeover. That kind of drastic difference isn't lasting. Don't change for him. Don't change for anyone but yourself. But don't push him away because you think you're not good enough or you think he won't like you. That's not fair to him."

"I know you're right. But not being ready for him isn't all of what's holding me back. We practically grew up together because he didn't have a family. And now, just finding out about us? Shawn has already cut Blake out, called him names. What if their friendship is wrecked for good? If we... If I fucked this up, there's no way things will be the same between him and my family. I can't do that to him. It's not fair. So I told him I can't be with him."

"So don't fuck things up. Give things a chance. Shawn will get over it."

"I want to be the person Blake deserves. But I feel like it's too late."

Her hand slapping my desk shocks me.

"Bailey!" I snap.

"That's bullshit, and you know it. You know the big difference I saw in you in Florida when we talked? Down there, you finally let yourself be happy. And maybe things fuck up, but there's a difference between things not working out and you not giving a good thing a chance to even begin. I haven't even seen you guys together, and I know you're perfect for each other. When you find that in life, Mel, you don't get to let it get away from you. Fuck what anyone else thinks. Do you know how lucky you were to get together? Most people will never find their soul mates. Don't you dare let him get away because you're scared."

I sit back. "Geez. When did you get so assertive?"

She bites her lip. "I don't know, but I sort of like it."

"Me too. But I'm pretty sure I already wrecked things. He was pissed at me for trying to protect him from losing my family."

"So? Do you want to be with this man?"

"Yes."

"Well? What are you going to do to fix your life and get him back?"

I prop my head on my hand. "I'm not sure yet, but you've given me a lot to think about."

"Good. Family is about love, Mel. And from the looks of it, you're the best person for him to have in his life. Fight for him—for both of you."

My phone beeps—message received.

"Go ahead and check it." Bailey leans forward. "I bet it's Blake."

I open it, hands trembling in fear and anticipation, but it's from Shelby. I laugh at the picture she's sent and show it to Bailey. She frowns. "Are they topless? What's that say on the ground behind them?"

I nod. Shelby and Ariella are sitting on the beach without tops on, just showing me their bare backs.

They'd never gone topless on the beach before. On the sand behind them, they've written *Wish you were here*.

Me too.

—————————

Nine p.m. rolls around. My fingers tremble when I call Blake, having had more time to marinate in my stupidity. I pace around the apartment while the phone rings, trying to work off some nerves. It's taken until now to decide what I'm going to say to him.

"Yeah." His voice is flat, but he picked up—a good sign.

My carefully planned script evaporates. "I'm an idiot. Please don't hang up on me."

He sighs but stays on the line.

"Blake, I'm sorry. I'm so sorry about what happened today."

"What *happened*? No, don't make it sound like something completely out of your control. It wasn't a random thing that occurred." His words are clipped and betray the fact that he's not as calm as he normally is.

I'm already fucking this up. "You're right. I'm sorry. Seeds were planted from my conversation with Shawn, and then I just panicked when Thaddeus showed up and saw us together."

"If you called to justify—"

"No! I take it back. I want to be with you. I overreacted today."

"You didn't overreact. You treated me like I'm nothing to you. Like I was an embarrassment or an inconvenience. I've had enough of that in my life, thanks."

I cringe. I hadn't even thought of it like that. This is

worse than I thought. "Blake, no, you have to know how much you mean to me."

"You have a great way of showing it." His anger is palpable, even through the phone. "Your family is the closest to a true family I've ever had, but I was willing to take a chance on you—on us. I risked the only family I know to be with you, and it kills me you didn't do the same. And the first time something… Hell, I don't even know what the hell it was, but you bailed over nothing. I was bringing you lunch, and you freaked the fuck out. What happens down the road when a real conflict comes up? Maybe that was just an excuse. Maybe it's all a big excuse because at the end of the day you just don't want to be together."

"That's not true. I do want to be together! I'm so sorry. I didn't want to fuck it up and ruin what you have with my family either. I didn't want to disappoint you. I was so stupid. Please give me a chance to try to do better." I feel about an inch tall.

"I'm sorry, Melanie. I can't do this."

The silence when he hangs up thunders through my heart.

Chapter 34

Blake

THE FUNNY THING ABOUT GETTING DRUNK IN PUBLIC BEFORE two o'clock on a weekday is that no one pays close attention to one another. None of us are here looking for hookups. I can be as pathetic as I want—though I'm not exactly crying into my beer, I've received more than one scowl—and no one judges.

Well, maybe they're judging, but no one's staring at me and that feels A-OK.

Where did it all go wrong? Not that it matters. I gave up my family for her, and what did she give me in return? Excuses for some legendarily shitty behavior.

If she'd overreacted and didn't mean the words she'd said, she would have followed me out of the office or called before she got home from work instead of blowing me off. Maybe she thinks she wants another chance, but how long until she gets buyer's remorse again? Actions scream volumes. Work is where her priorities are.

I shove my phone into my pocket and order another beer. Then I realize all that beer feels lonely sloshing around in my stomach, and I order some wings—not because I'm hungry, but because if I eat a little something now, maybe I'll be just drunk enough to pass out when I get home.

Jerry, the bartender, cocks his head when I order wings. "Don't you want the pizza? It's all you ever get."

Pizza reminds me of Mel now. The last thing I ate was the half a slice with her at lunch yesterday. Could I eat pizza again without remembering that night in Shelby's house, or yesterday when her face closed off and she... Nope, it's ruined. "I've gone off pizza."

Regardless of her intentions, I've lost her and my family in one fell swoop. Shawn's pissed and not returning my texts or calls. I can't look at her parents without seeing Mel's face. I can't be in their house without worrying about running into her or remembering her in the kitchen that last time...

I'm so close to tears that Jerry should put a rubber nipple on my beer bottle.

He nods. "Wings will be right out, then." He hightails it to the kitchen, not that I blame him. The rejection hangs from me, surrounding me like an off-putting poncho. Or a cloud of bad stench, like those assholes who wear too much body spray.

Is that the type of asshole who's going to take my place with Mel?

I squeeze more lemon into my beer, just to see something ruined, crushed like the future I thought would happen for us. She can say it was all about not taking her family from me, but maybe that's a lie. Maybe she really only meant for us to be a Florida fling, and I was the only one who didn't get that memo.

By the time the wings show up, I've drained another beer.

By the time the last wing is finished, I've waxed poetic with a stranger about New York women being ruthless.

By the time the stranger leaves, Shawn has perched himself on the stool at my side.

"Wow." I blink hard a few times. "Am I ever glad to see you, man. It's like you're psychic and knew I really needed a friend."

"Not really." He orders a rum and Coke. "You pocket-dialed me, and it sounded so uplifting I had to come find the party."

"Ah, a robust Sarcasm 2016. Great vintage." I take another gulp of beer, surprised to find this bottle's empty as well. I order another and pull out my phone, disengaging the call and turning the phone off. I should feel more embarrassed that Shawn heard my diatribe, but I can't scrape up enough sobriety to care. I'm just grateful I hadn't pocket-dialed Mel instead. Then again, maybe if I had dialed Mel, I'd have the ability to feel stupid. I shove her violently from my mind. "How's my best friend? You're still my friend, right? You haven't rejected me like Mel said you would?"

"I'm fine and not rejecting you. Right now, I care more about how you're doing."

"I'm fair to middling."

"Fair to bottoming." He flicks my bottle. "You don't drink like this. What's up? Look, if you're going to date my little sister, I don't want you doing shit like this. She deserves better."

"I'm better. I want the best for her. Wanted the best for her. Can you tell her that, please?"

He narrows his eyes. "What does that mean?"

"I tried." My sigh comes out. It feels good, so I do it again.

"What did you do?"

I glare at him. "Don't make it sound like I did something wrong. I didn't cheat on her or hurt her. I'm the innocent victim in all this. She's the one who stomped on my heart. She up and decided I'm not the one for her. Yeah. I literally have no idea what I did to change her feelings. This is all on her. I made a few reservations at places I thought we'd both enjoy. I didn't know reservations were evil. Are they? Are reservations a new faux pas? Because I never meant them like that."

Shawn frowns. "No, you're fine. What else did you do?"

I'm getting a little offended that he thinks I did something wrong, but it's good to have someone to talk to about this. Someone who knows exactly how frustrating and amazing Mel is. "I surprised her."

He grimaces. "Melanie's not one for surprises."

No shit. "It was just a picnic lunch—at her office so she wouldn't even have to leave. I know she had a lot to catch up on, but she basically threw me out."

"A picnic? If I'd known what a quivering pussy you were, I'd have made you date Melanie ages ago." He sips his drink.

"Shut up, Shawn."

"For real. I'm confident she'll be safe in your hands with your Amish wooing. You're a real smooth guy—reminds me of my grandpa's moves."

I gulp more beer in lieu of an answer.

His teasing side-eye turns to a full-on stare. "Wait, what's wrong? She didn't fall for your homemade preserves and hand-churned butter?"

"Why are you being a dick? I'm in real pain here, and

you're supposed to be my friend. It's over, Shawn. Stop joking about it."

His expression grows serious. "Sorry. I seriously thought it was a little tiff, not a real-deal fight."

"Well, now you know." I check my phone again. "She called me with a half-assed explanation, but it was all excuses. She's in love with her job, not me."

"Hang on. You guys made moony eyes at each other *the whole time* we were at my mom and dad's. She's stubborn but not impulsive. She wouldn't cut you out without a good reason. What the hell happened?"

I laugh. "Who the hell knows anymore? She said you were pissed at me too, and that validated her excuses, I guess."

He waves his hand. "Ah, you know Melanie. Give her a few days—she'll come around."

I shake my head. "There's nothing to wait for. I'm not going to beg someone to go out with me. We're both adults. If Mel wanted to be with me right now, she would be. I'm too old to be playing these games, man. Maybe she wants me to pursue her, but I'm not about the chase. I'm not a predator, and she isn't a trembling gazelle."

"That's for damn sure. My little sister's more like a frigging cheetah. She can cause a lot of damage in a very short time when she wants to."

"She's more stubborn than a cheetah. She's more like a rhino." A sexy rhino. But that's no longer my jurisdiction. I finish my beer and hold the empty bottle up, nodding at the bartender. He nods back.

"You're not giving up on her, though, right?" Shawn asks.

"What am I supposed to say? I love her and I thought she loved me, but she doesn't want—or isn't capable of—a relationship. She proved that by freaking out and then pushing me away."

Shawn scratches his nose. "Maybe she's looking for a sign or something. One of those big, romantic gestures. Chicks love that shit."

"What chicks? Ones like Shelby?"

"Maybe."

I slump farther on the stool. "Your sister's not the type. When she wants something, she goes for it. She's less about games than anyone I've ever met, and that makes this even more futile. No. If she's made up her mind, there's nothing I can do to win her back. And you know what? I shouldn't fucking have to."

Shawn slumps on his stool as well. "Shit."

"Yeah. I need to move on." Easier said than done. "So, take my mind off things. Tell me about you and Shelby and big romantic gestures."

"I don't know. I'm in a bit of a situation myself. You know she wanted me to come down there and check out her place."

"Wink wink."

He grins. "I know, but it's not just that. She shares everything, wants everyone to experience life to the fullest. I told you we went to Vegas, right?"

I nod, vaguely remembering something about a private jet. "Yes."

"She won twenty-six grand on the roulette table and gave it away. Just went around giving it to strangers—newlyweds, homeless people, and runaways. But she wasn't doing it to be a big shot. She brushed off their thanks and danced away from the gravity of what she was doing."

"Huh." Her place was nice, though. Maybe she's secretly loaded. She is… Ariella said something about that. I wonder if Shawn knows.

"I've never met someone with such a generous spirit, Blake." He laughs self-consciously. "It's clichéd as fuck, but she makes me want to be a better person. Like, I want to be successful so I can help more people."

Wow, Shawn with ambition? "I must be drunk."

He punches my shoulder. "I don't understand it either. All I know is I like it and want more of that feeling. I was with her when she gave the money away, and people thanked me like I was part of it. I *want* to be part of something important. Haven't figured out what that is, but when has common sense ever stopped me?"

"When did you become a grown-up?" I marvel.

He presses his lips together. "When I realized I'd rather be with one unique woman than chase all the pretty girls in New York."

I acutely know that feeling. Only, in my case, that unique woman pushed me away. And judging by the way she ran from her feelings yesterday, maybe she was just a girl after all.

Chapter 35
Melanie

BAILEY BUMPS MY SHOULDER WITH HERS. "I'M GLAD YOU came out."

I'm not sure if I am, but I manage a grin. "Me too." I haven't heard from Blake in three weeks. I called him once, but I didn't know what to say to his voice mail. Maybe he'll never pick up or read my texts again.

What if the only time I see him again is through Shawn—who also isn't answering his phone—and Blake looks at me with hurt or anger? Or worse, what if he looks at me like we were never lovers at all?

I deserve it, but it eats at me that he hasn't taken my calls for three weeks.

Three long, lonely, so-much-ice-cream-my-cat-is-getting-judgmental weeks.

The kicker? A little part of my ego had truly thought that once I called him, he'd pick up, I'd admit how much of an asshole I'd been, and he'd agree but forgive me. Everything between us had always been so easy that I guess I assumed making up would be too.

And when he didn't accept my apology or call me back, that part of my ego became a black hole of hurt. I should accept it and leave him alone. I've been trying.

"Melanie! How are you?" Jack sets a fresh screwdriver

on the table in front of me, a beer for Bailey, and something blue for Sarah.

"I'm OK. Thanks for getting us in." I gesture around the VIP section.

Jack winks at Sarah but replies to me. "You're welcome. I know a guy."

Jack and Sarah gravitate toward each other like two halves of a whole. When they're together, they touch. When one's away from the table, they find each other with their eyes and smile. I'm not normally one for public displays of affection, but they're so ridiculously in love it seems natural.

It reminds me of the hope I felt in Florida for a bigger life than the one I've been shrinking into. I want that bigger life, the bigger love. Not some lukewarm relationship that's nice or good.

I want what Blake and I had, but he's being painfully clear about his needs.

He needs me to go away.

He doesn't want to see me.

I blew it.

I gulp my drink, letting the alcohol burn my throat instead of the tears.

Bailey gives a frustrated growl and slaps her phone on the table. "Reese needs to see me about the Thaddeus cartoon idea I gave to Paulina. He doesn't like it and doesn't get it. Now I'm going to have to go into the office tomorrow and try to justify the whole idea with him breathing down my neck."

The funny thing is, for all the anger in Bailey's words, she glows while saying them. She and Reese are an amazing team, and they barely need words at this point when talking shop. Unfortunately, the unspoken things between them get in the way.

Seeing Bailey alone and frustrated tugs at my heart. If my amazing best friend can't find someone who's perfect for her, then what chance have I got? Only in my case, I had the perfect guy and I let him get away. I'd kick my own ass if I could reach it.

I take another sip of my drink.

"Screw work." Sarah slips off the stool. "Let's dance." We follow her to the dance floor.

It's crowded and noisy and just what I need. We smile and shimmy, and soon the pulsing music takes my mind off things. Bailey shakes her head when a guy gets into her dance space, gently pushing him away so she can continue dancing by herself.

She's always been so strong, but her speech in my office makes me think she's ready to find love. Sarah and Jack are meant for each other. I thought Blake and I were too. The fact that they've found the person they should be with is huge. Most people won't find that. Most people usually bounce around from unsuitable person to unsuitable person until they find someone with whom to settle. I don't know if soul mates are real, but seeing Jack and Sarah together almost makes me believe.

But what if we don't end up with the person we're supposed to be with? What if Blake and I spend the rest of our lives apart because I gave up? Will we both settle for someone completely wrong for us? God, we could miss out on the best thing that ever happened to us just because we were scared—or because I gave up.

I'm scared about Blake, but I sure as hell don't want to let unspoken things get in the way. I don't have a future stretched out in front of me, radiating with potential. I've already blown it with Blake.

Some people search their whole lives and never find the one. I found him. I found my person, and I lost him—and it hurts like hell.

But that doesn't mean I can't get him back. I just have to try harder.

I grin and throw myself into dancing. It's time to shake my life up for the better.

I want Blake, but there are a few things I need to take care of first.

It's really time for me to Switch things up.

···············

For too long, I've been governed by rigid control—policing myself to color inside the lines. Never to stray outside, for fear of being seen and judged and not taken seriously.

Fuck. That.

Starting now.

Why do we do this to ourselves? Why do I worry so much about judgmental people who probably wouldn't even notice me wearing something slightly brighter because the colors make me feel good? Why did I wait until I was in another state to get my tits out in public? OK, that one has real reasons, but metaphorically, I've been covered up by expectations, and they've done nothing but paint me into a corner until I broke up with someone I've wanted because I thought I should.

Because I thought I wasn't the type of person he needed. Because I was arrogant enough to think it was for his own good—but that was fueled by insecurity too because how could we last when he's so amazing and I'm just me?

We all need someone who will go out of their way to be the best person for us. Someone who cares enough to be good to us. To love us as we are. Blake knows me. I mean, how delusional is it to think he has no idea I can be rigid and stubborn? Even on vacation, he was coaxing me out of my shell, gently pushing my boundaries while letting me be exactly who I wanted to be.

He didn't fall for someone who doesn't exist. He was letting me be myself and accepting every shade of that.

You're goddamn right I'm not letting him go.

I stride into the office in a black pencil skirt and a flowy silvery-green top I bought with Shelby on my last day in Florida. The top doesn't hide every bump and imperfection—something I normally look for in a shirt—but it made me feel good. I bought it knowing I'd probably never wear it.

Now I care more about my authentic feelings than how I look to others. Maybe a black top would have made me more aesthetically pleasing to strangers on the train, but screw them. The one person I *need* to impress is myself. Being a bitch to myself is so last season.

Empowerment is a tough battle—knowing what to fight for and then mustering the courage to actually fight. Part of taking control of my life means knowing when to let things go. I did all I could about being robbed. I reported him to the police, and last night I signed up for Brazilian jujitsu lessons.

Will they turn me into a ninja? No. But if anyone tries to screw me over again, I'll know that I'm not helpless. I'll be able to fight back.

I hadn't realized how much that weighed on me until I hung up the phone after booking my private appointment and then burst into tears. They were cathartic—a release, a relief. That was a healthy focus on control.

But what I need now is nearly the opposite.

My stride slows on the way to Valerie's office.

This fight is a little less clear. My goal isn't to get Thaddeus fired. If he's doing it to me, he may be intimidating someone else.

I blot my palms on my skirt and knock on the door.

"Come in."

I enter, smiling at Valerie, seated behind her huge walnut desk. She's wearing a cream linen pantsuit that somehow doesn't have a single wrinkle. Her auburn hair is brushed back from her face, highlighting her strong bone structure, and her face unadorned with makeup. She's a handsome fiftysomething woman with kind, intelligent eyes like Sophia Loren's.

"Melanie, have a seat. How goes the battle?"

Appropriate words. I ease myself into the leather chair, searching for the right words. Two things have brought me to her office, and the order in which I broach the subjects matters. If Thaddeus is here to stay, my complaining will definitely cause friction. On the other hand, I refuse to take what he's dishing out any longer. Friction or not, I have to speak my mind, and I need to do that first.

"I need to talk to you about Thaddeus."

She frowns. "Oh?"

"While he hasn't technically crossed the line into formal complaint territory, he's been harassing me. Well, more haranguing, but—"

"What exactly has he been doing?"

I fill Valerie in about his actions, showing her some of the emails he's sent that he didn't cc her on. It's like lancing a boil. More and more comes out until I've vented it all. Just saying what he's done makes me lighter. "I didn't come in here to demand he be fired or even reprimanded. I'm just over being treated like his personal assistant, and I've had enough of his snide condescension. These emails he sends take up time and energy better used in dealing with company issues that actually need to be addressed."

Valerie sits back in her chair. "And you want what, mediation?"

"I'd definitely be open to that. I don't want conflict. I loved working here until he arrived. Maybe it's not all him—maybe it was timing—but something has to give. If we can all sit down and resolve these issues together, I'm completely willing to participate."

Valerie shakes her head. "That won't be necessary. Seems like on a fundamental level, one of you needs to go."

My heart drops. "I understand."

"I don't think you do. Thaddeus is the one who will be escorted from the building, not you."

"What?"

She smiles. "There's no way in hell I'd get rid of one of my best employees for a pain in the ass like Thad. You're not the first person he's annoyed—and worse. Honestly, he was on his last chance, and now he's fired."

"Seriously?" I'm one of her best employees? Pride warms my skin.

"Yes."

"Not to look a gift horse in the mouth, but why?"

Valerie sighs. "This never leaves my office, but I hired him as a favor to his dad. We were friends in college and he needed a favor. I owed him one for… Well, never mind what for. Suffice it to say, I owed him one. But I love this company, and no matter how good of friends I was with his family once upon a time, I won't sit by and watch someone shit where I eat." She winks at my shocked grin. "Between you and me, I'm over Thaddeus's emails as well. I need employees who don't need so much hand-holding."

My stomach goes hollow, but I'm determined to forge ahead with the second part of why I came here. "Valerie, I've also been meaning to ask you about moving to another area."

"You're great in Human Resources. Did you have somewhere specific in mind?"

I swallow. "Editorial. Features, maybe. I know it will be different from what I'm used to, but I think I've got the chops to do it. My attention to detail is impeccable, and I know the employees better than anyone, so you wouldn't need to worry about a new team member fitting in." My toes are balled into knots inside my shoes. I want this.

Her eyes twinkle. "I loved the ideas you came up with while on vacation. Jayla's going on maternity leave, as you know from her file. And if things work out with the newest planned expansion, Editorial's going to need someone like you." She taps a pen on her desktop, narrowing her eyes thoughtfully. "I pride myself on having started a company that keeps up with the fast-paced world we live in now."

If I were to take the position, I'd be in there, front lines, mingling with everyone for a change, but more than that, I'd be creating content. In a world of consumers, I want to be a creator. I shrug and go for a casual expression. "I'm already used to putting out fires. I want this, Valerie."

She smiles. "Let's call Jayla's maternity leave your test run to see if you like it—and if you can impress me."

If? She has no idea what I'm capable of when I put my mind to something. "I won't let you down."

Chapter 36

Blake

SEVENTEEN MINUTES.

Ziggy's bony knees stick out beneath his khaki shorts. It's weird, because he's active and has a decent build up top, but his legs are pale and scrawny.

He touches the tips of his fingers together. "I mean, it's not that we don't think you deserve a break. Everyone deserves a break. But what is a break?"

Fern nods. "If your life is something you feel you need to take a break from, something is fundamentally wrong on a cellular level, and you must change things up. Shake up the energy."

My gaze slides back to the clock.

Eighteen minutes.

Eighteen minutes of this weird hippie confrontation about my vacation.

"Right, and that's what I was doing," I say. "I went on a vacation to shake up the energy and recharge my batteries. I got some sun, did some sports"—fell in love—"and here I am, back when I said I'd be back."

"Right." Fern's voice and gaze are flat.

What is their problem? "Have none of your other therapists ever booked a couple weeks off for a vacation? I mean, I didn't just skip out with no warning and let clients down. This was arranged a month before I left so there was advance notice."

Ziggy swivels back and forth in his chair. "The thing is, you needed a break. But what about your clients? You had a responsibility to be there for them. They need you. They need you for a break from their pain, and maybe you need to weigh that need with your own. What's the greater good? I like to ask myself, 'What am I doing to make the world a better place? What can I do to make things better for more people? Am I letting my selfishness get in the way of my responsibilities?'"

This coming from a guy who once gave me shit when I wanted to work an extra day during the week—Fridays. Only that time, the speech had been, "Am I letting my ego get in the way of other therapists' opportunities? Do I need to be the one helping people, or are the clients better served seeing another massage therapist?"

Ziggy sighs. "We want people here who want to be here. That's what this is about at the end of the day."

The hypocrisy is astounding. Maybe I can bullshit this in a way they'll understand. "But how do you fully appreciate what you've got until you get away from it for some space and clarity?" My heart squeezes painfully as I think about Mel and me.

She left voice mails I've been unable to listen to. Hearing her voice again would undo me.

I don't need to be bludgeoned with the reasons why she doesn't want me.

Ziggy sits back in his chair, eyes widening. "You know, you're right. That's a very good point."

Fern glances at Ziggy. "We hadn't thought of it

that way. But I'm still feeling a tension from you, Blake. You should book in for an attunement with myself or Ziggy."

Ziggy's eyes light up. "You know, we have one of our weekend workshops coming up next weekend, if you're interested."

There are maybe three things in the world I'm less interested in than their weekend cult course. I looked online, Googling their names and course name because of professional interest in my colleagues. I found way too many message boards calling it a scam and a cult, with people asking how to get money back—or get their loved ones out of it.

"Wow, I'm flattered." And horrified.

Even if I believed in this energy business they're always talking about, there's no way I'd let these hypocrites anywhere near my chakras. Who knows what harm they'd do? I don't necessarily think they're bad people, but I know they're very much out for themselves.

If energy work is about helping others, their intentions aren't as pure as they pretend they are, and that's what grosses me out the most about them.

"I'd love to, but like you said, I've got a responsibility to the clients I overlooked while on vacation." Their words, not mine. "Their needs have to come before mine." I can't wait until I can quit this place.

"Fair enough." Fern glances at the clock. "Well, you're already twenty minutes late for your next client. Better hurry. I do hope you're taking your self-care seriously. You don't want to burn out by forty because you worked too hard."

For fuck's sake. First I'm an asshole for taking a

break and abandoning my clients, and now I'm an ass-hole for working too hard.

If they hadn't decided to haul me into their office for this idiotic little meeting, I wouldn't have been late. You can't win with people like this. They snag you with their good intentions and then sink you with their bullshit.

I'm out of here the first chance I get.

I close the door behind me and stride to the staff kitchen, taking a big slug of water and wishing it were something distilled. Fern and Ziggy would annoy the Dalai Lama. I've got enough stress in my life, and I don't need them breathing down my neck. They aren't even supposed to be here on Saturdays. If they're open-ing up their schedules so they're here when I am... Nope, I'm out.

The new receptionist, Laina, is an ally. She's not happy here either. They treat her marginally better than they treated Sarah. I'll sneakily encourage her to not book any clients into my schedule for the foreseeable future. Make Fern and Ziggy think no one wants to see me, and then maybe they'll be glad to see the back of me.

I don't necessarily believe they're able to tweak energy, but I don't want them gunning for me after I leave here. It's not worth the aggravation of keeping the door open on this chapter of my past.

The door to Fern and Ziggy's office is still closed when I leave the kitchen. They're probably chanting or doing couple's yoga. I hurry to the front desk, where Laina is sorting through a pile of files.

"Hey, Laina."

She startles. "Blake! I had your new patient do the intake forms and stalled as long as I could, but she seemed pretty agitated to be kept waiting so long. I stuck her in room three and told her to undress and lie under the sheet and that you'd be in right away." Her gaze is wild. "But that was fifteen minutes ago!"

"Whoa." I hold up a hand. "Don't worry about it. Fern and Ziggy put me behind schedule with one of their chats. Relax. I'll tell"—I look at the intake form—"Mae I was getting more oil or something."

"Thank you so much for understanding." Laina's relief is almost comical—or it would be, if I didn't know how hard she works.

I glance around to make sure we're alone.

"Listen, Laina, I'm not going to work here much longer, and I'd like you to not book anyone in with me for, well, ever. I'm done after today. I know this makes more work for you, and I'm sorry, but I need to get out of here."

She nods. "I'm not happy you're going, but I don't blame you."

"Why don't you leave too? Don't you have a degree in psychology?"

She nods. "But not a doctorate. Just enough to make me worry about everyone who works here."

I snort. "I'd better get in with my client. But take my contact information. If you need to get the hell out of here too, call me. I know a lot of people, and no promises, but I may be able to help you find a place that doesn't make you want to stab yourself in the face."

She sighs. "That sounds too good to be true."

"Anything's possible. You've just got to want it."

She hands me a pen. "Get out of here, vile tempter."

I set the form on the counter outside the room, stretching my fingers while I look it over. Mae Bell's history is pretty straightforward: no accidents, no major traumas, just regular tension from her desk job.

Most people expect physical workers to have more problems than office workers. But the people who sit at a desk and twist their upper bodies all day are usually in worse shape than any construction worker I've seen.

Athletes are another story.

Rotating my wrists one more time, I knock on the door, waiting a moment for a response.

Silence.

I roll my eyes. It's been fifteen minutes lying on a bed midday. She probably fell asleep on the table. It wouldn't be the first time. People are so stressed out that they're looking for release before they come to see me. It's good—those are the clients who want to put in the work and need the relief.

"Mae?" I step inside and close the door behind me. She faces away from me, but she's under the covers.

"Don't be mad," she says.

A jolt goes through my body like an electric shock.

Melanie Walker turns toward me, clutching the sheet to her body. "Hi."

THE SHOCK IN HIS EYES MORPHS INTO WARINESS, AND SUD-
denly this feels more like a bad idea than the genius one
it seemed half an hour ago.

I snuck in under false pretenses, since he obviously
wasn't taking my calls. I planned to pop up from the bed,
shocking him into giving me enough time to explain—
and blocking the door with my body if necessary.

I began having doubts when he didn't come into the
room right away, sure my cover had been blown. I won-
dered if he was going to leave me here in my underwear
without giving me the chance to explain, but no way
was I leaving before I knew for sure he was done with
me—after hearing me out.

Now it's all terrifyingly real.

If I pour my heart out and he rejects me, that's it. I'll
honor his feelings and leave him alone. I just have to
get the words out. That sounds a whole lot easier than
it is.

Clutching the sheets in my fists helps absorb the
sweat from them. My pulse races, adrenaline and fear
kicking my senses into a frenzy and I'm completely
tongue-tied. The soapy, masculine scent that's uniquely
his seems to fill the room, and I get a little warm despite

the fear coursing through my veins. How long has it been since we touched, kissed?

Can he feel the attraction between us? It hasn't dampened a bit. The force that pulls—

He crosses his arms.

OK, so maybe his anger dampens the force. But he doesn't storm out, and I cling to that fact like a life raft.

It's now or never. "So, this is the hippie place?"

His jaw tightens.

"It's pretty nice," I say. "I didn't meet the hippies, but at least the rooms are pretty." I focus on the crystals lying on the table nearby and the way the candlelight picks up facets in the rocks.

Seriously? You're bringing up the decor? What next, the weather?

Damn it. "How have you been?" I ask.

He narrows his eyes. "That's all you have to say to me?"

"No. Not nearly. God, I'm nervous as hell."

His eyes are unreadable. Normally I get him, and I can tell his moods like they're written on my heart.

Right now they're closed to me.

That stabs into my chest like a serrated blade, but it's all because of the way I treated him. I don't get to take his pain personally. Even if he rejects me now, I don't get to close down and not tell him the truth. I deserve his anger, and he deserves an explanation. He's not giving me anything, and that's fair.

It's all me. "I'm sorry. What I did was unmentionably shitty. You did nothing wrong. God, your picnic was so sweet and considerate. I was caught off guard, but that's not an excuse. You making reservations was an amazing thing. It meant you wanted to spend more time with me. I didn't feel worthy of that. The truth is, I don't want to ruin your relationship with my family, but that's not the root of the issue. It sounded nobler and forced the focus to external things instead of me looking at myself. I used my insecurities to push against us."

"You pushed hard."

"I did. But it wasn't because of you or anything you did."

The muscle below his left eye twitches.

I keep my gaze on his. "I pushed you away because I was scared of losing you. Because you'd find out I'm not the person I was in Florida. I even tried telling myself it was for your own good because I'd fuck up eventually, or you'd find out the real me, and I'd have cost you my family as well. That was arrogant and so none of my goddamn business. You were right about that not being my risk to mitigate. It was your decision. Then I lost you because of that, and it was so ironic and awful that right away I knew I'd screwed up.

"But I realized that I *am* that person you were with in Florida because who we are is a choice. The person I was doesn't fit me anymore. I can't go back to her life. Her narrow, cramped, boring little life. I want more. I enjoy doing things out of the ordinary. I love doing things without overthinking them. I'm still myself, but the fear is gone. You helped bring that out of me, but it was there all along. I was scared that if I needed you to feel like that, I wouldn't know who I was if we broke up. But I know who I am, and I don't need you to be that person."

"Not to be insensitive, but no shit. You were on a

nude beach when I saw you. You're not exactly a shrinking violet."

"I guess it took me a little longer to realize that than it took you. Even if you never speak to me again, I needed you to know that." My heart perks up. "I don't want to lose you, Blake. I don't need you—I want you. You're the only man I want to be with, and I know I don't deserve another chance to fuck it up, but here I am asking anyway. I'm throwing myself into one last attempt at earning the chance to make it up to you. Do you forgive me for being the worst person ever?"

Please, God. Please, please. I love him so much. Let him see my heart and know every word is genuine.

Blake's gaze drops to the floor and he sighs. "We've got twenty minutes left." He squirts some oil on his hands and rubs them together, agitation flowing from every pore. "I need to think."

He wants to massage me now?

Shut up. It may be the last time he ever touches you. Lie down and take it.

I ease down to the bed, glad that my tears are hidden when I put my face in the pillow even though I can see them hit the floor through the hole. The sheet slips down my back, cool air replacing it. Blake lifts my hair from my back and gasps.

"What's this?"

I sniffle. "A tattoo."

"It's a tree frog."

In a watercolor style. I nod. "Like the ones at Marathon. They symbolize transformation and authentic self. They're always themselves, even though they're constantly changing. I feel like that's something I can relate to. I thought I was losing myself if I changed too much, but who I am—the core of me—is always the same."

His touch, agonizingly soft against the edges of my week-old tattoo, sends shivers roaring across my body. He's so careful not to directly touch it in case it hurts. I can't breathe until he removes his hand, then I gasp at the loss.

"You got a tattoo for me?"

"No." My heart sinks. "I wish I could lie and tell you I did, but the truth is, I got it for myself. I realized I needed to change for me—not a man, or a boss, or because I thought I should to impress other people. I've done a lot of things these past few weeks to take my life back. To start being the person I want to be. To transform into the woman I know I am inside. You helped me see glimpses of her, but I wanted to tear her out of the chrysalis myself." I snivel. "Maybe I should have gotten a butterfly instead, but the frog felt right. It still does. You were willing to give up everything for me. I know I can't say anything to make it better, but I've been trying to change. Trying to be better."

"What else have you done to be better?"

"I told my boss about the asshole at work who made it his personal mission to make my life hell. It was hard because my boss was the one who hired Thaddeus and they were family friends." God, Blake probably couldn't care less.

His hands knead my lower back, and I melt into the massage table. He's touching me again, and it shouldn't feel this good. I shouldn't get to take pleasure from him even in this way, but I do.

"How did that go?"

I sigh. "It actually went well. I also made a case to switch to Editorial instead of HR. I got the position. She liked the story ideas I came up with on vacation."

"Congratulations."

"Thaddeus was a large part of the reason I did the Switch in the first place. Mostly to escape him and his bullshit. Anyway, that's done now."

He does something with his thumbs up my spine that curls my toes. "You said he was a large part of the reason, but not the whole part?"

"Yeah. I've also been taking a martial arts course since I got back. My shins are covered with bruises from learning how to block."

Blake actually checks them. "These are… I hope you've been icing these."

I bite my lip hard. "Yeah."

"Why did you sign up for martial arts?"

"Because before I left for vacation, I got mugged."

"Jesus."

"I filed a report and followed up. I wasn't hurt or anything, just shaken up. But I realized when I got home that the experience was seeping in, making my control issues come back with a vengeance. Again, I'm not trying to justify it or diminish my overreaction. I just wanted you to know I've been doing things to change. You said actions speak louder than words, and I want to prove to you that I'm… No, I want to *be* a better, stronger person. Trying to push you away was more about my own insecurities than about thinking I knew better what you needed."

"Jesus, Melanie. I had no idea you'd been under so much pressure."

"Mel." I sit up and face him, not caring if my tears make me seem weak. "Don't you ever call me Melanie. Even if you don't want me, I'll always be your Mel."

"I thought Mel was a boy's name."

A disbelieving squeak leaves my lips at his teasing. Does this mean…?

He closes his eyes. "I forgive you."

"What?"

"I love you and forgive you. I know you're a stubborn asshole sometimes." He shrugs. "What can I say? It makes life more interesting."

I reach for him, but he pushes me away and shakes his head. I'm such an idiot. He said he forgives me, not that he wants to be with me as well. That's it. I threw my Hail Mary pass and he caught it—but gave it back.

My heart sinks.

Chapter 38

Blake

SHE NODS AND STANDS UP, NOT LOOKING AT ME. "I UNDER-stand. You love and forgive me, but don't want to be together. If you ever change your mind…"

She thinks I'm rejecting her? I'd laugh if I could breathe. She couldn't be more wrong. I've spent every moment since her office in hell, sure I'd never have her in my life again and hating that idea with every breath I took. If she thinks she's walking out of here right now, she's got another think coming. "Lie down."

"What?" Her voice trembles with something—hope, maybe—but she lies on her stomach.

It takes every ounce of self-control to keep my hands moving on her back. "I want to kiss you so goddamn bad right now, Mel. You have no idea."

"I think I have some idea." Her voice is muffled by the face pillow.

"No, I don't think you do. I'm not going to kiss you right now, because if I kiss you right now, I'm going to get fired and possibly arrested for fucking you in public. At work."

"Oh." Her word comes out like a fucking moan, and I'm already hard.

"I'm not going to lie and pretend what you did didn't

kill me. But we're not children. We can work through anything life throws at us as long as we keep talking and don't shut each other out." I slip the sheet completely off the table.

Her simple turquoise panties match her bra. I'd rather they were off, but I'm already having a bitch of a time not kneading her hamstrings too hard.

"Do you have many clients after me?"

"You're my last one."

She looks at me over her shoulder. "Do you want to come over?"

"You angling for a ride home, Mel?"

"You wouldn't get me all hot and then make me ride the subway home alone, would you?" She spreads her legs, and there's a dark patch soaking through her panties.

"Fuck it." I flip her over and tear her panties down her legs. I need this woman. Now.

"You'll get fired or arrested! Is the door even locked?" she hisses.

"No." I kiss from her belly button to her pubic bone. "So you'd better keep quiet, Mel."

The tension leaves her body with the first long lick.

I missed how you taste.

I missed you.

I hated what you did.

I truly forgive you.

I love you.

I love you.

I love you.

I tell her with my tongue.

Her legs fall open, and her belly moves up and down faster with her increased breathing.

"God, I want to come so bad, but I can't, Blake—not when anyone could walk in."

I plunge two fingers inside her. "This is the first and only massage with a happy ending I'm ever going to give."

She moans, and I cover her mouth with my free hand.

"Shhh, baby. I love you."

Instead of moving my hand away, she nods and winds her fingers through my hair. She pulls my face back to her crotch, making me dip back down to taste her again.

I'm rock hard against the inside of my pants—my cock actually hurts, it's so hard—but all I want is to make Mel come on my mouth. Right here. Right now.

Her hips buck and her head tips back. I curl my fingers hard inside her, right into that sweet spot, and pulse against it. I never stop suckling and licking.

Her orgasm starts deep inside. The tension starts around my fingers and rolls outward through her body, unfurling like a flower bursting open until she's moaning into my hand. The last thing to move is her head, tipping backward as she smiles and gives one long exhalation.

I slide my fingers out of her. I clean them and her with a warm towel.

She smiles shyly. "Thank you. I can't believe you just did that."

"Me?" I nip her shoulder. "You're the one who left a wet spot on my table. Pervert."

"I should report you to the appropriate authorities."

I hand her the panties I took off. "The Better Business Bureau?"

"My best friends, so I can give them all the salacious details and make them jealous."

"Put your pants on, bad girl. I'll meet you outside, and we can get the hell out of here."

....

"You missed the exit to my apartment," she says.

I smile. "I know. It occurred to me you've never been to my place."

"Jersey, right?"

"Yup. You don't get out here much?"

"Not really."

"What's that tone? You're not a snob, are you?" I give her a teasing glare at the next red light.

"No. But it's weird how you can live somewhere and not really stray into the surrounding areas much."

"You work a lot."

She shrugs. "I guess. But even when we take vacations, we go somewhere else. We don't usually think about staying at home and taking the time to get to know the beauty around us. When's the last time you saw a show or went to the Met? Central Park? Why are you smiling?"

I accelerate and merge into the next lane. "I was planning to do just that. Stay around here and check out some new restaurants. Play tourist for a couple weeks before buckling down."

"And then Shawn sent you to Florida."

"Yup. Funny how I don't regret missing out on the beauty of home." I take her hand in mine, and she traces around my knuckles with her free hand.

"I'd kick his ass, but I'm pretty happy he meddled."

"He's pretty hung up on Shelby."

She whips her head around, facing me. "Really?"

"Maybe he was scared you'd meddle as well."

Mel scoots up in her seat. "You're goddamned right I will. First chance I get."

Whoops. Sorry, Shawn. "Then I'll have to keep you very busy, won't I?"

"I like the sound of that."

I park in my tiny driveway and turn to Mel, cautious hope blooming in my chest. It's important to me that she likes my place.

"This is your house?" She unbuckles and gets out of the truck.

"Yes."

"Do you have roomies?"

I laugh. "Rent's not quite as scary here as in the city. This isn't an easy commute neighborhood, so the prices stay reasonable-ish. It's just me out here." I unlock the door and lead her inside the foyer.

It's a bi-level, more narrow and long than sprawling, but it's a decent size. I follow her gaze and take things in, trying to see it with fresh eyes.

There are hardwood floors throughout because I tore out the psychedelic seventies carpet as soon as humanly possible. The walls in the hallway and living room are a light mauve—not my choice, but I haven't decided what I'd rather have yet—and it does brighten up the place during the crappy winters.

Mel trails a hand over the back of the black ultra-suede couch and continues down the hall to the kitchen. Light blue walls, granite countertops—a recent upgrade, along with the stainless-steel appliances—and neutral tile floors.

There's a nook for eating, but I don't have a dining room table yet.

"No table?" She turns to me.

"No, I mostly eat at the counter or in the living room."

"Hmm." She heads to take a peek in the bathroom and stands in the hall outside the last door. "What's upstairs?"

"Bedroom, bathroom, another room."

She nods at the closed, white door beside her. "Spare room?"

"No." I take her hands and press her against the wall.

Chapter 39

Melanie

MY HEART SOARS. IF MY PANTIES COULD TEAR THEMSELVES off, they would, because I want him inside me right now.

But he pauses and stares deeply into my eyes. "I love you, Mel. Actions matter to me, and you went out of your way to show me that. I appreciate that and I see you. I see you."

His tongue plunges inside my mouth and brushes across my tongue, sending sparks of lust through my body. His hand trails down my ribs, caresses the side of my waist, and moves to my hip. He grips it, and I press against him, clawing at his pants. He does see me. He knows me better than anyone, and I'm desperate with the urge to be closer to him, aware we dodged a bullet and that I probably don't deserve his forgiveness.

While I undo his pants and shove the material down his legs, he moves his mouth to my neck and teases my skin with gentle licks and kisses.

Blake slips my shirt over my head and undoes my bra with one hand. He strips it slowly off, gaze burning into mine the whole time. My nipples almost hurt when he palms my heavy breasts, and I groan and push my chest harder into his hands.

He flicks his tongue over my left nipple, then the right. He takes it into his mouth and sucks deeply, drawing tugs of pleasure that seem to come from straight between my legs.

Speaking of between the legs, I pull on his shoulders until he understands what I want and stands up. He's rock hard, and his hips thrust into my hand when I stroke him through the soft cotton of his boxer briefs.

His teeth clamp down on his bottom lip when I rub him, lightly but fast.

I kiss the corner of his mouth. "You're so hard."

"I've been hard since Inner Space."

"I really should have returned the favor while we were there."

He throws me over his shoulder in one quick motion. "You're right."

"Blake!"

His hand lands on my ass with a loud crack, and he rubs the sting away while walking.

I squirm on his shoulder. That was…surprisingly hot.

"It just occurred to me that I haven't shown you the most important room in the house yet," he says.

I grin against his back. "The library?"

He turns his head and bites my hip.

I moan.

"The bedroom, Mel. The one down here's bigger than the spare upstairs."

My feet gently hit the floor and I straighten, giving the blood a minute to leave my head. I shouldn't have worried. No dizziness comes because all my blood has rushed to more interesting areas.

He turns on the light and turns me around, wrapping

his arms around me from behind so I can look at the room. "Well?" He nuzzles my neck. "What do you think of my bedroom?"

I think I want you to fuck me in it.

I sweep it with my gaze, taking in the elegant mushroom-colored walls, the dark hardwood floors, and the bed—perfectly made with the fluffiest white blankets I've ever seen. "This is a very grown-up bedroom, Blake." I nudge my ass against his cock, making him suck in a deep breath. "It makes me want to do very grown-up things with you."

Keeping one arm wrapped around me, he spreads my legs with the other and pushes his cock through the gap. He rubs it up the full length of my slit, coating himself with my desire.

I sag against him and look down at the tip, peeking out below my clit before it disappears again. He pushes again and I drop my hand and rub it, releasing drops of pre-cum that I use to circle him faster.

He groans and nibbles my earlobe. "I need you."

The way he pushes against me nearly crosses my eyes. "Yeah. Give me a tour of your bed. Like, right the fuck now."

"I thought you'd never ask." He sweeps me up and sets me on the bed before I have time to blink twice.

I smile. "I don't remember asking."

He grins and rubs my pussy, revealing how wet I am. He spreads it all over, teasing me with it before inserting two fingers inside me.

My toes curl and my back arches, lifting my ass off the bed.

"Nice girls ask for what they want." He smirks.

I rotate my hips in time with his finger-fucking. "Do you really want me to be a nice girl?"

"Never." He bends and drops a sweet, almost chaste kiss on my mouth. "I love my bossy little Mel."

He takes his hand away to grab a condom from the nightstand. I rub his back, tracing light, impatient patterns while he rolls the condom on.

I spread my legs wide for him to settle between them. He does, but he caresses my face and gazes down at me with too much love, too many feelings, too much softness. My heart absorbs it all and radiates it back.

This is what they mean when they say "my heart is full to bursting."

It shouldn't be possible to feel so much for one person. How can I contain it?

I'm not supposed to. The point of love isn't to take and take and absorb it all. The point is to accept it and then give it back to that person.

Love isn't selfish. And with a love like this, you have to share the gorgeous burden. It's too much for one body.

I press my hand to his cheek. "I love you so much."

His delighted smile makes me smile.

I'm still smiling when he slowly enters me.

It's been weeks, not years, and yet it's like our first time. A joyous rediscovery of the bone-deep connection we share.

Maybe it's been the time apart, maybe it's that he's been tormented by desire since he got me off at work, but I need a minute to adjust to the way he stretches me.

I love that I don't need to say anything to him. He can feel it. He knows. He understands and waits.

Unlike the first time, we know each other's hearts and bodies. He knows exactly how to move to drive me wild. I know the precise tilt of my hips that whips him into a frenzy.

What we almost lost weighs on us for a moment. Poignant urgency claims our hands and lips, and it whispers against our skin. Joy turns to need, exploration turns to claiming, as though we're trying to imprint our souls against each other's skin so we'll always know we belong to each other.

With every thrust, that fades into something purer.

Soft sighs, tender caresses, deep, slow thrusts.

It took a little while, but we got here. And nothing's going to come between us again.

We make love, unafraid of rejection or worries or doubts, holding nothing back.

God, his hands and mouth and hips. Every inch of me is loved and cherished, and I know he feels the same.

We don't need words.

We just know.

_____

After we do a remixed version of the hotel shower sex that happened in Florida, I remember I didn't leave food for Buddy because I wasn't expecting to stay the night out here. Blake drives us to my place.

We order pizza and gorge on it, snuggling on the couch after and rubbing our full bellies.

Buddy has made himself at home on Blake's lap, and Blake obliges him by scratching under his chin—Buddy's favorite spot to be scratched. Blake looks around. "Buddy was an outdoor cat, right?"

I nod. "He was a stray. I feel bad about trapping him inside, but my landlord would kill me if she knew."

Buddy jumps off Blake's lap and heads to his spot on the windowsill. Blake nods. "He should really have more space. It's got to be culture shock."

"You trying to make me feel guilty, Blake Wilde? Because it's working."

He smiles. "You know, Buddy might really love having a house to prowl around in."

My heart kicks up. "Yeah?"

He nods. "And I have a backyard. The neighborhood's pretty quiet too. He'd be the badass of the back alley if he wanted to be an indoor-outdoor cat."

Is he asking me to move in with him? Do I even want that? *Yes, yes, yes!* I keep my tone casual. "Are you trying to steal my roommate?"

"Maybe." He kisses my shoulder. "I mean, you'd probably have to come along as well."

My throat swells with emotions. "Buddy has grown fairly attached to me."

"Yeah. He's not the only one who'd hate it if you weren't there too."

I clear my throat. "Are you asking me to move in with you?"

His lips pull into a mischievous grin. "I don't remember asking. That's pretty presumptuous of you, Mel."

I shriek and straddle his lap. "You jerk! Ask me nicely."

He wraps his arms around my lower back, locking me in place. "Melanie Walker, would you and your cat please invade my house and turn it into our home?"

"Mel." I splay my hands on his chest and rest my forehead against his. "Yes."

He swallows my whisper with a gentle kiss. "Thank you."

"Of course, we're going to have to discuss a few things regarding the decor."

"Is that right?" He smiles.

His house is perfect, but like Sammy Davis Jr., I gotta be me. "Yes."

"In that case, we should move negotiations to the bedroom. Buddy shouldn't see what's about to take place." He pulls me close, moving my legs over his lap and just holding me for a minute or twelve. Pesky things like time become meaningless when Blake is staring into my eyes like he's found forever inside them.

"I love you," I whisper.

"I love you more." He brushes my cheek with the backs of his fingers.

I nuzzle closer. "It's not a competition."

"Maybe not. But if it were, I'd win."

"Even though I had a head start?"

He nods and his eyes make me believe it.

Epilogue

Blake

I TRIP OVER ANOTHER BOX AND SWEAR, BUT THERE'S A HUGE grin on my face when I do it. Mel's finally here—all of her things instead of bits and pieces, and I'll gladly take the bruise on my shin because of that. My favorite person, moving into my house.

Our house.

It took five weeks to find someone to sublet her apartment, but we'd been bringing over boxes of her things in the meantime, trying to make it a casual integration.

Nothing about my feelings is casual.

Slowly but surely, my place has transformed into ours. We've started a photo collage of our own, adding pictures as we add experiences together. Last weekend we went to the Met. The weekend before, we headed out to the Hudson Valley. Making new memories together in a place we're both familiar with breathes new life into the area.

But to be honest, I just love spending time with her.

She leans over the counter, scribbling on her list. "What do you feel like for supper?"

I couldn't care less as long as she's sitting across from me at our new dining room table, gently bumping her feet against mine.

"Whatever you want."

"That's not an answer."

"Pasta?"

She scrunches her face and tilts her head in that way she does when she's trying to be casual. "How about we barbecue some burgers instead?"

She always asks me what I want, despite knowing full well she's already made up her mind. I smile. "Burgers sound awesome. Pasta tomorrow?"

"Deal." She grins. "Do we need paper towels?"

"You should use cloths and reduce your carbon footprint." I grab her from behind and nuzzle her neck, breathing in the mandarin and honey scent of her new shampoo.

"No way. That's cross-contamination and germ city. I'll find other ways to help the environment." She sighs and snuggles closer. "Mandatory dinner by candlelight. Sex with the lights off."

"Hey, now. Don't be hasty. I like seeing all of you."

She squirms out of my grasp and brandishes the shopping list at me like a weapon. "Shopping first. I don't want to get distracted again and end up eating cold cereal with no milk for supper."

I lean against the counter. "I'm pretty sure I saw a study that we Americans aren't getting enough fiber in our diets."

She smirks. "You're basically a hero."

A loud meow from the open back door gets our attention.

"There he is!" Mel croons and heads over to make a fuss over Buddy. "We've been worried about you, haven't we, Blake?"

"Sure."

She glares. "More."

I walk over to them and scoop Buddy into my arms. "We were very worried, Buddy-Wuddy."

Mel grimaces. "Too much."

I check him over. "He looks fine."

Mel scratches his forehead and he shakes his head, giving a flash of the new tattoo in his ear. We microchipped him as well, just in case. He's still not used to the collar, and he purrs when I scratch underneath it.

"He was only gone for two nights, but I'm glad he's checking in." Mel wiggles one of his paws. "I don't want to trap him inside, but he feels like my cat now. I like it when he's with us."

"He is yours now. But he's a wild one, not used to being in one place. Think of all the things he gets up to, all the fun he has out there with the swanky little alley cats."

Her eyes widen. "He'd better not be! I don't want him coming back here sick because another cat hasn't had its shots."

"Can cats get STDs?"

Mel punches my shoulder, careful not to hit Buddy. "You're the worst."

"You love me."

She shrugs a shoulder. "Well, you're also the best. You're a complicated man, Blake." She sashays to the counter and grabs her purse. "Are we going grocery shopping, or are you going to stand around holding my pussy all day?"

She's already laughing and sprinting to the door when I bend to set Buddy on the floor before chasing after her.

..................——..................

Melanie

Two weeks later

I LOWER MY HEAD, RELAXING SO I'M LOOKING AT MY LAP. It's an exercise Blake taught me to stretch the tension out of my neck when I've been on the computer too long.

I grab my coffee and take a sip. Unfortunately, it's another cold one.

Damn it.

I swallow and glare at the cup, like it's at fault for making my drink cold when it's really because I've been here for ten—shit, eleven hours. It can't be seven at night already.

I stride down the hall toward the kitchen, nodding at people as I pass.

Kojak's at her desk. She doesn't even look away from her computer screen.

"Winston, you good?" Winston gives me a wave and turns back to his sheaf of papers, furiously scribbling on the edge of a page with a red pen.

The thing I've learned about Winston in the last few weeks is that he's like a duck. You see a duck calmly floating on the surface of a lake, but underneath the water, where you can't see, they're furiously moving their legs.

Watching Winston might stress you out from how spastic he can get, but inside, he's calmly and methodically solving problems and working away. He's never missed a deadline yet.

Someone's using the fancy coffee machine when I reach the kitchen. Katka closes the fridge, revealing her identity. "Hey, Mel! How's it going?"

"Really well."

Seth emerges from the walk-in pantry with a bag of chips in hand. "I can't fucking believe our biggest advertiser pulled out with no warning."

"Yeah, I hate when that happens," Katka says.

I rinse my cup. "That's what she said."

Seth's eyes bug out and Katka laughs.

The ad change has made us scurry around for tomorrow's issue—hence the late night—but we're pulling together as a company, as a team.

My new position isn't only more satisfying—more creative, less listening to people bitch—but it lets me feel like I'm part of things. I can joke a little, be myself, let people realize I'm human.

It's amazing.

I don't need them to be strangers for them to take me seriously. In fact, they treat me more seriously and respectfully *because* they know me. With Blake at home and my job getting a thousand times better, I've never been happier in my entire life.

Other than the current hairy work situation, but we can sort this out and get the issue out on time.

"Seth, how are the—" My phone buzzes, and I hold up a hand and open the text—from Shelby. It's a selfie she's taken from a Jet Ski. Shawn flyboards in the background, getting way more air time than I ever did. Unfortunately, his trunks have slid down and half his ass hangs out. Shelby's smile in the foreground is huge.

I grin. He went down for the weekend, three days ago, and they're thick as thieves.

I don't know if it's forever, but they're good for each other.

And if they break up, I might keep her and get rid of him.

I reply: Just like my brother to half-ass it! I'm thankful he was facing away from the camera.

She replies right away: It's all fun and games until someone loses their bathing suit.

Don't I know it.

May the *Best Man* Win

Chapter 1

August

ON THE UPSIDE, THE PRELUDE HAD ALREADY BEGUN, AND chances were good that Mozart's Sonata in E-flat Major pumping through all those organ pipes would cover any sounds of distress emanating from St. A's sacristy.

Jase Foster crouched in front of Dean Skolnic, groom du jour, and cursed. This had to stop happening.

"You think she's gonna notice?" Dean asked, wincing as Jase pulled one strip of duct tape after another off the garbage bag of ice currently secured to Dean's shoulder.

"The arm?" Jase clarified, because while he wasn't an every-Sunday kind of guy, they were in a church so he couldn't flat-out lie. "No, man. I really don't."

Lena would take one look at her husband-to-be's swollen black eye, and she wouldn't see anything else.

Strike that.

She might notice the greenish-gray pallor of Dean's normally ruddy complexion, because coupled with the way he was gulping air like a goldfish, it didn't bode well for his stomach or anyone within splatter distance.

The door opened behind them, and Father John plowed in, five foot six inches of bristling irritation and grizzled holiness. Scowling at the scene in front of him, he snapped his fingers and pointed at the guilty-looking crew of lesser attendants—mostly Dean's cousins who'd driven in that morning—plastered to the back wall. "Crack the fucking window."

Jase steeled himself against the laugh clawing to get free. Because, yeah, Father John had a mouth on him. Something Jase had discovered when he, Max, Brody, and Sean were muscling Dean out of the limo, barely clearing the door before the driver peeled off. The priest had stopped dead in the mostly empty back parking lot, taken one look at Dean, and let loose with enough four-letter words that even the guys—seasoned professionals in the expletive arena—had been coughing into their fists, studying the thick canopy of trees above and the new asphalt beneath their feet, basically looking anywhere but at the pint-size priest with a bear's temper.

"How we doing, Father?" Jase asked, pulling the bag of ice free and stepping out of blast radius. "Need any help?"

More grumbling as the priest elbowed one of the groomsmen out of his way and opened the window himself. "Seems you've done enough already."

Probably. But Jase was chalking this morning up as a learning moment. No matter how bad the groom's nerves, a quick game of hoops on the way to the church was not the answer, especially when evening out the teams required bringing the limo driver into the mix.

Cutting a look over at Max, Jase pushed to his feet. "Let's get his jacket on."

Max Brandt was working his cop stance with his legs apart, his arms crossed over his chest, and a don't-fuck-with-me scowl firmly in place. He nodded down at Dean. "Get serious. He's gonna blow. We don't put it on him until he does."

Hell. Jase glanced around the tight confines of the sacristy to the cabinets stocked with candles, chalices, napkins, and the rest of the holy hardware, and he mentally amended *Fuck* with the requisite apologies applied.

Jase wanted to think Dean could pull it together, but when it came to hurling, Max could call it from a hundred yards away. Even before the Chicago police force honed his powers of observation to a sharpened critical edge, the guy had had a hinky instinct about when to clear a path. That, and about women too. Both handy skill sets to have.

Grabbing a plastic trash bin from next to the hanging rack of choir robes, Jase shoved it into Dean's good arm.

"You heard him, Dean. Make it happen, and we'll get you out there."

That was a promise, because unless one of his grooms had a definitive change of heart about marrying the woman waiting down the aisle, no-shows didn't happen on Jase's watch.

The door opened again, and Brody O'Donnel stepped

inside. He wasn't as tall as Jase or as menacing as Max, but the guy had presence. He was solidly built with a broad chest and a wild head of russet waves that fell well past his ears, which he'd only half bothered to tame for the morning's nuptials.

Whistling out a long breath, he eyeballed Dean, who was doing his best to manage the task assigned to him. Then nodding around the room, Brody grinned. "Father. Guys."

Father John looked up and broke into a beaming smile.

"Brody," he boomed like the guy was his prodigal son returned, even though the two had only met the night before. Then shaking his head with a warm laugh, he declined when Brody pulled a flask from the inner pocket of his single-button tux jacket and, shameless grin going straight up, held it out in offering.

"Aw, come on, Father John. It's the good stuff," he ribbed before passing it to one of the braver cousins.

Brody could always be counted on for two things: his uncanny ability to make friends with just about anyone and his propensity for always having a flask of "the good stuff" on hand for emergencies. Which made sense, considering he owned Belfast, one of Lakeview's most popular bars. Booze was, in fact, his thing.

"Brod, so what're we looking at?" Jase asked, knowing they had to be running out of time.

"The girls are about ready to go. Sean's smooth-talking the Skolnics, and I've got the safety pins, but...uh..."

Jase knew that drawn-out qualifier. Whatever Brody had to say, Jase was sure he wasn't going to like it. "What?"

"Maid of honor had the pins and wouldn't give 'em up if I didn't tell her what was going on."

Emily Klein. Fucking fantastic. Because after managing to avoid her throughout the entire engagement, now, with everything else that morning, Jase was going to have to deal with her getting up in his grill?

"She's coming?"

"Nah, I talked her down pretty good, so—"

And that was as far as Brody got before the sacristy door swung open again and that old familiar tension knuckled down Jase's spine. He took her in with one sweeping glance and then—just to piss her off—went back for a second, slower pass. She should have looked like Natasha Fatale from those old Rocky and Bullwinkle cartoons. She had the height, all right, but instead of the severe black hair, wickedly arched brows, bombshell body, and calculating scowl, Emily was every kind of soft. Soft strawberry-blond hair spiraling in loose curls over her shoulders. Big, soft-brown eyes. And a soft, shy smile that hid her poison-dart tongue. Even her body, tall and athletically lean, had a softness to its modest curves—curves that had distracted the hell out of Jase in high school but that he'd become immune to in the passing years.

Since he'd finally seen through her *soft* snow job to the cold, hard ice queen beneath.

"Jackass," she greeted, with a soft smile just for him.

"Emily. What can I do for you?"

"Brody mentioned Dean had—"

Dean coughed into his trash can, and Emily's superior scowl shifted to the man of the hour.

She looked from Dean back to Jase, her mouth gaping open in soundless horror. "*Is that dislocated?*"

The shoulder looked bad, Jase knew. And with anyone but Emily, he would have been all about the explanations, apologies, and assurances. Dean was going to be waiting at the end of that aisle, ready for Lena, even if Jase had to hold him up there himself. But since it was Emily… "No."

He waited.

Emily's toe started to tap, a nervous habit she'd had forever. One he took unhealthy pleasure in exploiting.

But Brody, a perpetual fixer fortunate enough not to have any history with Femily Fatale, stepped in with a reassuring shrug and his signature lopsided smile. "A little roughed up is all. Don't worry about a thing. He's fine."

Which was when Dean retched up the contents of his stomach and a round of applause sounded from the attendants stationed around the room.

Go time.

"Nice job, man," Jase offered, taking the trash-bag liner out of the bin and shoving it in Emily's direction. To his utter delight, she was so startled that her hands came up before she'd had the chance to think. And then she was stuck quite literally holding the bag.

Hauling Dean up by his good arm, Jase and Max worked the guy into the jacket and started pinning his sleeve to his coat. It wasn't perfect, but if ever there was a pinch, this was it.

"Oh… Oh no… Oh… What am I supposed to do with this?" Emily asked shakily behind him.

Jase didn't look back. "See if one of the groomsmen can help you with it."

He'd love to leave her hanging, but this was Dean's wedding, and he wouldn't be doing his friend any favors by screwing over his bride with a missing attendant. Even Emily.

"Uh-uh, no way," Brody said, laughing. "That has 'best man' written all over it. You know the drill, dude. With great power comes great responsibility, or some shit like that."

Not a chance. "Power to *delegate* responsibility. Hey, you with the braces, take this to the Dumpster out back and meet us up front."

The skinny kid let out a groan but hopped to, taking the trash bag from Emily and scurrying out the door just as Sean Wyse strode in. Smoothing back his immaculate hair, he flashed a picture-perfect smile at Emily. "Looking breathtaking today, but I think you're mixing with the wrong crowd here. Can I walk you back to the girls?"

Emily was chugging Sean's BS like it was a Starbucks mocha latte, cocking her head appreciatively but declining all the same. Then she was out the door, and the too-small space around Jase opened up enough that he could breathe.

About time.

Sean reached into Brody's pocket and helped himself to a swig of what was probably Jameson. "You ladies ready yet?"

Brody started lining the guys up in order for their trip to the other end of the church, while Jase took care of the sweat beaded on Dean's forehead with a handkerchief he knew better than to attend a wedding without. Then grabbing Dean by the side of his face, he looked him straight in the eyes.

"You good, man?" he asked, hoping like hell Lena

was in it for the duration. Dean was too good of a guy to get screwed over. "Ready to do this?"

Dean swallowed and nodded. "Yeah. I am."

The same thought that tore through Jase's mind every time he got one of his grooms ready echoed then—the thought Emily Klein had played no small part in reinforcing:

Better him than me.

Jase smiled his most confidence-inspiring smile, the one that closed deals, and jutted his chin toward the door. "Then let's get you married."

Chapter 2

STICKING TO THE FAR SIDE OF THE LEFT AISLE, A PINCH OF floor-length blush chiffon in hand and her smile straining at cheek-cramping proportions, Emily Klein skimmed past an usher seating the last of the late arrivals as she hustled toward the bridal room where Lena was waiting with the girls.

Best man her butt.

Seriously, how did Jase Foster keep getting this gig?

Obviously, the guys loved him. Couldn't get enough of the whole bromance business Jase had perfected back before it was even a thing. But the women? Come on, like they hadn't heard about the time Jase got Neil Wallace to the altar a mere two hours late—because the boat they took out that morning on a whim ran out of gas. Or when Jim Huang wore an eye patch to the altar because of some "epic" game of finger football gone wrong. Or when Trey Wazowski needed to start a suspicious course of antibiotics before leaving for the honeymoon.

Cripes, Emily had heard them all, and she hadn't even been at those weddings.

And now, because Lena had turned the same blind eye to Jase's questionable record as all those other brides, here *she* was, saddled with the task of preparing her friend for the fact that her husband-to-be looked like he'd been jumped in a dark alley on the way to the church.

Stopping in front of the paneled door not solid enough to muffle the twittering chatter within, Emily took a bracing breath.

A chuckle sounded from a few paces away, and she turned to find Paul Gonzalez shaking his salt-and-pepper head at her. "I thought the bride was supposed to be the nervous one."

Emily gave Lena's dad—who'd been her boss before his retirement—an affectionate smile. Like his daughter, the man was small in stature but big in heart, and Emily had always had a soft spot for him. "I don't know, Paul. Seems like someone ought to have a case of the nerves, and Lena's as cool as a cucumber."

Stepping over to her, Paul laid a reassuring hand on her shoulder. "Relax, Emily. Everything is going to be fine. Even if nothing goes according to plan—though something tells me since you had a hand in all this, it will—the day will still be perfect. Lena's marrying the man she loves. Nothing else matters."

He was such a sweet old guy. And so misguided.

But that's what she was for.

"You're right. Okay, I'll relax." And then flashing a wink as she slid into the bridal room, she quietly added, "Just as soon as the cake is cut and the bouquet is thrown."

"Yay! You're back," Lena sang out, delightedly rushing to Emily's side.

Dressed in formfitting raw silk with a mermaid flare that emphasized her curvy physique, the bride-to-be looked gorgeous, every lustrous mahogany coil pinned in place, her warm complexion flawless, lips glossed, and each lash curved in exacting detail.

Lena was ready to go.

"Is Dean nervous?" she asked in a hushed voice, leaning close like she was protecting the other bridesmaids from the truth. "Remember how he was before he got his car? With the pacing and all those lists—and that was just *leasing* a Bimmer. This is *forever*. He's got to be nervous. He is, isn't he?"

Emily stared into her friend's deep mocha eyes and shook her head. "Nervous? No way." Not anymore, she didn't think.

Lena bounced in her beaded pumps. "So tell! Is he completely devastating in his tux?"

Yes, completely. Only Lena probably wasn't talking about Jase, so no need to clarify the whole ugly-on-the-inside business.

And this was where it got dicey. Because while Emily knew Lena needed to be prepared for what Dean was going to look like—*before* she hiked up her skirt and started sprinting down the aisle barking out orders to call 911—she didn't want her friend freaking out before she'd even set foot down the aisle. So time to employ some of those well-honed public relations skills and put a little spin on the situation.

Emily took Lena's hands and pulled her friend over to sit on the floral love seat beneath the window.

"It's a gorgeous tux, Lena. We totally nailed it with the cut. The guys are all ready to go. But just so you're prepared, Dean took a little spill on the way to the church." When the limo driver got overeager for a rebound, started throwing elbows, and knocked him down. Yeah, she'd caught up with Braces, and he was a talker. "He has a bit of a black eye"—*a bit* because it was really way more red and blue and disgustingly swollen than actually black so far—"but he can't wait to marry you."

Lena looked past Emily to the door, like she was already considering that sprint. "He's okay?"

Okay would be stretching it. "He's waiting for you up front, hon. I guess his shoulder is banged up a smidge"—and his arm is safety-pinned to his jacket to hold it in place—"but it's nothing that would keep him from marrying you today." True story.

Satisfied, Lena smiled at Rachel, Marlene, Lorna, and the rest of the attendants hovering around the mirror, helping one another straighten straps and smooth hair. "Time to line up, ladies. I need one minute with Emily, and we'll be good to go."

The girls filed out the door, and then it was just the two of them.

"Today is because of you, Em," Lena said, squeezing Emily's hands. "If you hadn't been there three years ago…I don't think I would have been able to leave. I wouldn't have found Dean. None of this would be happening today."

Emily's heart gave a soft thud as she looked into her friend's sweet face. She was so happy, so confident: so different from those first months Emily had known her, when there'd barely been any light in her eyes at all. Emily had recognized in Lena the kind of quiet despair that had shaped her own life so significantly.

"No, Lena. You'd have gotten through it on your own." She had.

Lena shook her head. "You were with me through the worst days of my life. And nothing makes me happier than to have you here at my side through the very best one."

Blinking past her tears, Emily pulled Lena in for a tight hug. "You deserve this."

Lena pulled back and, with an arched brow, replied, "You deserve this too."

"Someday, maybe," Emily said with the smile she wanted Lena to believe. "But today's all yours. Are you ready?"

Her friend blinked back her own tears and nodded quickly.

"Then let's go."

Paul was standing at the door, his arm out, waiting to walk his only daughter down the aisle.

Emily adjusted Lena's skirt and handed her the bouquet before taking her spot in line ahead of them. The groomsmen who'd been waiting to the side paired up with bridesmaids.

A text alert vibrated the phone she'd managed to camouflage within her bouquet, in case of any wedding emergencies. Heart pounding, she checked and, seeing the message was from Jase, stifled a groan.

> You got your end done?

Jackass.
She texted back what was bound to be the truth.

> Better than you.

Then, with a tilt of her head, she flashed a winsome smile toward the front of the church, where Jase was waiting to walk up with Dean. He saw. The scowl said it all.

The music changed, and a hush fell over the church as the processional began.

Lena's words echoed through Emily's mind. *You deserve this too.*

She might, but that would mean inviting someone to get closer than she ever let people get. It would mean opening herself up to something she wasn't so sure she could handle again…whether she deserved it or not.

"I said it was an *accident*," Emily hissed beneath the celebratory din of laughter, big-band sound, and clinking crystal.

Cold blue eyes fixed on hers, hard and flat. Readable only in their blatant accusation.

Not surprising, considering first, she'd just skewered the butter-soft leather of Jase's tuxedo shoe with her stiletto, and second, when it came to Jase, who was groaning like she'd just run him over with a tractor, accusation was about the only thing he had to spare for her.

And after ten years of it, Emily had about reached her limit.

"I heard what you said," Jase growled through clenched teeth.

The implication being that he hadn't missed her omission either. He invariably considered an *apology* his due, but it absolutely, unequivocally, would *not* be forthcoming. Because if Jase hadn't been practically tripping over himself trying to avoid physical contact during this stupid, mandatory wedding-party dance, she wouldn't have nailed him. And while her misstep had, in fact, been accidental, after Jase's little stunt with the trash bag that morning, she didn't feel bad about it in the least.

The guy ought to learn to lead.

Or, better yet, take off. Get out of her hair, get out of her life—just get lost.

"Christ, lady!" Jase jerked back, his face blanching as he sucked a breath through his nose.

Oops. Now she'd nailed both feet.

She really wasn't a very good dancer—at least, not when it required coordinating shared floor space with another person.

"Oh, man up and stop being such a crybaby."

Jase seemed on the verge of apoplexy, so she flashed her widest smile and leaned in close—reluctantly conceding that it was nice to go onto her toes rather than lean down to whisper in a man's ear—to murmur softly, "Or do I need to get you a tissue, princess?"

He tensed, the air between them beginning to crackle.

The hand that had been barely hovering above her waist through the first half of the song firmed against the small of her back as he jerked her into hard contact with the solid planes of his body, the unexpected impact pushing her breath out in a whoosh. She barely had time to tell herself to breathe when the world spun. Suddenly, Jase had tipped her back into a dip so deep that she had no choice but to cling tightly to his shoulders and meet his unyielding stare.

His breath rushed over her jaw and neck, leaving a wash of unwelcome chills in its wake.

"Emily, you're going to apologize for stepping on not one of my feet, but both. *Nicely.*"

Like he'd apologized for the vomit?

"You're delusional."

"Oh, you'll apologize, all right, and you'd better make me believe it. Because if you don't, in about five seconds, I'm going to dump your sweet ass on this floor."

The breath froze in her lungs. "You wouldn't."

"*Test me.*"

Her fists tightened in the fabric of his jacket as her mind latched on to one thought: in the history of truly horrible bridesmaid gifts, Jase Foster was hands-down the worst.

Because, yeah, that's how Lena had sold him at her New Year's Eve engagement party eight months before. She'd been going on about how he was one of Dean's best friends and how much she loved him and how great he and Emily would be together. And since Emily's last interlude had been a while ago, the idea of a little masculine attention held a certain appeal. For about fifteen seconds, she'd entertained the idea of *maybe*. Maybe just for a few dates.

But then Lena had said it. "Dean was agonizing over who to pick as best man—you know how close he is to all the guys—but then I thought about the pictures, and this guy is tall, Emily. Like, way taller than you, even."

And right there, her spidey-senses started to tingle. Because coming in at five foot eleven and a half, she knew the list of guys who were taller than her by enough to earn a "way" qualifier was quite short. Sadly, Jase was among them.

Sure enough, when Lena had grabbed her arm and pointed to the six-foot-five stretch of broad-shouldered, lean, all taper-cut and tuxedo-fine male striding through a sea of formal wear... Ugh. Of course, it was him.

"His name's Jase Foster. And seriously, all tuxed up tonight"—Lena's voice had dropped to a conspiratorial whisper—"tell me he doesn't look *gift wrapped!*"

He might have, except that the bow tie dangling open at his neck, coupled with the roughed-up mess of dark-brown hair topping his ruggedly handsome face, suggested that at some point during the elegant engagement party the man had already been unwrapped and played with...*extensively*.

Typical.

"Any chance he comes with a gift receipt?" Emily had asked, keeping her voice light and teasing for her friend's sake.

And that's when he'd spotted her. She could tell by the way his steady progress through the crowd came to an abrupt halt and his mouth formed a four-letter word familiar enough to her own tongue that she recognized it on sight.

Real classy, Jase.

What a dickhead.

But then Jase had rubbed a hand over his mouth and jaw, wiping it clean of the flash of hostility he'd let slip. They were at an engagement party for friends close enough to slot them as the honor attendants in their wedding—and there was no place for a decade-old grudge in this celebration. Besides, she could rest assured that the depth of her loathing for Jase Foster was as clear to him as his was to her. And if not, she had the next eight months to reinforce it.

Now, staring up into the hard lines of Jase's face as he held her suspended precariously over certain humiliation, she couldn't believe she'd once thought this man could be her whole world. She'd thought he was her *friend*. She'd thought…

Well, lesson learned. Through bitter experience, she'd come to realize that Jase could only be counted on to let her down at the moment she needed him most.

Which meant she *really* needed to apologize—and fast.

Chapter 3

"SORRY."

One word. Grudgingly issued. But still, Jase was taking it for the victory it was. Not that he'd have actually followed through on his threat. Not a chance. And that she believed he would… Well, he wasn't quite sure how he felt about that.

"Very big of you, Em," he offered, prepared to pull her back up when her soft eyes narrowed on him.

"And typically *small* of you."

He sighed, looking down at the woman still caught in his arms, wondering when he'd finally be able to put her behind him.

Those damn legs of hers were the problem. Miles long and distracting as hell, they'd been strutting through Jase's life since he was sixteen, walking over whatever bit of peace he'd found and then strutting right back out, leaving nothing but a path of destruction in their wake.

Still, he was the lucky one. Thirty seconds had decided it. Thirty seconds difference, and maybe he'd be the one whose life never recovered.

His molars ground down, because that wasn't something he ought to be thinking about at Dean's wedding, but every time he saw Emily working that honey-and-sunshine routine of hers, he wanted to puke. Why did she even bother? It had to be exhausting to pretend you were someone you weren't 24-7. But maybe she liked the collection of friends that hiding the truth had garnered her.

Or maybe she actually believed her own bullshit, which was even worse, because how the hell was the population at large supposed to defend itself against that?

Jase pulled Emily up to standing, restoring the distance between them that he never should have breached.

"Thank you," she said, and then winced as if annoyed to have given him even that much.

"You bet," he answered, keeping the civil smile.

The song was almost over, and this dance was the last of the forced interaction with her—at least, until the next time their circles of friends happened to overlap in holy matrimony, and genetics once again threw them together as the tallest pairing in the wedding party. Maybe they'd luck out and it wouldn't happen for another year or so... or, better yet, ever again.

The song ended, and sure enough, Emily wasn't about to linger. No niceties being offered tonight. Without even looking back at him, she turned out of his hold. Fine by him.

Or it would have been, except that in her typical obliviousness to anyone beyond herself, Emily seemed unaware of how her body was lining up with his. Before he could pull out of the way, the bare skin of her arm met the back of his hand in a mesh of contact that could only be classified as a caress. Emily's sharp intake of breath had Jase's attention snapping to the widening of her eyes, then back to where his knuckles skated down the remaining length of her arm.

A second passed, and neither of them moved, both seemingly caught in the aftermath of a train wreck that never should have happened, in that jolt of electricity at first contact and the lingering low charge that seemed to sizzle through the duration.

Jesus, some things never changed.

———∿∿∿———

"You lying little hooker!" Lena gasped, her eyes bright with excitement. "You told me there was nothing between you and Jase, but then right there in the middle of everyone—"

Emily waved her off, walking past the new Mrs. Skolnic to the east bar, where the hunky bartender was as generous with his dimpled smile as he was with his pours. "That dip was just Jase being showy. Hey, Jimmy, could I get another glass of the pinot, please?"

Fresh drink in hand, Emily turned back to Lena, who was still staring at her with an all-too-smug look on her delighted face.

"I'm not talking about the dip, which was spectacular, by the way. I'm talking about after. When you guys had that"—Lena bit her lip and stepped closer, lowering her voice—"*moment*. It was like fifty shades of hot."

Taking a cool sip of the crisp white, and then a slightly heartier swallow, Emily shook her head. "That was no Jamie Dornan moment, please."

Lena's neatly sculpted brow pushed up, and then, pulling Emily by one hand, she led her back to the table where six of the bridesmaids were sitting, all of them with their eyes locked on her.

Trying not to slosh the wine, Emily went for another sip, because the second she sat down—

"Oh my God! You and Jase—"

"That touch. *Hawt*—"

"And the linger? Like a slow burn, only—"

"And when she was looking back all slow and stunned—"

Okay, so maybe she could have waited for the wine until she sat down, because apparently no response was required here. The girls were completely absorbed in this fantasy they'd concocted about some fictional *moment* that didn't exist.

"And he had that broody, WTF look—"

"Like he was *struck* by her—"

"I'm *super sorry* I half hit on him last night—"

"She is. Rachel had *no idea* you guys were—"

"But he totally wasn't interested, so don't worry about—"

"And if you get with Jase, you've gotta hook me up with Max—"

"Oh my God, you guys, let's agree: Emily gets the bouquet—"

The bouquet? Oh, no way. If that thing came hurtling in her direction, Emily was spiking it straight into the ground.

"Enough!" she pleaded, looking from one expectant face to the next. "It was *not* a moment. There is nothing, I repeat, *nothing* between Jase and me."

Lena crossed her arms on the tabletop, leaning forward and staring Emily down like a vendor trying to up their price. "So when did you guys meet? *Exactly.*"

As a rule, Emily wasn't a huge fan of talking about that part of her life—or her past in general, really. She'd much rather listen and focus on the now. But with all eyes on her, she could feel the heat creeping up her neck.

These girls were relentless. There was no way she was getting out of there without spilling something.

"High school. We were friends for a while, but it didn't stick."

Rachel leaned in then, same posture as Lena. "Friends, like friends who have something hot and unexplored between them?"

More heat crept up Emily's neck. Because for a few months, there *had* been something between them. Something that made her heart beat twice as fast when their eyes met in the hall, holding just that extra second. Something that left her a little breathless when he smiled at her. Something that felt like it was growing, getting bigger every time they talked. But whatever it was, one day it was there, keeping her up nights with her belly twisting and churning, wondering if he'd finally ask her—and the next day it was just gone. Jase was as *friendly* as ever, but apparently the guy's attention span toward females was the same then as it was now—not exactly the stuff of legend.

She'd been confused at first, but then she'd accepted it and moved on.

"Friends, like I dated his best friend for about a year."

This time, Marlene was closing the circle around her, her eyes gleaming. "So you were his best friend's girlfriend, but you're not anymore. Maybe he's thinking about a second chance?"

"No." In this, she was confident. Jase would never see her as anything *but* Eddie's girlfriend. The traitor who ruined Eddie's life. The scapegoat Jase blamed for everything, because if he didn't, he'd be forced to take some of the responsibility himself.

But she couldn't say any of that, so instead, she kept it simple. "Honestly, Jase and I don't get along very well. You'll just have to believe me. Neither of us would *ever* consider something more."

One by one, the girls sat back, and Emily relaxed.

"Sure, I believe you." Marlene nodded, casually smoothing a few strands of her jet hair back into place. "But just out of curiosity, why hasn't Jase taken his eyes off you the entire time we've been sitting here?"

———— ∿∿∿ ————

It was after midnight when the party finally shut down. Dean and Lena had said their good-byes a half hour before, and the band had already cleared out. The Skolnics had taken the gifts, and Emily was doing one final sweep to make sure nothing had been left behind when she came to the black tuxedo jacket hanging from a chair at the wedding party's table.

Someone would definitely be missing this.

Draping it over one arm, she caught the barest scent of cologne—good cologne—and raised the jacket to her nose. It was familiar, but she couldn't remember which one of the guys—

"Not going to lie, Em." The gruff voice from the doorway brought her head up in a rush. "The jacket huffing is kind of creepy."

Jase, he of the persistent, pointless glare. Of course.

Bow tie hanging loose from his open collar, sleeves cuffed to just below his elbows, he started across the ballroom with an easy, long-legged gait. "But I'm betting they've got some twelve-step program to help with it."

Not bothering with a response, she pinched the jacket between finger and thumb and held it out for him as they met in what had been the middle of the dance floor. "You leaving a mess for someone else to clean up. Why am I not surprised?"

Taking the jacket, he paused. "Sure you're okay? One more whiff for the road? Something to hold on to?"

"Pass," she answered, her heels clicking against the floor as she walked out. "I can't forget about you fast enough."

"Hey, Emily?"

She stopped and let out a weary sigh, because really, with this wedding over, all she wanted was to put Jase Foster behind her. She glanced over her shoulder to where he was frowning after her, a disconcerted look in his eyes. "What?"

"You're not friends with Sally Willson, are you?"

Her brow furrowed as something heavy settled in the pit of her stomach. "Sally was my roommate in college. We're like sisters."

She didn't want to ask; she didn't want to know. But by the way Jase was cursing into the palm of his hand and staring at her with those accusing eyes, she was fairly certain she already did.

Sally had been dating her boyfriend, Romeo Santos, for two years, and just this weekend, he'd taken her up to some cabin in Wisconsin.

"Oh no."

Jase shook his head and walked past her. "See you *soon*, Em."

Acknowledgments

To my amazing agent, Nicole Resciniti, for your guidance and support through everything. With you, I'm in such good hands. I could make a joke there, but I won't. I love you. <3

To Mary Altman and Laura Costello, my amazing editors who made this book so much better than it would have been without their patience and insights. You ladies rock, and I appreciate you so much! Also to Diane Dannenfeldt and Heather Hall for helping my books shine!

To the team at Sourcebooks—you've consistently blown me away by being outstanding! Thank you for all you do!

To Jessa Russo, for always being the Chunk to my Sloth. I can't wait to see you again outside the Internet in 3-D! I love you. Without you, I'm not sure where I'd be in this writing business. I'd quote a bunch of song lyrics here, but that would cost too much in permissions and royalties. I'll call you and sing them to you instead because I know how much you love that!

To Cait Greer, who is a way better person than I'll ever be, but still talks to me every day. I love you! *snugs*

To Amber Tuscan-Clites and Heather Griffin, for the laughs and the hugs and the rants and e-shanking of our enemies. I love you both so much! Someday we'll get to PEI for our *Anne of Green Gables* retreat, but I'll settle for anywhere as long as we get to meet in person!

To Brandi Lynch, for always making time for me and for having the cutest accent ever. You're amazing and need to come see me in Canada!

To Roselle Kaes, who is so talented in so many ways. I marvel at you every day! You're one of my favorite people ever. Thank you for being a bright part of my life.

To Gracie West, for reading this and giving delightful feedback. My life is richer for having met you. <3

To JC Nelson, for the critique and the laughs. You're one delightful motherfucker—and that's the highest of compliments!

To Genevieve Kennedy, Leanna Klyne, and Brett Willisko, my best friends since we were too young to know better—I love you so much.

To Lydia Aswolf, for the emails that are so support-ive and pick me up more than I can say, thank you! <3 Please make more words.

To Emmie Mears, for being my Gummy Bear. <3 You're outstanding.

To my family—thanks for understanding when I get salty about deadlines and stressed about life and health and worries. You're the best, and I love you all more—even though it's not a competition.

Because we know that if it were a competition, I'd totally win!

And to each and every reader who picks up my book and leaves a review—thank you so much. You are as important to my stories as any characters in them. Thank you for supporting me! <3

About the Author

Tamara Mataya is a *New York Times* and *USA Today* bestselling author, a librarian, and a musician with synesthesia. Armed with a name tag and a thin veneer of credibility, she takes great delight in recommending books and shushing people. She puts the *she* in That's What She Said and the *B* in LGBTQIA+.